THE GIRLS' WEEKEND

Also By M.I. Hattersley

The Ex

The Girl She Was

My Daughter is Gone

THE GIRLS' WEEKEND

M.I. Hattersley

embla books

This edition published in the UK in 2026 by

embla books

An imprint of Bonnier Books UK
5th Floor, HYLO, 105 Bunhill Row,
London, EC1Y 8LZ

Originally published in 2023 as The Bachelorette Party.

A CIP catalogue record for this book is available from the British Library.

ISBN: 9781471420160

Also available as an ebook and an audiobook

3

Typeset by IDSUK (Data Connection) Ltd
Printed and bound by CPI Group (UK) Ltd, Croydon CR0 4YY

FSC www.fsc.org MIX Paper | Supporting responsible forestry FSC® C013604

The authorised representative in the EEA is Bonnier Books UK (Ireland) Limited.
Registered office address: Block B, The Crescent Building
Northwood, Santry
Dublin 9, D09 C6X8
Ireland
compliance@bonnierbooks.ie
www.bonnierbooks.co.uk

For AJH

PART 1

Chapter 1

Thursday

This was a bad idea.

Chloe had known it was a bad idea the moment Keren's email pinged up on her phone inviting her to Alison's bachelorette party. She'd even known it was a bad idea when she'd replied to say she was free on that particular weekend and was super excited to attend.

It still felt like a bad idea.

Yet, here she was, in a car only half an hour away from the secluded cabin near Salt Point where she would spend a long weekend with four girls in their early to mid-twenties, most of whom she didn't know that well.

It could be fun.

It could also be an absolute nightmare.

She reached over and fiddled some more with the car radio's auto-tune controls, turning her nose up at the tame middle-of-the-road music she was met with. It sounded sort of familiar, but these sorts of songs always did.

"Man, why do they never play any decent music on the radio these days?"

Rob, in the driver's seat, didn't take his eyes off the road, but Chloe noticed the smirk playing across his face. "Maybe it's not just the music."

"What do you mean?" Chloe asked, twisting around in her seat to look at him.

Rob shrugged. "Well, from everything you've said since I picked you up, it sounds to me like you might be wearing a pair of shitty glasses."

"What? I'm not wearing glasses."

"Not actual shitty glasses," Rob continued. "Metaphorical ones. It's like we always see life through the frame of our own internal experiences, right? So, some days when everything that happens to us feels shitty – the music on the radio, the fact they didn't have the soda you wanted at the last gas station, that you're going on a weekend away with people you don't know that well – then it's important to remember we're adding a lot of our own baggage to the equation." He glanced at Chloe and his smirk grew into a smile. "The outside world is pretty neutral. Often, its not what we're looking at that's shitty, so much as we're looking at the world through shitty glasses. It's our own thinking about things that colors our experience of it. It's just something my therapist said to me once that really stuck with me."

Chloe had been readying herself to argue, but Rob made a good point. She had been feeling negative about this weekend and it wasn't fair. She liked Alison and even if she didn't know her that well – and the others attending the weekend even less – they were no doubt lovely people. But there were other reasons why the prospect of spending four days in a log cabin surrounded by trees, wildlife – and lakes – made her stomach twist in knots. She watched Rob for a few moments, wondering if she should open up about what was worrying her, but decided against it. She didn't want to open up that can of worms now, not with Rob. She hadn't spoken about her past for many years. She wanted to keep it that way.

"So, what do I do about these shitty glasses?" she asked. "Can I take them off?"

"Hopefully," Rob said. "But the first step is acknowledging they're there."

Chloe smiled. "Ahh. Good old acknowledgement. It's always the first step, isn't it?"

"You know it."

Rob laughed and Chloe did too. She reclined in her seat, her gaze drawn to the window where the early evening light bathed the landscape in a stunning, pale orange hue. With a bit of effort, she realized, she could perhaps muster a sense of excitement. After all, escaping New York's chaos for a few days, leaving behind the relentless stress of her daily routine, was a welcome change. By now, they had definitely left the city behind, having passed the threshold of civilization at least twenty minutes ago and the view outside the window shifting from houses and buildings to an expanse of trees and lush greenery.

They'd been traveling along the Taconic State Parkway for over an hour at this stage, heading for Clinton Corner, where they would take Route 115 to Salt Point and then a series of smaller, winding roads to the cabin. Assuming they could find the cabin at all. From the map Keren had provided, it looked to be in the middle of nowhere.

Chloe leaned over and checked Rob's phone screen in the plastic holster attached to the windshield.

"Do we still have a signal?" she asked.

"So far. But I imagine it will go at some point. It usually does when we get deeper into the wilderness. But it's cool. I've got a good idea where we're heading."

"Okay, I trust you," she said, giggling. "And thanks again for driving me. You're a total star."

Rob grinned. "It's no problem. It gives me a good excuse to visit my mom. I've not been up to visit her this year, and she's really looking forward to my visit. Apparently, she's been baking all day. Apple pie . . . cherry pie . . . I'll be twenty pounds heavier on Sunday when I pick you up."

Chloe giggled some more. Rob was dropping her off at the cabin and then driving north up to Scranton, where his mom lived with her second husband. Initially, Chloe had felt awkward accepting his offer of a lift. Paying for this weekend away had destroyed her financially, and she had little money to put toward gas. But Rob had talked her into it and seemed more than happy to drive. Chloe was grateful to have him as a friend. He was one of the good ones.

"We should be there in about twenty minutes," he told her. "And I've got to say I'm pretty envious of you."

"I bet you are. Spending Thursday to Sunday with four pretty girls in a secluded log cabin. That's your idea of heaven, right?"

"Come off it. That's not what I meant." He glanced over, his expression turned serious. "You don't enjoy being in the woods? All that fresh air, being able to walk around in nature?"

Chloe turned back to the window. The truth was, she enjoyed all those things. She had previously, at least. But this was the first time she'd been somewhere like this since . . . well, that holiday. To say she was feeling apprehensive about the weekend away would be an understatement.

She'd done enough work with her own therapist over the years she no longer woke up in a cold sweat after vivid nightmares related to what happened. Yet, she could still feel the deep-seated trauma inside of her. She pictured it like a malicious entity, lying in wait within her soul and ready to reawaken at the slightest provocation.

"You're right," she told Rob, shaking away the image. "I'm just being stupid. I bet I have a great time. In fact, I know I will! And I do so appreciate you doing this for me."

"I told you. It's fine."

"Work didn't mind you taking the afternoon off?"

"Nah. I start with a new client on Monday, so I'd only be surfing the net today, counting the minutes."

Rob was a graphic designer and a damn good one, by all accounts. He'd recently wrapped up a campaign for an innovative energy drink, a project that had not only been successful but had also earned him a prestigious industry award. Now, he was preparing for his next big challenge: a rebranding project for the Lilian Vernon corporation.

Chloe had felt a twinge of envy as Rob had relayed this to her at the start of the journey. It was never easy hearing how well someone else was doing, and how much they had their shit together when you were still floundering in life. But Chloe was genuinely pleased for Rob. He worked hard, and he deserved all his success. Even if his achievements made her impact on the world appear all but indistinguishable.

Chloe had been living in Sheepshead Bay, Brooklyn, ever since graduating from Columbia where she'd majored in Visual Arts. That was six years ago, and she was still yet to get what her parents called a 'real job'. Her life was a juggling act of various creative pursuits and she still wasn't sure entirely what she wanted to do with her life.

She ran a moderately successful Etsy shop, selling her handmade jewelry, and supplemented her income with occasional gigs playing guitar and singing in coffee shops. Acting gigs were another source of income, but they were few and far between.

She still attended auditions, however. Indeed, the reason she was traveling to the cabin with Rob and arriving later than the other girls was due to an audition she'd had that afternoon. It was a two-pager for a short film about werewolves that sounded pretty lame but paid well. Not that Chloe held out much hope of getting the part. The other actresses in the waiting room had all been a few years younger than her and were all blonde. They probably invited her to audition just to provide contrast. She imagined she'd have to speak to her mom and dad in a few weeks and tell them – no, she still didn't have any acting work. Then would come the inevitable intake of breath and Mom's soft voice as she suggested that perhaps it was time Chloe considered moving back home and helping in her father's shop.

Chloe knew her parents were supportive, or at least they had been, but they worried a great deal about her chosen path in life – or the lack of one. They feared she was squandering her life away in New York and viewed her diverse pursuits – the Etsy shop, the singing, the acting – as indicators that she was flighty, that she didn't stick to anything. Yet, for Chloe, these ventures were all pieces of the same puzzle, pathways to achieving her longstanding goal of making a living through her creative talents and being her own boss. Only, that ambition was fine in your early twenties, but she was twenty-six now and while she was still scraping together a living, the fear and doubt were beginning to gnaw at her.

But, no, she mustn't think that way.

It wasn't helpful.

Take off the shitty glasses, Chloe!

It had been at an acting audition – a commercial for dog food, of all things – where Chloe had first met Alison a year earlier. Usually at these castings, you nodded politely at the other people in the waiting room and then sat in silence waiting for your name to be called. But as Chloe had taken a seat beside one of the younger and much prettier (and blonde, again!) actresses, they'd turned and smiled, engaging her in friendly conversation. Chloe had been rather taken aback initially, but Alison – for it was she – was so bubbly and carefree she'd found herself relaxing quickly into her company.

Neither of them got the part but Alison mentioned a new acting class she'd started attending – run by Andre Clarendon, the famous off-broadway director – and invited Chloe along with her. It had been a great class, but it was also expensive, and Chloe couldn't afford it after the first term. Still, she and Alison had remained friends, and Chloe was glad to have Alison in her life. She was positive-spirited, fun to be around, and often brought out the best in Chloe.

So why was she feeling so anxious about this weekend?

Was it just the location, or was there something else?

"Hey, Chloe? You okay?"

Rob's question snapped her from her thoughts. She looked over as he flashed her a smile. His expression suggested he'd been talking to her and she'd not heard.

"Oh, yeah, sure. Sorry! I was just lost in my thoughts. Did you ask me a question?"

"Don't worry about it. You were just muttering to yourself and looked angry."

"Did I? Shit. Sorry."

Rob smiled and shook his head, turning his attention back to the road. "We're almost there, I think. What did the directions say again?"

"Umm. To get past Pleasant Plains and then take the left at the sign for Deer Ridge. From there it's a winding road then an unmarked dirt track for about two miles."

"That's what I thought. Well, we should be getting up to that final turn-off soon enough. The GPS has gone I'm afraid, so we're driving on good old-fashioned word of mouth and instinct."

Chloe checked her phone, which she had clutched in her hand as usual. "Yeah, I'm the same – no bars, no Gs, no signal.

Do you think that's how it's going to be out here the whole time? Geez, how am I going to call Alison if we can't find the place?"

And how am I going to call you to pick me up early if I hate it there?

"We'll find it," Rob told her. "I'll find it."

Chloe sat back and released a long breath. Rob was a good guy and she knew he liked her. As in, *liked her*, liked her. But even if she'd felt the same – which she might, given the right situation – she couldn't even consider starting a relationship right now. She didn't know if she'd be in New York this time next year.

The thought twisted her stomach some more, so she pushed it down and adjusted her position, sitting up straight and rolling her shoulders back.

Off with these shitty glasses.

She was away for the entire weekend and had paid a lot of money to be – so she might as well try to enjoy it.

However, as Rob took the next turn the road became a bumpy, uneven track that snaked deep into a forest so dense it felt as if night had descended. The unpleasant sensation in Chloe's stomach intensified as they drove on, and she started to wonder if they'd gone the wrong way. Or maybe that was just her wishful thinking because there was secluded and there was *really freaking* secluded. Attempting to ease her doubts, she dialed Alison's number to double-check she was going the right way, only to be greeted by her voicemail. No signal. Of course.

"I'm starting to have second thoughts about this," she said, pressing her forehead against the passenger seat window as she gazed out through the trees. "It looks pretty sinister out there."

"You're going to have a great time," Rob assured her. "You worry too much, you know that?"

Chloe scoffed. Yes, she did know that. But she also knew what happened when people didn't worry enough, or when they were too relaxed.

"Look, there we go," Rob said, pointing to a gnarled old sign nailed to the trunk of a huge pine tree. "Ravenwood Hollow, 3 miles. That's the place, right? We're all good."

Chloe nodded. "Yeah. Cool."

Despite this, the sight of the track ahead, growing darker as the canopy of trees thickened, did little to bolster her confidence. Nor did the fact that the bottom of the sign had been blasted out with buckshot.

But she was here now. There was no turning back.

Chapter 2

The cabin was bigger than Chloe was expecting, standing in the center of a clearing about the size of a baseball diamond.

"Thank God, they're already here," she said, taking in the bright red Ford, parked out front, a stark contrast to its leafy surroundings.

She took in the scene as Rob brought his car to a stop. The cabin was built from dark-stained timber and fitted in perfectly among the rich greens of the surrounding trees and shrubs. It was raised up on stilts with three wooden steps leading up to a covered deck that spanned the front of the building and stretched down one side.

Over to the left, a few yards away from the main structure, was a smaller outbuilding built from the same dark wood. Its door hung slightly ajar, revealing a few logs inside, presumably to be used for the hearth within the main dwelling. But it was cold out here, and there was not enough fuel to cover the weekend, Chloe noticed.

A stone pathway, littered with leaves and other natural debris, stretched from where the car was parked up to the cabin's steps.

"It looks great," Rob said, killing the engine. "You're going to have a great time."

"Yeah," Chloe replied. "I will."

"I mean, the other option is you could come up to Scranton with me for the weekend."

"Hmm. Maybe I should."

She was only half joking.

Rob chuckled. "Believe me, Chloe, even if this bachelorette party turns out to be a complete disaster, it'll still be a walk in the park compared to being cooped up with Mom for three days."

"Oh, come on. From everything you've told me about your mom, she sounds cool."

"She's okay, I guess. But she's constantly on my case about settling down. Me going home with a pretty girl in tow is just throwing fuel on that fire."

Chloe averted her gaze, feeling a warmth spread across her cheeks. An uncomfortable silence enveloped the car, broken only when she reached for the door handle. "I should probably, you know . . ."

"Yeah, sure!" Rob said, popping the trunk. "Let me get your stuff."

He got out and circled the car to fetch Chloe's bag as she opened the door and stepped out, her boots crunching lightly on the gravel and leaf-strewn ground. Stretching her arms high and arching her back, she took in the tranquil scene. It was so still here, the air so fresh, it was almost a shock to the system. The constant cacophony of New York City, which she had grown so accustomed to, was utterly absent here.

She closed her eyes and took in a deep breath. The city's pollution now replaced by the pure, heady scent of untouched wilderness. The air was crisp and carried the distinct aroma of pine and dry earth. A rustling noise over to her left made her open her eyes, but there was nothing to see. Just some critter going about its life. Above her, birds tweeted and chirped as they roosted down for the night.

"Yay! Chloe's here!"

The shout drew her attention back to the cabin, where Alison was bounding down the steps, a red cup in her hand, its unnaturally pink contents sloshing over the side.

"My god, it's been forever!" Alison squealed, throwing her arms around Chloe and enveloping her in a too-tight embrace.

Chloe laughed, pulling back slightly. "Honestly, Ali, what's it been – a few weeks?"

"Almost a month. And it feels like forever without my home-girl. Come here, let's do it." She leaned forward and they did the exaggerated 'air kissing' thing they always did. It was supposed to be their way of mocking the way other actresses could be with one another, but Chloe often wondered what the difference was.

"You look amazing," she told Alison.

This was no exaggeration. Alison always looked good. Eternally breezy and energetic, she was one of those annoying women who could throw on any old thing and make it look like a carefully curated outfit. Today, she'd embraced what Chloe mentally dubbed 'Outdoorsy Barbie' – and boy, had she nailed it.

She was wearing a pair of khaki cargo pants that would have looked dorky on most people but on her, looked downright chic. The cuffs were rolled up to her ankles, revealing thick woolen socks peeking out from practical yet stylish hiking boots. The hip pockets on the pants were bulging on both sides, probably stuffed with essentials like lip balm, moisturizer, and sunscreen. On her top half, Alison was wearing a forest green shirt under a light, water-resistant jacket.

"Did you have a pleasant drive up here?" she asked. Her naturally blonde hair was pulled back into a practical ponytail, though a few stray tendrils had escaped, framing her face as she smiled.

"Yeah, not too bad," Chloe replied.

"And who do we have here?" Alison asked, flashing her eyes, along with her perfect white teeth, as Rob appeared around the side of the car with Chloe's bag.

"I told you Rob was giving me a ride, right?" Chloe replied, feeling her cheeks flush some more. "He's on his way to his mom's house."

"You sure you don't want to stay?" Alison asked.

Rob chuckled. "No, I think I'll leave you girls to it."

"That's a pity."

"Hey, leave him alone," Chloe said, surprised at the twinge of jealousy she was experiencing. "You're about to get married in a few weeks, Ali. Remember Noah?"

"Oh, yeah. *Him*." Alison sneered, then laughed. "Well, it was nice to meet you, Rob. And Chloe, come on in. Everyone's inside waiting."

With that, she swayed back up to the cabin, sipping at her drink as she went.

"You're going to have your work cut out with her this weekend," Rob whispered.

"Don't I know it," Chloe replied, straightening up as she turned to him. "Well, I guess this is goodbye for now."

"You'll be fine," Rob assured her. "Come here."

They hugged. "I won't be able to contact you," she said. "You were right, the reception here is non-existent."

"It'll be good for you," he said, pulling away and tilting his head slightly as he looked at her. "Some time in the fresh air, playing some drinking games . . . you might actually have fun. Remember what that's like?"

"Yeah, you're right." She mimed taking off a pair of glasses. "Here, take these, will you?"

Rob looked puzzled. "Huh?"

"The shitty glasses I've been seeing things through. You were right. Thanks for the pep talk. I needed it. And the ride. You're a star."

"I do what I can," he said. "But I had better get going. My mom will be wondering where I am. I'll see you on Sunday at three, right?"

"Perfect. See you then."

She watched Rob as he climbed back behind the wheel and started the engine, raising her hand to wave as he reversed the car and pulled it around in a turn.

"See you Sunday," she called after him, still waving as the car drove away and disappeared around a bend in the track.

She shivered and it wasn't entirely from the cool air. She felt very exposed and alone all of a sudden, standing in the clearing. But Rob was right, this would be good for her, and it was all about how you looked at things. It would be fine, she told herself as she hoisted her bag over her shoulder and headed for the cabin.

No! It wouldn't be fine.

It would be FUN!

Three nights in a cabin with nothing to do but drink and bitch, with no phone reception and miles from anywhere . . .

Hell, what could possibly go wrong?

Chapter 3

The cabin door creaked ominously as Chloe pushed it open, finding herself in a short, narrow hallway that opened out into a much larger room. Laughter and murmurs of the other girls echoed from within the cabin as she tentatively made her way down.

Alison and two other girls that Chloe vaguely recognized were lounging on a three-seater orange couch in front of a vast stone fireplace. Alison saw Chloe as soon as she entered the room and, placing her cup on the coffee table beside her, she hurried over, an almost manic grin spreading across her face.

"Hey everyone," she said, turning to address the other girls. "You remember Chloe, right? My friend from acting class."

"Hello," Chloe said, waving self-consciously as the girls turned to look at her. "How are you all doing?"

"Hey!" they responded in unison.

"Welcome to the fun house!" the dark-haired one added, a note of sarcasm straining her husky voice. "You're going to love it!"

The open-plan living area of the cabin held a certain rustic charm, but it wasn't what Chloe would have described as cozy. In front of her was a mismatched collection of couches and chairs, some draped in throws and blankets, others displaying the well-worn original material. The seating had been arranged in a circle around a large soot-streaked fireplace, with small windows on either side looking out into the dense forest beyond.

Further into the room stood a grand, aged dining table, its surface scratched and faded, encircled by a set of eight chairs. A bunch of pink and white balloons had been tied together and served as a fitting centerpiece and a banner declaring 'ALISON'S BACHELORETTE PARTY' hung down from a gnarly wooden ceiling beam. Beyond the dining area, the back wall of the cabin housed a simple kitchen setup. Cabinets crafted from weathered wood, their knobs chipped and mismatched, sat above a countertop of gleaming metal, more reminiscent of a workshop than a kitchen. Copper pans, their bases blackened from years of use, dangled from another overhead beam.

Adjacent to the kitchen, a gigantic metal refrigerator stood next to an old bureau, the two pieces of furniture so incongruous next to each other. Next to the bureau was a closed door which presumably led to the back of the cabin, to the bedrooms and (hopefully!) a decent-sized and functional bathroom.

"What do you think?" Alison asked. "I know what you're going to say – it's not as luxurious as I was expecting, either, but it's authentic, don't you think? It's real. The guy who owns it is some old woodsman, been living out here alone for like thirty years or something."

Chloe nodded, wide-eyed, as she continued to take in the place. Against the wall to her right was a large table on top of which stood a vast selection of liquor bottles – gin, whisky, vodka, wine, plus mixers – along with a stack of red plastic cups. Above this, and around the walls of the living area were a selection of stuffed hunting trophies – a stag, a wild boar, a gnarly old wolf whose eyes seemed to meet hers as she looked on. She supposed they added to the cabin's 'authenticity' but she found their presence creepy and distasteful. Also hanging on the walls were a series of landscape paintings that looked to be originals, depicting dark woodland and grey skies, each more desolate than the next.

"Yeah, it's . . . quaint," she said. "So, is the owner around?"

"No. He's got another cabin a mile or so due north of here where he stays while he rents this place out. He won't bother us," Alison said. "But anyway, come on, I'll introduce you to everyone."

She took Chloe's hand and eagerly led her over to where the other two girls were lounging on the main couch opposite the hearth. Despite Chloe's initial reservations, she found herself smiling and relaxing in the moment. While Alison's vivacity could be dizzying for some, Chloe usually found it grounding and today was no different.

Rob was right. This weekend could be just the distraction Chloe needed, and who better than Alison to provide that distraction? Always the life of the party, always the center of a whirlwind.

"This is Keren, she's my beautiful Maid of Honor," Alison announced, standing in front of the brunette girl with the husky voice. "She's amazing."

Keren sat the cup she'd been holding down and got up off the couch. She and Chloe hugged awkwardly for a moment before stepping back and regarding each other.

"Ali has told me all about you," Keren said, looking her up and down. "She says you're incredibly talented."

"I don't know about that," Chloe replied. "But it's good to meet you. I've heard all about you, too. Nice to finally put a face to the name."

And what a face it was. Although Alison was undoubtedly pretty, Keren was nothing short of stunning. Her thick dark hair shone in the light, making her appear as if she'd just stepped out of a shampoo commercial. As she stood, it fell forward, framing her face but obscuring one eye. With a casual sweep of her hand, she tucked the strands behind her ear, smiling warmly as she studied Chloe with a confident, quietly assertive gaze. Her outfit screamed urban chic, melded with cabin comfort – a pair of skintight black jeans that highlighted her shapely legs and an oversized black mohair sweater.

"Did you find the place all right?" she asked.

"Just about. We're certainly out in the wilderness, aren't we?"

"Oh yes," Keren said, raising her eyebrows. "Don't we know it? It's going to be a few days of roughing it and no mistake. You know we can't even use our phones!"

"Well, even if we could," Alison butted in, "I want to make a rule that we have a cell-free weekend, okay? We can take some photos later, but for most of the time I want us to go analog and focus on talking and being with one another."

Chloe grinned. That sounded like a great idea to her. But Keren's snorts signaled she perhaps didn't share that view.

"What's the point of taking photos if we can't even get on Insta?" she moaned, sitting back down and grabbing up her cup.

The fourth girl, whom Chloe definitely recognized, had been watching the exchange with a smirk on her face and now leaned forward. "Poor Keren, the Instagram queen of New York City. How will she ever cope?"

Keren gave her a hard stare. "I'm just saying . . ."

"I'm sure you can live without it and your phone for a few days, sweetie," Alison said.

"Can I? We can't even message people."

Alison tilted her head to one side. "Who do you need to be messaging?" she asked.

Keren shrugged. "No one. But my public needs me! They'll miss me."

Chloe let out a soft chuckle, unsure how much of all this was a joke, but choosing to take it as one to appease her nerves.

"I take it there are bedrooms and a bathroom?" she asked.

"Yeah, of course. I'll show you the rest. The bathroom is all plumbed in and we've even got hot water," Alison said. "What more do we want? And we're all here together. That's what's important."

Keren threw Alison a sardonic look, but there seemed to be warmth beneath it now.

"Yes, I suppose Ali has a point," she conceded, giving Chloe a conspiratorial wink. "It will be nice to go off-grid for a few days. It feels like forever since we all caught up properly. Life just gets so busy, you know? But for the next three days, we'll all be together. Just us girls. It's bound to be a blast—we'll make sure of it!"

"Well, I'm glad you invited me," Chloe said. "I'm really happy to be here." She didn't know who she was trying to convince most, yet at that moment she realized it was true. Her anxieties about returning to the woods now seemed trivial. What happened was so long ago. It was a different time; she was a different person.

"You and Alison met at Brown, that right?" she asked, refocusing on the conversation.

"Sure did," Keren said, grinning. "We hit it off in our freshman year and have been besties ever since."

"Kappa Delta forever, baby," Alison said, raising her fist.

At this, Chloe noticed the fourth girl shifting in her seat.

"And over here we have Jess," Alison said, motioning for her to join the introductions.

"Hey, how's it going?" Jess said, getting to her feet, speaking in that resigned way only true New Yorkers can manage. "Good to see you."

"Likewise. We've met before, haven't we?" Chloe said, her smile friendly as she nodded in recognition.

"That's right, at the Madame Starlight after-show," Alison said and snorted. "Gosh, what a train wreck that production was!"

"I thought it was fun," Chloe said, moving in for a hug but pausing as Jess extended her hand for a shake instead. "Great to see you again, Jess."

"Yeah, you too," Jess said with a timid smile.

She had a more muted, gentler presence than her friends, but was still pretty in her own way. Her hair, a sandy blonde color, was pulled back into a low ponytail and her light blue eyes were big and sparkled with intelligence. Alongside Keren and Alison, her style was more practical and unpretentious. She was wearing a pair of faded denim jeans and a large grey hoodie that swamped her small frame. She'd rolled the sleeves up her arm and as they shook hands Chloe noticed her slender and delicate wrists.

"Remind me again how you know each other?" Chloe asked.

Jess glanced at Alison, scratching at her neck as she did. "Hell, we've known each other forever, haven't we?"

"Absolutely," Alison replied. "Jess and I have been friends since we were kids. We grew up in the same neighborhood. We were inseparable all through school. She's my wing girl, my ride or die."

Jess snickered at this, but the laughter stopped so quickly that Chloe couldn't help but feel it was forced. She relaxed her shoulders. Despite picking up on some slight tension between the three girls, she was relieved to discover Alison's friends seemed pleasant enough. They certainly weren't the bunch of *Mean Girls* clones she'd imagined on the ride up here.

"Well, this is everyone," Keren said, clapping her hands together. "I guess we can get the party started now!"

"Wasn't there someone else?" Chloe asked. "Your roomie, Hannah?"

Alison rolled her eyes like a bad sitcom character. "Hmm. *She* might not be coming now."

"Oh, that's a shame," Chloe said. "How come?"

Alison made her way to the window, dismissing the matter with a wave of her hand. "Hannah's a cool girl, but she's *sooo* flighty. She's going to make her own way here, she says. If she comes at all. She had unexpected work commitments. Or something. *Whatever*."

"Ah, I see," Chloe said, exchanging a look with Keren. She didn't know Hannah that well, but she knew Alison well enough to know she was pissed that her roommate wasn't in attendance. She'd met Hannah a few times when she'd called for Alison on the way to acting class. Hannah was in her mid-to-late twenties like Chloe – unlike the rest, who were around twenty-four – and now Chloe felt rather out of place again suddenly. She was the elder of the group. The matriarch. But wasn't a matriarch supposed to have their shit together and impart words of wisdom to the younger people in the tribe?

She wasn't sure she'd be much use to any of them in this regard.

"Hannah might still come, Ali," Keren interjected, trying to lighten the mood. "But either way, we're going to have SO. MUCH. FUN! Right girls?"

"Definitely," Chloe chimed in.

"Totally," Jess concurred.

Alison, her mood instantly lifted, spun around with a playful glint in her eyes. "You know what? You're absolutely right!" she exclaimed. "Keren, why don't you show Chloe to her room, and then we can kick this party into high gear! It's getting late. We've got some drinking to do. And we've got games to play!"

Chapter 4

The cabin boasted three bedrooms and a spacious bathroom, complete with a bathtub that had shower attachments, a basin, and a toilet.

"Your room is down here at the far end," Keren said, leading the way, the old floorboards groaning under each step. "You'll be sharing with Jess. I hope that's cool. I'm next door, with a bed made out for Hannah, too, if she ever turns up. Alison has the big room to herself across the corridor."

"It's too bad about Hannah not making it," Chloe said, still trying to figure out the group dynamics. "Is Alison upset about it?"

Keren hesitated before responding. "A little. I think. You know Alison – she's super loyal, so whenever someone lets her down, she feels it more. Plus, she's on this manic, high-energy kick at the moment. One of her episodes. You've been around her enough to know what that's like, right?"

Chloe didn't know Alison that well, not really. But she nodded her understanding, regardless. "Yeah, I get it."

"I just think she's super stressed and anxious with all the wedding planning and stuff," Keren continued, reaching the end of the hallway and pushing open the door to reveal the room. "But we're all here now, so we're going to make sure she has an unforgettable time, right?" She flashed a reassuring smile as she gestured at the room. "So, here we go. This is you."

"Oh . . . nice."

The room was spacious but gloomy, the only natural light provided by a tiny window on one wall. When Keren flicked on the light switch, the low-watt bulb did little to illuminate the place. Two beds, parallel and separated by a small bedside table, occupied most of the floor space. The blankets were haphazardly thrown on, as though the last occupants had left in a rush, and the slightly sunken mattresses hinted at their age. A small red suitcase was sitting on the left-hand bed, which she assumed had been claimed by Jess. Chloe lifted her bag onto the second bed and perched on the edge of the mattress, feeling a gentle give in its springs.

In front of her, adjacent to the door, an old mahogany closet leaned slightly askew, its dark wood marred from years of use. Hanging beside the window, an ornate mirror with an oxidized silver frame seemed to reflect a subtly distorted image, its surface wavy and irregular. The only other piece of furniture was an empty bookcase that stood waist-high against the opposite wall.

On the surface, the accommodation was nice enough, but there was something about the place that made Chloe uneasy. It could have been the dated furniture, the slightly musty smell. It could just have been the fact she was still wearing her shitty glasses. Or maybe even glasses colored by what happened to her two decades earlier when she was staying in a cabin not unlike this one.

"So, what's the game plan?" Chloe asked, trying to shake off her discomfort, watching as Keren ran her finger across the top of the bookcase and pulled a face.

"You get settled in as quick as you can and come join us," she said. "You need to catch up. Alison has already finished off three Cosmopolitans!"

"That's Alison, though. Always the life of the party."

"Yeah. She's great." Keren smiled but Chloe sensed a certain coldness behind her eyes. "We've had some wild times together she and I."

Chloe smiled back.

Don't worry, hon, I'm not trying to steal your bestie or anything.

She might have been overthinking Keren's response. But this was exactly the kind of situation Chloe had been dreading. She had plenty of female friends, Alison included, but she also knew a group of girls together could quickly descend into a total bitch-fest if you weren't careful. Particularly with a group that had known each other significantly longer than she'd known them. She'd be very surprised if there wasn't a ton of petty grievance and past rivalry to overcome at some point over the weekend. Yet, she reasoned, it was all part of the territory. As long as she remained prepared, she'd navigate through it just fine.

"You're going to be an amazing Maid of Honor," she told Keren, aiming to pre-empt any potential negativity, killing her with kindness. "Alison is lucky to have you."

"Thank you." Keren rolled her eyes. "It's hard work, though, I tell you that. Especially when Bridezilla changes all the plans at the last minute and won't listen to reason. She's stressed? What about me?"

She glared at Chloe, who didn't know how to respond to this outburst. She grinned and forced a laugh. "I'm sure it'll all be great."

"Yes. It will be. IT WILL BE!" Keren said, throwing her hands up to the ceiling as if encouraging the gods. "Anyway, I'll leave you to it. Get changed, freshen up, do what you need to do, and then join the party."

"Will do, thanks."

Chloe remained sitting on the bed, as Keren exited and closed the door behind her. She took a moment for herself, eyes closed, tuning into the buzz of lively conversation and the unmistakable sound of Alison's high-pitched laughter filtering through the cabin walls. Drawing in a deep breath, she consciously relaxed her shoulders, letting go of any lingering tension.

All right. Time to have some fun.

With a renewed sense of purpose, Chloe unpacked. She hung a couple of sweaters and a hoodie in the closet alongside Jess's already-hung clothes and placed her jeans, shirts and underwear in one of the drawers underneath the main closet space. Glancing through the window she saw dusk had now given way to night, the sky an inky rectangle in the wall of the cabin. She changed into a pair of fresh jeans and an old sweater that had belonged to her father and, feeling more like herself, made her way back to join the others in the main living area.

The room was dimly lit, bathed in the soft glow from a couple of strategically placed table lamps that cast long, dramatic shadows across the space. Alison was standing in front of the main couch, where Jess and Keren were huddled up on either end. A drink in one hand, Alison was gesticulating dramatically with the other, as if acting out a one-woman show. Noticing Chloe's arrival, she paused, breaking into a warm grin.

"There you are! Cool. You haven't missed much. I can start over. Get yourself a drink first." She pointed at the table on the far side of the room laden with liquor bottles. "The rule this weekend is just help yourself whenever you want a drink. There's plenty more where that came from in the refrigerator too. Whatever you want – we've got it. As long as it's not beer. Ugh."

Damn, a cold beer would have hit the spot right about now. But after the long drive, Chloe would take anything.

"What was going on just then?" she asked, walking over and selecting a bottle of gin. She poured herself a decent measure along with a slug of tonic. "It felt like I walked in on some kind of performance just now."

"Ali is trying to scare us with a lame ghost story," Jess called over.

"It's not lame, *Jessica*!" Alison snapped back. "And it's not a story. It's all totally true!"

"Yeah, sure," Keren said, laughing. "Come on then, *Tales From The Crypt*, continue."

Alison glared at Keren and for a moment Chloe felt the atmosphere in the room shift. But then Alison laughed, and it shifted again. "Okay. Here we go."

Chloe settled down between Keren and Jess, sipping at her drink as Alison lowered her head and got back into character.

"It was a night just like this – dark and misty and with an eerie chill in the air." Her voice had dropped a few octaves and she was relishing her role, giving the word eerie at least twelve 'e's. "When a weary traveler came knocking on the door of this very cabin, desperate for shelter from the relentless, ghostly fog that had consumed the entire forest. With trembling hands, he knocked on the door, the sound echoing through the quiet cabin."

Chloe brought her legs up onto the couch and clutched them to her chest. She felt cold suddenly and was glad of her dad's old sweater. She wondered for a moment if she should suggest making a fire, but Alison was well into her story now and she didn't want to disturb her again.

"The cabin was inhabited by a man named Jebediah Walters, who lived alone, isolated from civilization. The people in the next town would whisper about the 'Man of the Woods', but always with fear in their voices." Alison paused for a moment, her eyes landing on each of the girls in turn and grinning maniacally. "Jebediah was once a respected hunter, providing animal hides and meat to the villagers. But there was something dark festering within him, something that yearned to explore the sinister depths of human depravity. And that fateful night that darkness overcame him."

"Jesus, Ali," Jess whined. "Get on with it, will you? This is terrible."

"Yeah, why are you shaking, then?" Alison replied.

"Go to hell."

Alison laughed and her face dropped once more. "The weary traveler, exhausted and desperate, saw nothing but a sanctuary from the menacing wilderness. Jebediah, however, saw an opportunity to quench a morbid curiosity that had lingered within his twisted soul for far too long. No longer satisfied with the skin and bones of mere animals, that night, beneath the inky blackness overhead, Jebediah succumbed to his base desires, subjecting the traveler to an agonizing death as he skinned him alive and carved up his flesh for meat."

"Aw, gross. Come on, Ali. This is bad." Keren got up and walked over to the drinks table. "I thought you were supposed to be a good actress."

"Get lost. I'm a great actress," Alison called back.

"Yes, you are. Come on, keep going," Chloe urged. She could sense Jess beside her growing more anxious, but despite the wind whistling through the trees outside and the branches scraping against the side of the cabin, she was rather enjoying the unsettling story. "What happened next?"

Alison, the consummate actress, continued. "Over the next few days, Jebediah provided this new meat to the unsuspecting town. But his insatiable darkness had not been calmed. In fact, it only grew. One by one, the townspeople began to vanish, their disappearances shrouded in mystery. People suspected Jebediah, but many were too scared to even voice their suspicions out loud. It was too ungodly a thought, too horrific to contemplate. But eventually, a group of villagers, driven by fear and desperation, approached the cabin, only to be confronted by a macabre tableau of human heads mounted upon the walls and furniture crafted from bones, and human skin."

She paused for effect. No one spoke. Keren had returned to the couch with her drink and all three girls were waiting with bated breath for Alison to carry on.

"But Jebediah was nowhere to be found," she went on. "The townsfolk searched the entire forest but never found him again. They hoped he'd died out here, taken by wolves or the elements. Yet every so often someone would go missing, never to be found, and they knew it was Jebediah, still up to his old tricks. They say his evil spirit still permeates these very walls, a ghastly reminder of the grotesque atrocities committed within. And so, on nights like this, when the mist claws at the windows and the air turns disconcertingly chilly, Jebediah's spirit revels in the horror that clings to this damned place. And . . ." here she dropped her voice to a whisper, ". . . if you listen very carefully, sometimes you can hear his ghoulish laughter and the tearing of skin from flesh, and tonight as you sleep, if you hear a banging on the door don't answer it, because it could well be Jebediah returning home looking for new blood."

"Shit!"

As Alison's words lingered in the air, there was a sudden banging on the front door that made all four of them yell out in surprise. Keren gripped Chloe's arm. Jess physically jumped out of her seat.

"What was that?"

Alison stared wide-eyed at the girls. It was hard to tell whether she was scared too, or this was just part of the act. "I don't know," she gasped.

"Could it be Hannah?" Chloe asked.

"No. She's not coming," Alison muttered. "For sure."

The banging went again, louder now, more insistent. "What do we do?" Jess whined. "What if it's some crazy person come to kill us? Jebediah?"

"There is no fucking Jebediah, idiot," Keren said.

"Then who is it?"

Alison turned to Jess. "I guess we need to answer the door and find out."

"Okay, after you then," Jess replied.

But before anyone could move, they heard the front door crash open and felt an icy wind rush in from outside.

"Hello there?" Alison called out, her voice trembling as she shifted around the side of the couch, putting the furniture between her and the doorway. "Who is it?"

Chloe froze, an intense feeling of dread settling in her stomach as the sound of heavy footsteps shuffled down the corridor from the front door. Whoever this was, they were now in the cabin, and they were heading their way.

Chapter 5

Chloe sat bolt upright, gripping her knees and ready to move, as a man appeared in the doorway. He glared at the four girls and growled.

"You found the key, then?"

Alison made a sound that was half nervous laughter, half like the sound of a balloon deflating.

"Oh, it's Jerry. Right?" she exclaimed, lowering the hand she had pressed to her chest. "I forgot you said you might call in on the first night."

The man, Jerry, muttered something under his breath and gestured at the stone hearth. "I gots ya some firewood outside. You want it?"

"Jerry is the owner of this place," Alison told the rest of them. "And, yes please, Jerry. That would be awesome."

The old man nodded, casting a suspicious gaze over at Chloe and the rest of them as he did so. Chloe guessed him to be in his early sixties, but he could have been younger. It was hard to tell under the bushy eyebrows and thick gray beard. Physically, he was a thin, wiry man whose features looked as if they'd been carved by many years in the wilderness. His skin was tanned and weathered and, despite the bushy beard, the hair on his head was sparse. Long strands were combed back from his face, revealing troughs of tanned scalp beneath. His eyes, although recessed with age, shone with a sharp and scrutinizing gaze that lingered uncomfortably long, especially as he looked Keren up and down.

"I got ya some birds too," he muttered, still staring at Keren.

He was wearing a red and black flannel shirt, its fibers worn thin, and the colors faded by time. His jeans were stained with grass and mud and his boots were scuffed, the leather molded to his feet from years of use.

"Some . . . birds?" Alison repeated, laughing nervously, exchanging a glance with Chloe. "O—kay. Cool."

Jerry muttered something else under his breath and turned, retracing his steps out of the cabin. The girls watched him in silence, not able to even breathe until they heard the front door close.

"Jesus," Keren exclaimed, once Jerry was out of earshot. "Creepy much?"

Alison snickered. "I know! Apparently, he's a real character. A bit of a Jebediah himself, some would say." Chloe noticed her glancing at Jess as she said this last part.

"Whatever. Don't talk dumb," Jess said in retort, shoving Alison on the arm. "Did you know he was coming? Is that why you told us that stupid story?"

"No. I swear," Alison said. "It was a pure coincidence. Funny though, right?"

"Sure, real funny," Jess sniffed. "I almost had a freaking heart attack."

They shut up as a shuffling sound in the hallway announced Jerry's return. He entered, carrying a sack of logs and two dead birds, their necks dangling limp as he held them up. He dumped the logs unceremoniously in front of the hearth and slung the birds on the low table in front of the fireplace. The birds were still feathered, and their vacant eyes seemed to fixate on the horrified girls.

"Here ya go," Jerry said. "That should last ya for the few days you're here."

"Awesome. And what sort of birds are those?" Keren asked him, giggling to herself, making a joke of it.

"These here are ruffed grouse," Jerry replied, his eyes darting from girl to girl like a kid in a candy store. Chloe pulled her sweater down over her legs as his eyes landed on her. He sneered but didn't look away. He didn't even blink. "I don't like other folk hunting around here. This is my land, my woods. So if you see any more birds, you leave them be. You hear me?"

Keren held her hands up. "Absolutely, no worries there, Jerry," she said, eyeing her friends with a twinkle in her eye. "No hunting Jerry's birds. You got that, girls?"

Chloe chewed on her lip. She didn't like the way Keren was acting. Jerry might have been an old man, but he had a way of holding himself, a sort of unsettling calm, that suggested a deeper, possibly darker side. She didn't think it was a good idea to mock him.

"Now that you're here though, Jerry," Keren said, not picking up on any of the hard stares Chloe was throwing her way, "Alison said there was no Wi-Fi mentioned on the website – but I don't suppose you have it, do you?"

It was Jerry's turn to laugh. "Nah, I don't have any of that modern stuff here. I have a man in the next town who sorts the listings out on that website for me. He does it all. I just go to town once a week and get told who's coming and when."

Jess shifted nervously. "But what if we have an emergency?" she asked. "What if we need you?"

The old man smirked, his eyes flickering with sardonic amusement. "Emergencies don't happen out here unless you make 'em, Miss. You city folk are always expecting to be connected. Up here, you ain't. And that's the beauty of it." His eyes lingered on Jess a second too long before his lips twisted into a distorted, unsettling smile. "I'll be up in the north of the woods, in my other cabin. You won't see me, but if you really have a problem, you can find me there. But no phones. I don't need you girls calling me every time you hear a branch snap."

"But it's all safe, right?" Alison asked. "There's nothing around here we need to be . . . aware of?"

Jerry's face dropped, the laughter ceasing. "What do you mean?"

"If we go for a walk in the woods. That's cool, right?"

Jerry grumbled to himself. "Had too many damn poachers and trespassers messing around these parts recently. It gets my goat. Any more, and I'm ready to sort out the problem myself."

"Right, but we do want to go for a walk at some stage," Keren told him. "The woods are so pretty this time of year. You aren't going to shoot us if we head on out, are you?"

"As long as you stick to the paths, you'll be fine," Jerry replied, straightening up. "I'll know it's you girls from all the chatter. If you like, there's a lake over to the east but it can be treacherous this time of year. The same goes for the old quarry over to the west. That's a long drop if you're not careful. What you have to realize is this place is isolated, very isolated. Ain't no one gonna hear you scream if you get into trouble." His eyes glinted with something indefinable. "Not that you should be screaming, long as you don't wander too far."

At this, he let out a long throaty laugh which sent a shiver down Chloe's back and made her look away. But it wasn't just Jerry's creepy presence that made her uneasy.

The mention of a lake, treacherous at this time of year . . .

Alison took a half-step forward, her voice feigning confidence. "I'm sure we'll be fine."

"Sure thing," Jerry replied, revealing a row of blackened teeth as he took in her ample chest. "By the way, make sure you look after that key. It's the only one I supply to guests. I've got a master key up at the other cabin. But that's for me."

Another shiver ran down Chloe's back. She didn't like the way he said that. As if he was going to use it to let himself in, to sneak around and . . .

No! Don't be thinking that way.

You're here to have fun. To kick back and enjoy yourself.

"We'll be careful with it, we promise," Alison told Jerry, risking another step forward. "But if that's all for now, we don't want to keep you."

"Yeah, thanks Jerry," Keren said, moving over to stand next to her friend. "You're a star. These birds look . . . mmm, tasty."

Jerry looked them both up and down and shook his head. "All right then. And you know I like the cabin left as clean and tidy as you found it."

"No problem. We're clean freaks, aren't we girls?" Alison said.

"Oh, sure," Jess added.

Jerry harrumphed to himself but finally headed for the door. As he did, Chloe sighed, releasing the tension in her shoulders. She hated being judgmental, but the guy was odd. The way he was looking at them made her feel uneasy.

"I'll be doing work around the area over the next few days," Jerry called back as he got to the front door. "Felling a few trees and the like. But I won't disturb you. So long now."

And with that, he was gone.

Alison waited a moment, then turned back to the girls, giggling. "Well, then," she said. "Wasn't Jerry a treat?"

They all laughed, and Chloe did, too. But Jerry's words were still echoing around her head as she finished her drink and walked over to fix herself another large one.

This place is isolated, very isolated.

Ain't no one gonna hear you scream if you get into trouble.

Chapter 6

After Jerry's departure the atmosphere in the cabin was heightened and the unease palpable. Alison and Keren made lighthearted jokes, commenting on the way the old woodsman had been ogling them, giggling to themselves about it – yet it was apparent to Chloe they too felt uncomfortable after his visit.

"I don't think it's right he just burst in here unannounced," Jess said. "It's not cool. At all!" She took a big gulp from her cup, shuddering a little as she swallowed it down.

Each of them had made fresh drinks and they were now sitting around the dining table at the back of the cabin. The fact they'd instinctively chosen the spot furthest away from the front door was probably not a coincidence, Chloe thought.

"I'm sure he's completely harmless," Keren added. "Just a lonely old man. He probably doesn't see a lot of people day-to-day. Especially not groups of hot twenty-year-olds? Can't blame the guy for staring." She tossed her hair over her shoulders self-consciously and giggled some more, receiving a hostile glance from Jess.

"Did you have much contact with Jerry while booking the place?" Chloe asked her.

"I didn't book it," Keren said, the humor fading from her face. "Alison took over and did it all."

Alison coughed. "Yeah, well, it was a last-minute thing," she said. "When I decided I wanted this place for my party I had to move fast – book this weekend before anyone else could get it. My mom stayed here last year with my stepfather and wouldn't stop talking about how amazing it was. It sounded perfect for what I wanted. Plus, she still had the link to the booking site, so I made the arrangements. Shoot. That's not bad luck, is it?"

"I don't think so," Chloe said, relaxing once more into the group. "I've never heard of that. Besides, it sounds as if you and Noah are perfect together. You don't need to worry."

She'd only met Alison's fiancé, Noah, once, when she'd bumped into them in the street a few months earlier. He had seemed nice enough. He was everything she'd expected Alison's boyfriend to be – tall, broad-shouldered, chiseled jaw, with piercing blue eyes and a knowing smile.

"I know. I'm being silly," Alison said, but Chloe noticed her left eye twitch slightly. "He's perfect. We are perfect together."

"Oh, here we go again," Jess mocked. "Another Alison monologue about how she and Noah are the dream couple."

"Aw, now come on, Jess," Keren replied. "She's not mentioned him much. A lot less than I'd expected, actually." She glanced at Alison as she said this who stuck out her lip and shrugged.

"It's another rule for the weekend. No talking about boys." She grinned. "This party is about me and my girls."

"Well, that suits me just fine," Chloe replied, although she wasn't sure how convincing she sounded. Images of Rob flashed up in her mind – his smile, the twinkle in his eyes as he looked at her. He was a good guy. She was already looking forward to spending time with him on the ride home on Sunday.

"I'm surprised you're saying this, Jess," Keren said, snapping Chloe from her thoughts. "You're the one who's been getting all gooey to me about your new man."

Jess glared at Keren who turned to Chloe. "Jess has a new boyfriend," Keren announced.

"What?!" Alison cried. "When did this happen? You never told me!"

"I was going to," Jess said, still glaring at Keren. "It's all very new and I didn't want to jinx it by telling everyone. We've only been seeing each other for a month or so."

"I got it out of her because she couldn't stop smiling when we met up to talk about this weekend," Keren added. "He sounds cool. He sounds hot!"

Jess looked down, but her shyness couldn't hide her smile. "He's called Ethan. He is hot."

"Oh my God, this is huge! *Jess is getting laid!*" Alison sang. "That's awesome babe. Really."

Jess sniffed. "Yeah, well . . . Can we leave it now, please? Like I said, I don't want to jinx it."

A sudden hush fell over the table. Chloe's gaze flittered between the others as they sipped at their drinks. Their shared history stretched back years and there were obviously many levels to their friendship, both good and bad. They knew each other inside out. Knew which buttons to press and which levers to pull to get the best and worst out of each other. Still, Chloe thought, with any luck the mood in the cabin would remain pleasant and enjoyable.

Or maybe not . . .

"I'm not sure you're totally accurate about Jerry, though, Keren," Alison said, breaking the awkward silence. "You said he was a harmless old man. I'm not sure that's true."

"What do you mean?" Chloe asked, sitting upright.

"Well, I don't want to scare anyone, but I did read a few rumors about him online after I'd booked the place."

"Oh, great. Now she tells us!" Jess exclaimed. "What rumors?"

"Nothing major. I joined a Facebook group for Deer Ridge and the surrounding area, including Ravenwood Hollow. Jerry Washington has been mentioned a few times on there over the last few years. People are wary of him. It seems he's got himself a reputation in the town as a bit of a scary loner. Apparently, he was a doomsday prepper around the time of the millennium. He had these cabins packed full of weapons and canned foods waiting for the zombie apocalypse." She glanced at Jess. "He's a real conspiracy nut too – a flat-earther, an anti-vaxxer. There are stories of him pulling guns on people he's found near his land. He's got a real temper."

"Oh, wonderful," Keren said, her apprehension now showing beneath her robust confidence. "You didn't think to tell us this before we got here?"

"I didn't want to put anyone off," Alison said. "And it's just rumors, probably all made up. You know what people are like. Besides, he's making money off us and that's what counts, even to grizzled old woodsmen. As long as we act respectful of him and his property, it'll all be fine."

But Alison's revelation left the girls silent once more. Chloe finished her drink and glanced around the cabin. Jess had already checked that the front door was locked, and the windows were all sealed shut. The cabin seemed secure enough. But if Jerry had the other key . . .

Ain't no one gonna hear you scream if you get into trouble.

They were in the wilderness, after all. Miles from anywhere.

"But we're staying?" Keren asked. "I mean, we have to, right?"

"I guess," Jess replied.

"Come on," Keren told her. "We're not going to let silly stories get to us, are we? Besides, Jerry might be a creepy old man. But the emphasis here is on *old.* You saw him, right? He's all skin and bone. I reckon the four of us could easily take him down if we needed to." She laughed, and so did Alison. Jess forced a smile.

"He said he's going to be up at his cabin the whole time," Keren continued. "I don't care what he's doing up there as long as he doesn't bother us. And he won't. I'm sure of it. So, let's do this. Alison's bachelorette party, baby! It's going to be a total blast." She gulped back her drink and slammed the cup down on the table.

"Is anyone hungry?" Jess asked. "I've not eaten since lunch, and my stomach is rumbling."

"There you go, hon," Alison told her, pointing at the dead birds Jerry had brought them. "Go for your life."

Jess shuddered. "I wouldn't know where to even start preparing something like that."

"I could do it!"

The words were out of Chloe's mouth before she'd even realized what she was saying. The other three turned to her with questioning faces.

"Prepare the birds, I mean," she added, realizing she had to follow through with her pronouncement. "If you did want to eat them, we could. When I was younger, my dad taught me how to pluck and butcher a bird."

"No way. I didn't know you were the outdoorsy type," Alison said.

"I'm not. Not anymore. But when I was young, we used to go on family vacations to a cabin similar to this in Acadia National Park. My dad is from Maine and he liked to go back there whenever he could. We'd hunt, go hiking, pick berries, swim . . . It was fun."

Sure it was fun. Right up until the point where it wasn't anymore.

Buoyed by the gin, Chloe almost said this part out loud but held herself back. She hadn't talked about what happened for such a long time and this wasn't the time to start doing so.

"Anyway, what I'm saying is I can cook those birds if we want to eat them."

The girls were all staring at her open-mouthed. Then Keren scowled. "Um, no, you're okay, Chloe. We've got a ton of food in the trunk of Jess's car that doesn't have feathers. Chips and dips, pizzas. I'll go fetch it in."

"Be careful out there," Jess told her.

"Oh, come off it, Jess," Alison said. "Keren can handle herself. I reckon if she did encounter Jerry out there it'd be him who was begging for mercy first."

Keren winked. "He wouldn't know what the hell to do with me."

They all laughed, the tension easing again. But, even so, it was now apparent to Chloe that this would be a weekend of ups and downs – of watching what you said, how you said it, and who you said it to. But that was often what it was like when a group of young girls got together. She was prepared for it.

She was prepared for anything.

"Then, when I get back," Keren said, heading for the door, "We'll have a good old-fashioned game of Truth or Dare. No back outs!"

Jess groaned, and Chloe did too.

She was prepared for anything. But not Truth or Dare.

Chapter 7

Chloe built a fire using the logs that Jerry had brought and as she lit it and joined the girls on the couches, a playful chatter filled the air, punctuated by the creaks and groans of the wood in the hearth as the flames took hold.

"Here you go, doll," Alison said, handing her a fresh drink. "This will lubricate the old Truth or Dare muscles. Don't worry, it won't be that bad."

Was it that obvious she didn't want to get involved?

Chloe puffed out her cheeks unable to ignore the bubbling enthusiasm on Alison's face. "I just think it's a bit of a cliché, that's all."

"It's a bachelorette, Chloe. Cliché is practically a requirement," Keren said, her words slurring slightly. "Don't worry. We'll keep it all in good spirits. Right, girls?"

"Absolutely!" Alison said, her eyes sparkling mischievously. "Who wants to go first?"

Jess, her nerves evidently fraying, hesitated before chiming in, "I'm not so sure about this either. I mean, it's getting kind of late. Maybe we should check all the doors are locked and turn in for the night."

"Little Jess, always the worrier," Alison teased, but there was a bite to her tone that straddled the line between playful and mean. "Just forget about Jerry. We're safe here in the cabin. But are any of you safe from . . . .The Truth!" She let out a manic, over-the-top laugh, pointing at Jess and then at Keren. "Are you? *Are you!?*"

Keren rolled her eyes. "Calm it down, Meryl Streep! There are no casting directors in the room as far as I can tell." She raised her chin. "And don't worry about me, baby. I'm ready for anything you can throw at me. Don't worry, Jess. It'll be fine. It's just a game. I want to play."

"Of course you do. And Alison and Keren always get what they want." Jess mumbled this to herself, and Chloe wondered if she was the only one who'd heard her. Neither of the other two reacted to the comments.

"Okay, let's start with Keren, then, seeing as it's her idea." Alison's voice kept its usual cheery timbre but there was a distinct coolness in her eyes as they met Keren's.

"Fine," Keren said. "Truth."

Alison gulped back her drink. "Okay. Let me think . . . Yeah, I've got one. Truth: Are you jealous of me?"

Chloe almost spat out her drink. "Woah, Alison. Let's keep it friendly, huh?"

"I am," Alison replied. "Keren knows I'm only messing around."

"Do I?" Keren smirked. "But the answer is no. I'm not jealous. Why would I be?"

"I don't know. I always assumed you'd be the one getting married first, the one to bag a hot guy like Noah. I just wonder if it bothers you at all."

Jesus. Tense much?

Chloe sat back as a hush fell over the room. She met Jess's gaze, both sensing the jagged edge beneath Alison's playful exterior. Keren's expression remained composed although the flush that rose to her cheeks betrayed a flicker of emotion.

"You know me, Ali. I'm a big supporter of everything you do," she replied, though her voice held a thread of tightness. "I don't even know if I want to get married. So, again – no. I'm not jealous of you. I'm *happy* for you!"

"Good!" Alison said. "That's what I thought."

Chloe looked from one to the other, feeling the undercurrent of something unpleasant bubbling beneath the surface.

"Shall we move on," she said.

"It's all good," Keren said, winking at Alison. "She knows I can take it. What about you, Chloe? You want a truth?"

She sighed. "Sure. Why not? Let's get this over with."

"Okay," Keren said, as a wide grin spread across her face. "What one thing don't you want any of us to know?"

Alison and Jess gasped dramatically. "Ooh, that's a good question," Alison said.

Chloe frowned. It was a good question, but not one she wanted to answer. She could tell them she didn't want anyone to know how down on herself she'd been these last few months, how she felt as if she was wasting her life and should maybe get on the career ladder like her folks kept telling her to do. She could tell them she worried she'd lost her moxie completely and would never get it back. She even thought about telling them what happened twenty years ago when she was staying in a cabin such as this.

But it was probably best to keep it light.

"Hmm. Let me think. The one thing I don't want any of you to know is that . . . I snore real loud, especially after I've been drinking." She turned to Jess with a sympathetic grin. "Sorry, babe, I hope you've got earplugs."

"Ahh, Chloe, that's such a lame answer," Keren said.

"Leave her alone, it's fine." Jess butted in. "And don't worry. I don't have earplugs but I'm a very deep sleeper. So, no worries."

Chloe gave her a friendly nod as Keren continued to make disappointed spluttering noises.

"Now it's my go!" Alison announced. "I'll have a truth as well. And make it a good one."

"All right," Keren said, her eyes flashing as if she already had one in the barrel. "Do you ever feel like you sacrificed a part of yourself for Noah?"

Alison's exuberant expression dropped. She glared at Keren. "What do you mean by that?"

Keren leaned forward. "You know what I mean. You were all set to move to L.A. But then you met Noah and decided to stay in New York. I'm asking – do you ever regret not moving? Do you regret not pursuing your dreams of being a movie star?"

The questions hung in the air for what seemed like forever. Next to Chloe, Jess fidgeted and muttered to herself, as if she'd rather be sitting anywhere else but in this room with these people. She knew how she felt.

"Nope. No regrets," Alison whispered after a pause. "I love Noah."

But as she was saying this her voice broke and she looked away, blotting at her eye with the edge of her finger. Jess sighed audibly, her discomfort seemingly growing.

"Are you okay?" Chloe asked. "Shall we move on?"

"No. It's fine. I'm fine." Alison blew out a breath and fanned her face. "I'm just being over-emotional. You know how I can be! Silly emotional Alison. But no, I don't regret staying. I don't regret any decision I make. Life's too short for that. My therapist said it's important to keep looking forward."

"Oh yeah? Which therapist is this again?" Jess chimed in. "You've had so many it's hard to keep up."

Chloe snapped her head to look at Jess. She felt this was a particularly cruel jibe. Alison had made no secret of the fact she sometimes suffered with her mental health. She'd never gone into too much detail but had hinted to Chloe about a past traumatic relationship as well as problems at home when she was younger. It didn't help if even her oldest friend was unsupportive.

"She's taking care of herself," Chloe stated. "Doing the work. That's admirable."

"Sorry, Alison," Jess mumbled. "I didn't mean to sound like such a bitch. I guess I'm still a little anxious." She finished her drink.

"It is getting late," Chloe said, glancing at the old clock hanging over the hearth and seeing it was almost eleven. "Maybe we should turn in for the night. That way we can get a good night's sleep and wake up—"

"Not yet!" Keren interrupted. "Jess hasn't had her turn."

"I don't want a turn."

"You have to. Come on Jess."

She glared at Alison. "Fine. Okay. Dare!"

Alison's eyes glimmered as she swiveled towards Jess, no doubt a dare already formulating in her mind. "Jess, I dare you to go outside alone and walk slowly around the cabin, barefoot. Twice."

Jess's eyes widened, her gaze darting from Alison to the nearest window. Outside it was pitch black. "No way," she replied, her hand involuntarily clutching the arm of the couch. "I'm not going out there tonight."

Alison stuck out her bottom lip and flashed her friend those big Bambi eyes of hers. "Aww, come on, Jessica. Don't be such a little scaredy cat."

"I'm not scared. But that's stupid. We don't know what wild animals are roaming around out there. And what if I fall and twist my ankle or something? I'll be no good for the rest of the weekend with my foot all swollen."

"Poor baby Jess." Alison continued, mocking her in a silly voice. "She's terrified of the dark. She's scared that the ghost of Jebediah Walters is out there."

"Get lost. I just don't think it's smart to go running around in the dark when I don't know the area! If you're so brave, why don't you do it?"

"Fine!" Alison said, jumping to her feet. "I will."

Chloe and the others watched as Alison marched confidently down the hallway to the entrance.

"Be careful," Jess called after her.

"Bare feet, remember!" Keren added, but Alison didn't turn around. She yanked open the cabin door and stood for a moment, framed in the doorway. Then with a murmur of nervous laughter propelling her forward, she stepped out into the misty night.

As the door slammed shut behind Alison, Keren turned to the others and grinned. "Let's hope Jerry isn't out there waiting for her."

"Don't even joke about it," Chloe said. Lowering her voice, she added. "Is Alison all right?"

"How do you mean?" asked Jess.

"I don't know, maybe it's me, but I feel as if she's coming across really manic tonight. More than usual. And she's drinking a lot. I mean . . . I know it's her bachelorette party and all, but I don't want her to overdo it on the first night."

Keren smirked. "Well, Ali isn't one to do things by half. I think we all know she can, like you say, be pretty manic at times. But that's just who she is. Let her enjoy herself. She's cool."

"Yeah, okay," Chloe replied. "You know her best."

"Well . . . *I* know her best, *actually*," Jess added.

"Yes of course."

"The longest, at least," Keren added.

"Same thing."

"Um, not really."

Chloe held her hands up, not wanting to be the instigator of another fight. "Hey, girls, I'm sure you both know Alison extremely well and you're both equally important to her. I think it's awesome she has all her best friends here with her. It's going to be a great weekend. Yes?"

"Yes. It is," Keren agreed. "It will certainly be eventful."

Just then something banged against the window making them all jump.

"What the—Shit!" Jess cried out, then released a laugh as Alison's face appeared at the window. She pressed her face against the glass, her cheeks and nose squashed and distorted as she grinned at them.

"Heeeelp mee . . ." she groaned.

"Get lost!" Jess yelled. "And get a move on. You said two laps of the cabin. That's only once around."

Alison stepped back and flipped the bird before disappearing into the mist.

"What a dork," Keren said.

"She's such a fun person to be around when she's in this sort of mood," Chloe said. "I'm so glad she invited me to join you all this weekend."

And at that moment, she meant what she said. It was good to be away from the city, away from the four walls of her tiny apartment and all the everyday problems life liked to throw at her. She now felt more determined than ever to make the most of her time away. Because despite the wilderness conjuring up troubling memories of her past, she did enjoy being in the outdoors. She always had. Maybe tomorrow she'd slip away and grab some time alone. A long walk in the forest, with all that good pine air, could be just what she needed to get her thoughts in order.

She sat back on the couch, smiling to herself as Keren and Jess teased each other, much more light-heartedly and warmly now. They were all tired and a little worse for wear with drink but the camaraderie felt strong between them again, the cattiness of the past hour all but forgotten as light laughter filled the room. Tomorrow was a new day, and after a night's rest there was no reason why Alison's bachelorette party couldn't be the very thing Chloe needed.

She thought suddenly of Rob, who had said pretty much these exact words to her on the ride up here. Good old Rob. He was a great friend. Hell, if she managed to sort her life out and found a way of staying in New York then maybe they could . . .

Shit!

Chloe's warm fuzzy thoughts were shattered as a blood-curdling scream rang out from outside, dragging her swiftly back into the moment.

Jess jumped to her feet. Keren too.

"Was that . . . ?" Jess gasped.

"Yes!" Keren replied, running to the hallway and grabbing her coat from the back of the door, beckoning for Chloe and Jess to follow. "That was Ali. She's in trouble!"

Chapter 8

Alison's screams sliced through the night air as the girls bolted from the cabin – Keren first, followed by Chloe, and then Jess skipping along in the rear.

Chloe felt her heart pound against her ribcage, racing as she navigated the steps, her breath catching in her throat as the sudden chill of the night embraced her.

Was this Alison messing around?

Drawing on her acting skills to prank them?

Chloe hoped to hell that was the case, but she didn't think so. Those screams sounded as if they came from the very depths of Alison's soul. And as much as Chloe loved Alison, dearly, she didn't believe her friend was that good an actress.

Casting her gaze around in a desperate search, Chloe strained to see through the darkness. The cabin door stood ajar, its light spilling out and throwing elongated, unsettling shadows across the ground. The air was heavy with cold mist, which only added to the eeriness.

"Alison!" they cried out in a chorus of desperation, their voices echoing amid the trees as they peered into the dark, seeking any hint of movement, any silhouette that might be their friend. "Where are you?"

The sounds of woodland creatures, startled by the commotion, rustled in the undergrowth as the girls moved around the side of the cabin, huddled together for safety. Jess had pulled out her phone and switched on the flashlight, waving the light across the forest floor in front of them. Keren had picked up a large stick and was clutching it in front of her like a sword.

"Alison?" Chloe's voice carried through the night, laced with urgency. "Where are you?"

The screaming had stopped but had been replaced by the soft, haunting sounds of sobbing coming from the back of the cabin.

"Over there," Jess hissed. "It's Ali!"

They sprinted around to the source of the noise where they found Alison, standing in front of a row of huge pine trees, her eyes wide with terror.

"Alison," Keren said, her voice trembling. "What the fuck is going on?"

"There was . . . Someone . . ." Alison's voice was barely above a whisper as she pointed, her hand quivering, into the trees. "A man . . . He was . . . Right there . . ."

"Jerry?" Jess whispered.

Alison continued to stare into the trees. "I don't know. Maybe. He was just standing there. Tall. Thin. Dressed in black."

Keren threw a skeptical glance toward Chloe, her forehead creased in a scowl. "Ali, are you sure? It's pitch dark out here. Even if there was something, how could you be certain of what you saw? It was probably a deer. Or, more likely, just a trick of the light."

"I know what I saw!" Alison shot back, her voice edged with frustration. "There was someone out there. They were watching us."

Perhaps fortified by the large stick she was holding – or her disbelief in Alison's story – Keren walked over to the tree line and parted the branches. "Hello! Anyone there?" She waited a second before turning back towards them, shaking her head. "Nothing. No one there."

"Oh, right, because if someone is lurking in the trees, they're just going to answer back when you call out to them!" Alison snapped. "You ever see that happen in a horror movie? 'Hey, is anyone there?' 'Yep, just me, your friendly neighborhood axe murderer.'"

Chloe couldn't help giggling at this. It was a nervous release. "Sorry," she said, as Alison spun around. "I didn't mean to make light of the situation."

"There's no one out there," Keren assured them. "I promise."

"Well, there was," Alison insisted, her voice still shaky.

Chloe placed her hand on her friend's quivering shoulder. "Why don't we get you inside," she suggested. "Whether or not there was someone out there, we're all better off in the safety of the cabin. It's warm in there. Come on, let's go." She carefully guided Alison back around the side of the cabin.

"I know what I saw," Alison muttered, in a small voice, almost unrecognizable as hers. "There was someone in the trees. A tall, thin man with long, wild hair."

"Well, like I say, let's get inside where it's safe and warm," Chloe told her. "The cabin is secure as far as I can tell. Nothing can get to us in there."

Behind her, she could hear Jess and Keren muttering to each other.

"Do you really think there was someone out there, watching us?" Jess asked, her voice laden with concern.

"No. Of course I don't," Keren replied. "It's just Ali's overactive imagination. She got herself all worked up with that stupid ghost story and then Jerry's visit made the whole thing worse. You know what she's like – a total drama queen."

They made their way down the side of the cabin, each of them tense, glancing over their shoulders just in case and Jess yelping as a twig snapped beneath someone's foot. Chloe was all but sure Keren's assessment of the situation was correct but – keeping with the horror movie analogy – it was usually the ones most dismissive of the threat that got picked off first. The cabin, with its warm interior glow, suddenly appeared more vulnerable than comforting.

"Let's get inside, quickly," Chloe said, herding the three younger girls through the door before taking one final, thorough sweep of the surroundings. But there was no one there and no sounds except for those of the forest – the organic rustle of critters, the distant hoot of an owl.

Once inside, Chloe didn't waste a moment. She shut the door firmly behind them and turned the lock, feeling a wave of relief as the heavy metal bolt slid into place. She tested the handle, giving it a few firm shakes, but it held securely. Satisfied, she pulled the key from the lock and carried it into the main living area.

Here, the once lively atmosphere was now somber. Alison sat on the large orange couch, her posture slumped, while Jess and Keren stood over her, exchanging uneasy glances. The playful laughter and light-hearted banter that had defined the start of their evening now felt like a distant memory. An unsettling silence lingered heavily in the room.

Jess looked up as Chloe approached and placed the key on the mantelpiece above the hearth.

"Is the door locked?" she asked, striving for casualness in her tone but failing.

Chloe nodded. "Everything's cool. I double-checked; there's no one outside."

"Look, Ali," Keren said. "It's been a long night. Let's not let this get to us. It was probably just an animal, nothing more."

Alison's eyes, red and swollen, sparked with a sudden anger at Keren's words. "Do you think I can't tell a man from a wild animal? I know what I saw!"

Keren met Chloe's gaze and gave her the sort of thin-lipped smile you might offer another guest at a funeral. Turning back to Alison, she continued gently, "Ali, sweetie, we looked around, and there was no one there." She leaned down and rested her hand on her friend's shoulder. "Is it possible that maybe, just maybe, you might have been seeing things? We've all had quite a bit to drink tonight, after all."

The atmosphere in the cabin seemed to drop a few degrees as Alison rounded on Keren, her face contorted in a mixture of fury and despair. "So now I'm just a dumb drunk girl who's imagining things? Is that it, Keren?"

Chloe stepped forward, lowering her voice. "No one is saying that, Alison. We're just trying to make sense of things and stay calm, okay?"

Keren and Jess gave her an appreciative smile. But Chloe couldn't help but feel a little annoyed at her burgeoning position among the group. When had she become the de facto mediator, the sensible one?

Didn't they know she was as anxious and messed up as the rest of them?

And regardless, Alison was still crying and muttering to herself, unresponsive to Chloe's attempts to calm her. She jabbed her finger towards the window at the imposing dark forest beyond.

"There was someone there, a man, he was watching me. Watching all of us!" she hissed.

The room fell silent once more as the flickering flames from the hearth cast shifting shadows across the women's faces. The pop and crackle from a moisture-filled log did little to soothe their frayed nerves.

"Maybe we should just call the police or something. Let them handle it," Jess suggested.

"No!" Keren quickly retorted, a firmness in her voice. "That would completely ruin our weekend. Besides, the nearest station is at least thirty miles away. I highly doubt they're going to send a patrol car out because some girls in a cabin thought they saw something in the woods." She sat back and folded her arms, giving Jess a withering glance. "And I don't know about yours, my phone doesn't have any signal."

Jess looked as if she was about to say something else, but before she could Chloe stepped in, taking on the role of mediator once again. "Okay, everyone, let's just take a step back and breathe. It's late, and we could all use some rest. I'm even willing to bet everything will seem a lot less frightening in the morning. Hell, we'll probably find ourselves laughing about the whole ordeal."

"Laughing?" Keren scoffed, her voice dripping with sarcasm. "You mean like having fun? Can you remind me again what that feels like?"

Ignoring Keren's remark, Chloe turned her attention to Alison, who was still visibly shaken. "Hey, Alison, what do you say we head to bed, yeah?"

Alison, sniffing and wiping at her face, nodded reluctantly. "Yeah, okay. Thanks, Chloe."

Chloe offered her a reassuring smile as she helped her to her feet. "I'm sure whatever was out there is now long gone. The doors are locked, and the windows are sealed. We're completely safe inside the cabin. Nothing can get to us. I promise. Everything is going to be just fine. Besides, this is your bachelorette party! We're here to celebrate and have a good time, remember?"

"Yeah. Sure," Alison replied, though her voice lacked conviction. "Thanks."

But as Chloe led Alison away from the living area and toward the bedrooms the knot of anxiety in her stomach told a different story. And as she continued to offer words of reassurance, she couldn't help but wonder: who was she really trying to convince? Alison and the others – or herself?

Chapter 9

After the exhaustive events of the day, Chloe had fallen asleep relatively quickly but had woken with a start around 2 a.m., wide awake and unsettled.

Rolling over, she checked her phone for the fourth time since awakening, noting that it was now just past three.

Darn it.

She'd been tossing and turning for over an hour and the old mattress beneath her seemed to have grown more uncomfortable with each minute that passed. It was too soft and lacked support, but there was also a sharp bulge near her left hip where the springs were damaged, causing a jagged piece of metal to protrude.

She lay on her back and pulled the worn sheets up to her chin, her senses heightened as she listened to the nocturnal sounds of the cabin. Jess was sound asleep in the bed beside her – breathing in deep, rhythmic sighs like she hadn't a care in the world. Every now and then she'd mutter something in her sleep, but it was nothing Chloe could make out. Elsewhere, every creak and groan from the old cabin, every gust of wind and rustle of leaves outside the window only served to amplify Chloe's anxiety. As the minutes ticked by the realization dawned on her – she wasn't going to fall back asleep any time soon. She reached out for her Kindle, hoping a little reading might settle her when a loud creak resonated from the main living space.

She froze, a breath caught in her throat, her heart pounding. "Jess," she whispered. "Did you hear that?"

But Jess remained in a deep slumber, oblivious. Chloe stared at the door, willing it to remain shut. Moments passed in tense silence, but no one entered her room, there were no more noises. It was probably just the old wooden beams contracting in the cold, she told herself. However, the nagging uncertainty wouldn't let her be, and she knew she wouldn't find sleep again without investigating.

Throwing back the sheets, she sat up and placed her feet on the chilly hardwood floor. She was wearing panties and an oversized tee brought specifically for sleeping in, and here in the back of the cabin away from the hearth, the air sent a shiver down her body leaving her legs dappled with goose-bumps. Grabbing her jeans from off the floor, she gave them a brisk shake – just in case any unwanted critters had taken up residence – and slipped them on. Moving over to the door, she scanned the room, searching for something to use as a makeshift weapon. The only item she could see that vaguely approached that definition was a golfing umbrella Jess had brought. That would have to do. Gripping the handle, wielding it like a sword, she left her room and moved slowly down the corridor.

Pausing by the door to the living area she listened intently, and her heart almost stopped. She could hear footsteps.

She'd checked and double-checked the front door was locked before going to bed, but Jerry had told them he had another key.

Was this him?

Before she could talk herself out of it, she clasped the door handle and eased it open.

"Oh, crap. It's you!"

A wave of relief washed over her at the sight of Keren standing by the dining table, her stern expression illuminated by the phone in her hand. She looked up and shoved the phone in her pocket as Chloe entered.

"Hey! Couldn't sleep either, huh?" she asked. Then, on noticing the umbrella, "What are you planning on doing with that?"

"I heard a noise. I thought you were . . . Well, never mind." She lowered the umbrella, feeling a bit of a dummy all of a sudden. "You were trying to get a signal?"

"Yeah, and failing miserably. I just wanted to . . . Forget about it. Doesn't matter."

Chloe approached her. Before Keren had pocketed her phone it looked to her as if she'd been on WhatsApp. But who the hell was she trying to message at this time of night?

"Is everything okay?" Chloe asked.

Keren scoffed. "Apart from us being stuck in the middle of nowhere in this creepy-ass cabin and everyone on edge you mean?"

Chloe responded with a playful grin. "It could be worse?"

"Could it? You know I wanted us all to go up to Montauk for the weekend? I had a boutique hotel in mind. It would have been idyllic. Walks on the beach, delicious seafood, fine wine, massages, pampering . . . and decent cell phone coverage! But for some unknown reason Alison insisted on us coming to this place. Said her mom adored it here, and we'd bond better in such a secluded cabin, free from distractions." She sank into one of the chairs around the table with a groan. "Well, let's see how she gets on without those distractions. I'd say it's going spectacularly well so far wouldn't you?"

Chloe took a step back, surprised by the intensity of Keren's outburst. She watched her for a few moments, but her expression was hard to read. She was certainly angry but there were undercurrents of almost grim satisfaction, Chloe thought.

"I'm sure it'll get better," she offered but received only a grunt in response.

Chloe had suspected Alison's friends were the sort of girls who were super sweet and chilled, right up until the point where they didn't get their own way, but she hadn't expected such a blatant display of self-interest. After all, this was supposed to be Alison's special weekend. She was about to point this out to Keren when the door creaked open, and Jess's head peeked nervously around the side.

"I was wondering where you'd gone," she whispered, her voice tinged with concern. "What's happening?"

"Nothing much," Chloe replied, forcing a smile. "We both couldn't sleep and ended up chatting."

Jess padded over to them. "Weird night. I just checked on Ali. She's sound asleep and snoring."

"That's good," Chloe said. "I think we can chalk up last night's scare to a few too many Cosmos and ghost stories. Tomorrow's going to be a new day with a whole different energy. We'll make sure of it!"

Jess and Keren both nodded in agreement but neither seemed that convinced. "I am a bit worried about Ali though," Jess said. "I've not seen her for a few weeks, but she seems . . . How do I put it . . . ?"

"Crazy?" Keren interjected. "Like she's almost *too* happy."

"Hey, come on. That's not cool," Jess said. "But, yeah, I guess. And have you noticed she's barely mentioned Noah at all? Do you think something happened between them?"

"She did say she wanted to focus on us girls this weekend," Chloe added. "I'm sure everything is fine."

"I don't know, Chloe," Keren said. "You don't know Ali like we do. She's not herself."

Chloe felt a twinge of irritation. While she hadn't known Alison as long as the others had, she still considered her a close friend. And wasn't in the mood for condescension.

"Maybe she's just feeling the pressure of the wedding," she suggested. "She's hardly the first bride to feel stressed out. And to be honest, she doesn't seem that different to me. She's just Alison – high-energy, funny, wants everyone to have a good time."

Jess shook her head, settling into a seat next to Keren. "I know. But I'm worried about her. I'm just not sure Noah is the right guy for her."

This piqued Keren's interest, causing her to shift in her seat to face Jess. "What makes you say that?"

Jess hesitated before answering, her fingers unconsciously playing with her necklace. "I've known Ali almost my entire life and she does tend to latch onto men quickly. Too quickly. Her dad left when she was young, and I think it had a big effect on her. Then there was Tony, her college boyfriend. He died in a car crash when we were eighteen. Alison wasn't in the car with him when it happened but his death hit her hard. She didn't get out of bed for weeks. She didn't want anyone to see her grieving and upset. But that's Alison for you, Little Miss Perfect. She wants everyone to be happy, constantly. And herself most of all. Maybe because she's scared of what happens when she's not. She puts too much pressure on herself, and even more so on her relationships. I'm worried she's jumping into marriage too soon."

"I get what you're saying," Keren replied. "I mean, I know Noah, he's a great guy. But are he and Alison really meant for each other? I'm not so sure."

Jesus.

Chloe looked from Keren to Jess and back again. What great friends these two were. Could they not have, maybe, addressed these concerns directly with Alison, preferably before her bachelorette weekend?

"What's your take on this, Chloe?" Jess asked.

Caught off guard, Chloe stammered momentarily before halting herself, deciding to step out from her usual peacemaker role. "I think maybe you should trust your friend's judgment a little more," she stated firmly. "Alison is a grown woman. She's smart and, as far as I can tell, she's done enough work on herself to understand all of this on her own. If she believes marrying Noah is the right decision, then I trust her choice."

Jess nodded, seemingly taking Chloe's comments to heart, while Keren diverted her gaze and let out a pointed sigh. "Whatever. All I know is that tonight was a total wash-out. I'm heading back to bed." Standing, she raised her hand in a half-hearted wave. "Later, losers. Let's hope tomorrow is more fun."

Chloe and Jess watched as she wandered away. Once she was out of earshot, Chloe sat down. "Poor Alison," she said. "I didn't realize all that about her dad and her boyfriend dying."

Jess shrugged. "It happens. Alison is one of those lucky people who always seems to bounce back from things. Plus, she's never had to worry about getting attention from guys."

Chloe's eyes narrowed slightly at this remark. "It sounds as if things are going good for you too, though. This new guy you're with sounds like one of the good ones. Ethan, right?"

Jess's eyes dropped to her lap, her demeanor shifting. "Yeah," she murmured, her voice softer now. "He was a good guy. But, we're not together anymore."

"Oh? I thought . . . ?"

"I didn't want to tell the others yet. I knew Alison would make a big thing about it and I'm not ready to talk about it." She puffed out her cheeks. "I think it's probably why I've been in a bitchy mood. It's hard, you know, to hear of how great everything is for her . . ." She sniffed and wiped at her eyes. "I'm fine. It is what it is. I loved him. I thought he loved me. He didn't. You see it's not as easy for girls like me, Chloe. Alison is so pretty, so carefree. So much fun."

"Don't be so hard on yourself, Jess," Chloe told her. "You're fun and pretty, too. Alison isn't trying to hurt anyone being how she is."

"Oh, yeah, totally!" Jess replied. "I'm just feeling sorry for myself. I can't help feeling a bit used, I guess. But what can you do? I'll get over it."

Chloe offered her a genuine smile. "Good for you. Men, huh? Who the hell needs them?" But as she said this her thoughts drifted to Rob. She wished she could find the same ease in dismissing these feelings, wished she could comfort herself as effortlessly as she did others.

"Yeah, screw them all," Jess replied, laughing as she stretched and got to her feet. "We should probably head back to bed, too. I feel super tired suddenly and it sounds like Alison has a whole day planned out for us tomorrow. Keren will probably be miserable but she should have put her foot down if she didn't like the plans. She is the Maid of Honor, *after all*."

Chloe paused, detecting a layer of bitterness behind Jess's words. "Were you hoping Alison would make you Maid of Honor?"

Jess turned back, her face contorting in disgust. "God, no. That's way too much responsibility. I'm much happier staying in the background." But Chloe couldn't help noticing the strain in her voice as she said this.

"Got it. I'm with you there," Chloe responded, aiming to keep the conversation light. "Come on then, let's get some rest. Like you say, it sounds as if tomorrow is going to be a fun-packed day."

That was fine by Chloe. Fun-packed meant busy. Busy meant she stayed out of her own troubling thoughts and would hopefully keep the bitching and jealousy at bay. However, as she walked back to her room, she couldn't help but wonder if expecting a drama-free day was too optimistic. Especially with this friendship group.

Chapter 10

Friday

Chloe's eyelids fluttered open, battling against the insistent throb that underscored her temples. The room, basked in the morning light, seemed too bright, as if it was mocking her, playing tricks with her groggy senses. After a few futile attempts to reconcile with sleep, she wrestled out from under the bedsheets and sat up.

She licked her lips, detecting a faint, metallic taste. She hadn't drunk anywhere near as much alcohol as the others. Why was she feeling so out of sorts?

Her mind flickered back to the events of last night, the ghost story, Jerry's visit, Alison's screams still rattling around in her memory. She glanced at her bedside table where the glass of water she'd taken to bed with her remained untouched. She was probably a little dehydrated, that was all.

Leaning over, she picked up the glass and gulped down the contents. In the bed beside her, Jess stirred but didn't open her eyes. Being as quiet as she could, Alison pulled on her jeans and headed for the door. As she passed Alison's room, she wondered how her friend would be coping this morning. Certainly, she would be battling a monstrous hangover after last night's antics. But as Chloe staggered into the main space of the cabin, she found Alison standing in the kitchen, her hair washed and combed back from her face, frying pan in hand. In front of her, the table was set for breakfast.

"Good morning," Alison greeted her, a radiant smile on her face. "I hope you slept as well as I did!"

Chloe's stomach performed a nervous dance at the sight of the scrambled eggs in the frying pan. "Yeah, morning," she mumbled, trying her best to emulate Alison's upbeat demeanor. "So, you feel okay?"

"I feel fantastic!" Alison said, gesturing for Chloe to take a seat. "I made eggs and toast, plus I've got some grits on the stove and I can whip up some hash browns if you'd like."

"Eggs are fine, thank you," Chloe said, still struggling to get her head around the shock of seeing Alison so upbeat. "What time did you wake up?"

Alison glanced at the clock above the fireplace. "I've been up and about since seven. Almost two hours. I was worried you three lazy bones were going to sleep all morning. Ah, cool, here's the others." Chloe turned her head just in time to see Keren and Jess entering the room. They didn't look as bad as she felt, but they didn't look as good as Alison was acting.

"Morning," Keren said, giving a half-hearted wave. Her mascara from the night before was now a smudged mess around her eyes, and her thick hair was stuck up all over the place. "Something smells good."

"I made breakfast!" Alison announced with a beaming smile. "Come on, grab a seat, I'm about to serve. I made coffee, too. I'm guessing everyone could do with a cup?"

"Hell yes!" Jess said, taking a seat beside Chloe.

"Coming up," Alison said, shoveling piles of scrambled eggs onto each of the four plates and then turning back to the kitchen counter.

Chloe exchanged subtle glances with Keren and Jess. The atmosphere felt tense and awkward as if everyone was holding back from saying what they were really thinking, all the while trying to comprehend Alison's drastic change in mood.

"How are you feeling, Ali?" Keren asked. "After last night I mean?"

"I'm perfectly fine," Alison called over her shoulder, busying herself with something on the counter. "I know, I know, I was acting a bit crazy. But I'm okay now."

"Good to know. I think it's best we just put it all behind us," Chloe added, giving Keren and Jess a meaningful look, silently urging them to go along with it.

"So, what's on the agenda today, Ms. Bachelorette?" Keren asked, poking at her eggs with a tentative air as if psyching herself up to eat. "I was thinking maybe we could do face masks and—"

"Hiking!" Alison said, triumphantly, turning around to face them. She held a tray containing an assortment of mismatched mugs and a large French press. "Let's embrace the great outdoors and breathe in some fresh forest air! Trust me, it's way better for your skin than any face mask."

"Sounds like a plan!" Chloe responded, throwing another glance at Jess and Keren. It was annoying that she'd had this parental role thrust upon her, but she was unable to stop herself. Jess and Keren both looked as if they'd rather spend a night alone with Jerry than take a walk in the forest, but neither voiced their concerns aloud.

Alison poured out the coffee and the four of them tucked into breakfast, sharing sparse words and avoiding eye contact. It was a weird atmosphere, but it was still early and Chloe hoped once they were out in the fresh air tensions would fade and they'd all start to enjoy themselves.

After showering and dressing in their warmest clothes, they assembled in the driveway in front of the cabin. It was a clear spring day, and the sun was even threatening to appear through the clouds, unusual but not unwelcome for late April. Nevertheless, the air was brisk, and Chloe found herself grateful for the thermal underwear she'd thought to wear beneath her clothes.

Armed with the compass app on Alison's phone and an old map they'd found in the cabin the group set off. They battled through the long grass and dense undergrowth until they came to a trail, which, according to the map, would take them past the quarry and around the nearby lake.

Learning of their intended destination stirred unease in Chloe, but she consciously stilled her breathing and pushed the dark thoughts away. This was Alison's weekend, and she was determined not to be another dissenting presence. Besides, she was no longer a child; she was fully capable of handling whatever lay ahead.

As they walked deeper into the forest, the overarching trees seemed to close in around them, shrouding the path in a subtle darkness. Behind her, Chloe could hear Keren's sarcastic mutterings and Jess's mumbles of uncertainty, but she tried her best to dial them out. The ground beneath their boots was muddy in places, soft and mossy in others and the smells and sounds of nature – the scent of earth and pine, the flutter and chirping of birds – were both enriching and welcome. As she pressed on, Chloe was transported back to her childhood – to a time when walking in the woods with her dad was one of her favorite pastimes – and before long she was starting to feel like herself again. In fact, she was feeling better than that. She was feeling optimistic for once – as if all the stress she'd brought with her had been left behind in the cabin. She hoped it stayed there.

Having advanced ahead, Alison paused in a small clearing to allow Chloe to catch up. "Look at the two of them," she said, with a smirk, gesturing toward Keren and Jess. "It's as though they've never been out of the city before."

Chloe turned to watch as they waited for them to catch up. Keren was the first to reach them, her arms scrunched up to her chest to avoid snagging her sweater on low-lying branches.

"Are you not enjoying yourself?" Chloe asked.

"Oh, absolutely. Isn't it evident?" Keren replied her tone dripping with sarcasm.

Suddenly, Jess halted, her eyes darting nervously through the trees. "Did anyone else hear that?" she asked.

"I heard a bird, or a rabbit, maybe," Alison replied. "Honestly, Jess, I never realized you were such a coward."

Visibly tensing, Jess glared at Alison. "I'm not, but you guys all heard Jerry telling us to stay on the path, right? Well, we haven't been walking on any sort of path since about ten minutes back. What if he mistakes us for poachers and shoots us."

"I seriously doubt that'll happen," Chloe told her. "I expect Jerry just said that to scare us. Or to stop us from delving too close to his other cabin. He might present as a bit of an eccentric, but he does understand the modern world, laws and all. His cabin is on Airbnb, for God's sake. I don't think he's the unhinged wild man you guys all think he is."

"I don't know . . ." Alison added. "He sounded pretty serious last night when he was expressing his dislike for trespassers."

Chloe shot her a stern glance.

Good one, Alison. Here's me trying to calm the situation, and you're still stoking the flames.

Jess pulled a face. "Can we head back, please? I need to pee!"

"Go behind a tree," Keren told her.

Jess squealed. "No way. I can't do that."

"You're going to have to," Alison told her. "The route we're on is a circle and it's quicker to carry on than turn back – but we're still thirty minutes away from the cabin. Go on. You'll manage."

Jess grimaced. "What about bugs? Or snakes?"

"They won't bother you," Chloe said, putting on her most reassuring voice. "Just be careful of poison ivy. It often starts to grow around springtime. The leaves grow in clumps of three and are reddish brown."

Alison leaned back and pouted as if impressed. "Seems like we've got ourselves a true nature enthusiast here. I didn't know you were such an expert."

Chloe chuckled. "I wouldn't say that, but I did go camping a lot as a kid. Not so much as I got older."

"See, Jess. You'll be fine," Alison said, playfully nudging her friend. "Squat down behind that big oak tree over there."

Jess looked over to where she was pointing. "That one? It's pretty far away. What if I—?"

"Jess! Just go and take a piss, will you?" Alison snapped. "It's going to be dark before we get back to the cabin and we've still got loads of activities to get through."

"Ooo, yay!" Keren quipped under her breath, receiving a dark look from Alison.

"But you'll wait for me, yes?" Jess asked, setting off, her need to pee clearly overriding any fears she might have. "I'll be as quick as I can."

The three others watched as Jess hurried through the long grass and ferns toward the shelter of the oak tree. At one point she stopped and flapped around wildly at a cloud of flies that were buzzing around, eliciting giggles from Chloe and Alison.

"Poor thing," Alison said, as Jess disappeared around the side of the tree. "I didn't think she'd find it this hard. She's not cut out for the wilderness."

As if to perfectly highlight this point, the tranquility of the forest was suddenly shattered by a blood-curdling scream.

"Jess?" Chloe called out, her instincts driving her towards the oak tree as a couple of stout pigeons flew out from the undergrowth.

As Chloe rounded the tree, she discovered Jess, frozen in shock. She was staring at the ground with her hands up in the air as if recoiling from something. Getting closer, Chloe saw why. A gruesome display of blood and entrails lay scattered on the ground. Her heart raced as she saw the intestines, a heart, what could have been a kidney, all splayed out in a grotesque tableau. It looked as though a large animal had met a violent end. Or even . . .

"What is—Ew!" Alison squealed, appearing alongside Chloe. "What the hell is that?"

"I- I- d-don't know," Jess stammered. "I finished peeing and turned around to pull up my pants when I noticed wet blood on the tree trunk. I followed it around and found . . . this!"

"What in the—" Keren's words stalled in her throat as she joined them, her eyes wide with unspoken dread. "What sort of creature does something like that?"

Chloe shook her head. She had no clue. The way this animal had been torn apart and its insides left here to rot was unlike anything she'd ever seen before. The best-case scenario was that a wild bear or some kind of mountain cat had violently gutted its prey and then dragged the carcass away. That thought alone was unsettling.

But the worst-case scenario?

Right now, she didn't even want to think about that.

Chapter 11

Chloe's heart raced as she wrestled for answers, to explain the gory details at her feet. She was trying to keep a level head, trying to stay focused on what she knew, not what her imagination was telling her, but any way she looked at it, this was weird.

No, forget weird.

Try downright unsettling.

"That's a big old heart," Keren said, staring unblinkingly at the strewn guts. "Are we sure this was an animal?"

"What the fuck?" Jess wailed. "Shut up, Keren! Of course it's an animal. What are you trying to say?"

Keren held her hands up. "I'm not saying anything. But this looks like some creepy ass ritualistic shit if you ask me."

Well, no one is asking you, Chloe thought, grinding her teeth together.

"Come on, guys," she said, grabbing Jess's arm and guiding her away. "Let's not keep looking at it."

"But what happened here?" Alison asked, trudging along after them as Chloe led Jess back to the path.

"I don't know," Chloe replied. "But that's nature for you. It can get a little grizzly up close."

But the truth was Keren had a point. The way those intestines and blood were laid out back there, it did look like a macabre sacrifice had taken place.

Shuddering, Chloe shook the thought away. She was hungry and thirsty, and she wasn't thinking straight. That was all.

"I'm parched," Chloe said, turning to Alison. "Could you hand out the water and snacks? We probably all need a pick-me-up."

"Good call." Alison slid the backpack she was carrying onto the crook of her arm and unzipped it. Taking out two water bottles, she handed one to Chloe and the other to Jess. Chloe drank well before offering the bottle to Keren.

"Drink something," she urged her. "We don't want to get dehydrated."

Keren took the bottle with a smile and took a big swig. "Please tell me we're heading back to the cabin now," she said, once finished.

"Yes. We are," Alison said. "Follow me. I know where I'm going."

They set off again, the girls all walking at a brisker pace than before, with Chloe marching on behind Alison. As they wound their way through the trees, she noticed a shift in the atmosphere. The bitching and moaning, the muttered asides and dramatic sighs had now ceased and each of the women was focused on the task at hand. Namely, getting back to the safety of the cabin as quickly as possible.

Chloe remained vigilant, scanning the undergrowth for anything else untoward. But she saw nothing. She did, however, notice that they appeared to have walked past the same cluster of tall pine trees more than once.

Shit.

She quickened her pace to reach Alison, lowering her voice as she walked alongside her. "Hey, Ali, I think we might be going around in a circle."

Alison didn't look at her. Her face was rigid with concentration. "Really? You think that?"

"I'm afraid so. We've passed that circle of trees back there already, about twenty minutes ago."

Alison turned to look at Chloe. Her face fell, and her eyes welled up. "Damn it! I was so sure I was leading us the right way."

"Hey, it's okay," Chloe said, giving her arm a playful nudge. "We can figure it out. I've got a pretty good sense of direction. I think if we keep veering left from now on, we'll reach the path leading to the cabin."

A smile tugged at Alison's lips. "Thanks, Chloe, you're a lifesaver. I'm so glad you came away with us."

"Me, too," she said. And she meant it. "Thank you for inviting me. It means a lot."

"You sound surprised that I did. Of course I'd invite you."

Choosing her moment, Chloe decided to bring up something that had been niggling at her. "Speaking of invites – what happened to Hannah?"

Alison stopped walking. "What do you mean?"

"Just that she didn't turn up, that's all. I thought she was looking forward to the trip." She left unsaid how she, too, had been anticipating Hannah's presence this weekend. Being closer to Chloe's age, Hannah never seemed quite so emotional or self-obsessed as the others. Although they'd only met a handful of times, the subtle maturity that arose in those few years between the mid- and late-twenties was noticeable.

"She did want to come," Alison replied. "But she had work obligations. Her boss called her at the last minute, and she couldn't get out of it. It sucks but it can't be helped."

"That's a shame."

Alison sighed. "Yes. It is. I was pretty hurt when she told me." Her voice hardened a bit. "In fact, I was downright pissed at her! But just between you and me I think she's jealous of mine and Noah's relationship."

"Oh? I see."

"Yeah. People see us together and they want what we have. It happens a lot," Alison continued, jutting out her chin. "Also, Hannah's annoyed because she's going to have to find a new roommate soon. Once I move into Noah's place."

Chloe bit back a response. She wasn't sure if these things were true or if it was just Alison venting. Either way, it was best not to get involved. She sensed some of Alison's claims might be amplified by her past experiences and insecurities, creating a distorted perception – her own version of Chloe's shitty glasses.

"But enough about Hannah," Alison said, nudging Chloe back. "We're going to have a fun weekend without her. You can count on that."

Chloe grinned. "Of course."

They walked on, Chloe now leading the way. Behind her, she could hear Keren and Jess, who were still discussing their gruesome find. They talked of Jerry, of grizzly bears and of roaming wildcats. They still sounded antsy but there was a giddiness to their conversation now too, as if they were starting to revel in the situation. That was a good sign, Chloe felt. People enjoyed being a little scared so long as they felt secure. It was why people enjoyed scary movies and rollercoasters.

She turned around, walking backward to take the two of them in. Keren was hunched over, her hands out in front of her like claws, perhaps doing an impression of whatever animal it was that had caused the scene back there. Beside her Jess squealed, playing along. It was good to see.

"Come on, you two," she called after them. "We're almost there. If we carry on in this direction, we should reach the cabin in about ten minutes."

"Thanks, Chloe," Keren said, as they hurried to catch up. "I don't know what we'd do without you."

It was a rare moment of seriousness among Keren's usual cynicism, and it made Chloe smile. She allowed Keren and Jess to pass by in front of her and waited a few moments, breathing in the fresh air and the smells of the forest – the mingling scents of leaves and fresh wood. She felt more grounded than she had in a long time. Plus, by getting them lost Alison had inadvertently avoided taking them past the lake. That was a good thing. Chloe was feeling hopeful right now and she didn't want to spoil that by putting herself in a potentially stressful situation. Maybe they'd go there tomorrow, or the next day but she'd deal with that then. For now, the cabin beckoned, along with a well-earned meal. She might even roast up the birds Jerry had brought them.

But as Chloe resumed her walk, she noticed something out of the corner of her eye. She halted, focusing on a silhouette discernible among the trees about three hundred yards away. It was too far to identify, but whoever it was they were just standing there, staring at her. Could it be Jerry? Hoping to ease the tension, Chloe held up her hand to wave.

"Hey," she called, trying to sound casual.

The figure remained eerily still. Chloe blinked, then opened her eyes wide. Was it even a person? Maybe it was just a shadow or an oddly shaped tree trunk playing tricks on her eyes.

But no. As she looked on the figure raised its hand, mirroring her gesture. It was Jerry. It had to be.

"Chloe! Hurry up!" Alison's voice pulled Chloe from her thoughts.

"I'm coming!"

Although she wanted to move forward, she couldn't tear her gaze away from the figure as they knelt and picked up something from the ground. It was a shovel, which they began to use, digging into the earth with enthusiasm.

Chloe's mind raced.

If this was Jerry – was he burying something?

And if so, what?

The unsettling thought sent a jolt of nervous energy down her spine where it blossomed in her belly making her nauseous. She really needed to eat.

Pulling her phone out of her pocket, she set off after the others. As she walked, she swiped open the phone but a glance at the screen confirmed her fears: still no signal. The battery indicator was also showing just fifteen percent. She longed to call Rob, if only to hear his reassuring voice, or to know she had an escape route if needed.

"It's okay," she whispered to herself. "Everything will be fine."

Gritting her teeth, she shoved the phone back into her pocket and set off at a rapid pace. All at once she felt very vulnerable out here in the wilderness away from the others, away from civilization.

Chapter 12

Warmth and the comforting scent of timber enveloped Chloe and her friends as they entered the cabin. Chloe made sure the door was securely locked behind her, giving it a good shake, before joining the others in the living area. The hike had been a good idea of Alison's, but Chloe was grateful to be back indoors, away from the unsettling wilderness of the forest. Her socks were damp, and her hair was stuck to her forehead from the mist and sweat.

Jess and Keren collapsed onto the couch as if they'd just got back from climbing Everest rather than walking a few miles on relatively level terrain. They were city girls through and through, but Chloe understood, smiling to herself as she sank into a low armchair and began removing her boots. Although the cabin's scratchy wooden walls and dim lighting provided a stark contrast to the vibrant, unpredictable outdoors, it offered safety, and after a few minutes, she felt herself relaxing. She watched as Jess and Keren shed their outer garments and huddled back into the warmth of the couch. They both seemed a little nervous still.

"Did you think all that blood had come out of you at first?" Keren asked, eyeing Jess with an impish expression.

Jess looked horrified. "Ew, no! Seriously, grow up?"

"You shit your panties," Keren sang, her smirk widening. "It was so funny."

"No, it wasn't," Jess snapped. "It was scary. You were scared too."

"Nah. I knew it was just some dead animal. I didn't like looking at it, but I wasn't scared like the rest of you."

"I think we should leave," Jess said, sitting up and looking at each of them in turn. "I'm serious. There have been too many weird things going on. I'll drive us to the next town. We can stay there. Get a motel for the rest of the weekend. We can still do all the things we want to and—"

"Hey, hey, hey!" Alison walked over, patting the air in an attempt to calm Jess's heightened outburst. "It's fine, hon. We're safe here."

"Please, Alison," Jess continued. "This isn't cool. I'm not having fun."

Alison caught Chloe's gaze, a look of pleading in her eyes.

"Come on, Jess," Chloe said. "This is Alison's bachelorette party. And we're all adults. Let's try and keep a healthy perspective here. Nothing has actually happened."

"Hasn't it?"

"You're just imagining it," Keren told her. "We're here now, Jess. We might as well stick it out."

"You won't be saying that when we're all dead, being eaten by Jerry."

"Well, no, I won't," Keren said, shaking her head with a smirk. "Because I'll be dead. But at least I won't have to listen to your pathetic whining any longer."

Alison giggled at this. Jess turned away. "You're all total bitches. Do you know that?"

"Bad bitches forever!" Keren called out, raising her fist in a show of triumph.

Chloe shook her head in mock dismay. But regardless of Jess's paranoia, it was probably a good sign that the group was reverting to its usual dynamics. Teasing and bickering were clearly the default methods of communication between Alison and her friends, and the banter indicated a return to some semblance of normality. Jess would calm down now they were back in the cabin. Here it was much easier to rationalize the gory scene they'd encountered for what it most probably was – a small animal falling foul of a larger predator. As Chloe had said, it was just nature at work.

Yet as she pulled off her sweater, she couldn't shake that image of Jerry, shovel in hand digging in the dirt.

Most likely he was just digging for truffles, she told herself. She'd done the same with her father when she was younger. She also knew Oregon white truffles were common to the area, and often found near oak trees, of which there were plenty.

Yes, that had to be it.

Either that or he had a vegetable patch in the clearing where she'd seen him. Both were completely normal and valid explanations for what he was doing.

"Who's up for some hot chocolate?"

Chloe looked up to see Alison standing with a pan in one hand and a big grin on her face.

"Sure, that would be awesome," Chloe replied.

The others agreed and Chloe watched as Alison skipped over to the kitchen to prepare the drinks.

"I'm so sweaty," Jess shrilled, eliciting a snicker from Keren. She glared at her. "Oh, please! Do get a life, will you? Jesus. I'm going to get changed." She got up and headed for the bedrooms, Keren's mocking giggles following her.

"Don't be long, Jess," Alison called after her from the stove. "The hot chocolate's almost done."

"Yeah, yeah."

"And be careful of any boogeymen lurking under your bed," Keren called after her.

"Go to hell."

Keren met Chloe's gaze and grinned. "She's fine. She knows I'm only joking. We all love each other really."

Chloe nodded and smiled. She hoped Keren was right, but she didn't get the impression these girls even liked each other for most of the time. She was thinking about how to respond when an idea sparked in her mind, distracting her.

"You know what?" she said, slapping her thighs and getting up. "I am going to cook those birds. How about it? You want roast pheasant for lunch?"

"Totally!" Keren said, as Chloe went to the hearth and picked up the dead birds. "If it's not too much of a pain in the ass for you?"

"It's cool. I've handled game plenty of times over the years."

Alison regarded Chloe as she joined her in the kitchen. "You really are a star at all this outdoorsy stuff, Chloe. I never knew."

Chloe couldn't help but feel the remark was more of a jab than a compliment.

"How would you know?" she replied, keeping her tone light, choosing to give her friend the benefit of the doubt. "It was a long time ago when I used to do this sort of thing. But I guess you never forget."

An image flashed in her mind. That day, down by the lake. The blazing sun overhead, the shouting, the screams, the confusion. Then his hand grabbing for hers . . .

No! Don't!

She shook her head to try and disperse the image. It didn't help to think about such things. It never did.

"I'd best get on with preparations," she said, slapping the birds down on the counter. "Hope you don't mind me working alongside you."

"No worries, Chef!" Alison replied, saluting her. "I'm pretty much done now anyway."

"Great."

The hot chocolate smelled amazing, and Chloe's stomach hadn't stopped rumbling since they got back to the cabin. She began plucking the feathers from the first bird as Alison opened one of the cabinets and took out four mugs. Placing them on a tray, she leaned into Chloe, whispering conspiringly.

"Once we've warmed our bones with the hot chocolate, I'll get the cocktails flowing again."

Chloe carried on plucking. "Don't you think it's a bit early to be drinking?"

"Um. Never!" Alison replied, picking up the pan of hot chocolate from off the stove and dividing it between the waiting mugs. "It's my bachelorette party. Besides, I think we could all do with a strong drink after the events of this morning."

"Yeah, but it was nothing to worry about, Alison. Right?"

"Oh, absolutely." She placed one of the mugs next to Chloe and took the tray over to the hearth where Keren and Jess – now dressed in fresh dry clothes – were sitting. "Here we go, ladies. Drink it while it's hot."

Chloe grabbed her mug and took a large drink. It burnt the sides of her mouth, but she was so hungry and parched she didn't care. It was also super sweet and very tasty. She blew across the top and took another sip, turning to watch Alison as she settled on the couch beside Keren. They were laughing at something she couldn't hear but observing the scene from this distance there was something about the exchange that felt strained. They were both smiling and seemed pleasant enough but there was a brittleness behind both their eyes that betrayed them.

Chloe leaned back against the counter. It was probably nothing. It was just what happened when you were both competing to be queen bee. It was Alison's weekend, but Keren clearly didn't want to relinquish the top spot. Chloe, being the outsider of the group and a little older, was glad she didn't have to concern herself with such petty rivalries and powerplays. Chloe knew both Keren and Alison were a lot more attractive than she was, but she'd made peace with her looks a long time ago and would never have let someone's appearance be a factor in whether she was friends with them. And that wasn't to say she was bad looking. If she did her hair and make-up – not like today – she'd describe herself as a solid seven. But apart from when she went for acting jobs, she didn't care too much about her appearance. She was happy with who she was. Externally, at least. All the internal stuff was another matter and a complete shit-show most of the time.

A loud cackle from Alison snapped her from her thoughts and she glanced over to see her heading for the makeshift bar area. Drinking again.

Should she be worried?

If this wasn't Alison's bachelorette party, her alcohol consumption would have been cause for concern, but it was probably her way of dealing with the pressure of all the wedding arrangements. Chloe remembered reading how getting married was one of the top ten most stressful life events. So, it made sense Alison would want to kick back this weekend. And Chloe didn't want to be a buzz kill.

She even accepted the large Cosmopolitan Alison offered her once she'd finished plucking the birds. It was strong with vodka but – *screw it* – it was also needed. Plus, she needed a little liquid courage because as the birds had been plucked now came the icky bit. Placing the first bird on its back she removed the crop – the fleshy food sack next to the wishbone – which she yanked out before chopping off the head and neck with a sharp knife. These all went into the trash along with the plucked feathers, wings and feet. Next, she stuffed her hand up the poor thing's bottom, trying not to think too deeply about it as she pulled out the liver and guts and then washed the bird inside and out ready for roasting, and moved onto its mate.

As she worked small bursts of laughter carried over from the hearth, the other girls now suitably lubricated and having fun. She caught snippets of the conversation, Keren and Alison teasing Jess about some boy she used to like. She remembered what Jess had told her last night about Ethan dumping her and felt bad. But she seemed okay and was giving it back to the other two with just as much gusto.

As the subdued chatter continued, Chloe found her gaze drifting over to the window half-expecting to see Jerry's dark form emerging from the trees outside. It was an unsettling reminder and she wondered if she should tell the others what she'd seen.

But then, what exactly had she seen?

Jerry going about his business? Looking for food? Tending his land like he'd told them he would be doing? He was hardly standing in the forest with a smoking gun, and without concrete evidence of anything sinister, she chose not to alarm her friends. The ambiance in the cabin was now lively, and she didn't want to cast a shadow over their merriment.

After setting the birds in the oven to roast she was sweating and ready for a shower. Excusing herself she grabbed a towel from her bag and headed into the bathroom. Under the warm embrace of the shower, Chloe tried to relax. She let out a deep sigh, concentrating on the feel of the warm water as it cascaded over her body, washing away the layers of sweat and grime.

But it wasn't enough of a distraction. Alone with her thoughts, she soon found herself focusing on the same infernal questions she'd been wrestling with for the past few months.

Chiefly, what the hell was she doing with her life?

She was going to turn thirty in a few years. That wasn't old, but it was too old to have nothing to show for your three decades. She might have been able to navigate her way through a dense and unforgiving forest but when it came to her career path or her life plan, she found herself lost and roaming. Her self-worth, once so robust, had eroded over the years, leaving her unsure of herself and what to do for the best. She closed her eyes, putting her head under the water, hoping it might somehow clean out her troubled mind.

It felt good under the warm jets. She didn't have to think about this now.

Beneath the comforting hum of the water, Chloe barely registered the escalating voices filtering through the wooden walls. It wasn't until she heard yelling, loud and high-pitched, that her eyes snapped open, and she twisted off the shower unit.

What the hell?

Leaning around the side of the cubicle she listened. Yes, that was yelling all right. It sounded like Jess. She sounded hysterical.

Wrapping the towel around herself, Chloe stepped out of the shower, picking up more frantic chatter and raised voices as she moved to the door. She hurried down the hallway towards the main space to find Jess, visibly trembling, in front of the hearth with Alison and Keren flanking her, trying to calm her down.

"What's going on?" Chloe asked.

Jess glared at her with red, teary eyes, her face gripped with tension. "The worst thing has happened," she hissed. "We're stuck here, Chloe. We're trapped."

Chapter 13

Chloe looked at Keren and Alison for answers. Alison was too busy trying to comfort Jess to respond but Keren stepped closer and lowered her voice.

"It's not as bad as she's making out," she said. "You know Jess . . ."

"I know we're stuck here!" Jess snapped, spinning around to face them. "I know someone has sabotaged my car!"

"What?" Chloe asked.

Keren rolled her eyes. "We don't know that."

"Okay, can we all calm down and explain to me what happened?" Chloe said, gripping the towel tightly around herself.

Jess gulped back a deep breath, a futile attempt to calm her erratic breathing. "I . . . I was still feeling a bit shaky after this afternoon," she started. "I was going to drive into the next town to pick up some supplies – chips and soda and a salad to go with the birds – I figured being around civilization again would stop me worrying so much, remind me we're not too far away from other people. But . . . But when I went out to the car just now, it won't start. So, it is as bad as I thought. We're trapped here. In the middle of nowhere with no phones and no way of getting away."

Chloe paused. It wasn't an ideal situation, but she couldn't help but think this was Jess overreacting a little, perhaps even a subconscious plea for attention. The group dynamic between Jess, Alison and Keren was complicated. It couldn't be easy for her to play second fiddle all the time.

Yet, if her car really wouldn't start . . .

"Did you check everything?" she asked, addressing the whole group. "And the car definitely won't start?"

Keren cleared her throat. "Yeah, we did. It's screwed. I don't know if it's a dead battery or something else, but it won't start at all."

"If it's just a dead battery, then that's easily fixed," Chloe told Jess. "My friend, Rob, is picking me up on Sunday afternoon around five. He's pretty good with cars. I'm sure he'll be able to get it started no problem. You can still drive out of here."

"But not until Sunday?" Jess said. "What if we need to get out of here before then?"

"We've got enough supplies, Jess," Alison said, rubbing her friend's shoulder affectionately. "I don't think we need to worry."

"I think it might be too late for that," Jess whined as if she was about to start crying again. "You need to let me go!"

"She wants to walk into the next town and find someone to come out and fix it today," Keren muttered in Chloe's ear. "We're trying to talk her out of it."

Chloe nodded. "Hmm, yeah. I don't think it's a great idea to set off walking anywhere, Jess. It'll take you over two hours to walk to the nearest town and it's getting late. You might not find anywhere open."

"And like we all keep saying – it is Alison's party, guys," Keren added. "Can we all try and calm down and go back to having fun? I know what we saw earlier was super gross, but it was just nature. Come on, Jess. Let's have a drink and settle down. After a few Cosmos things will seem a lot less scary."

"Please, Jess," Alison said, lowering her head to look Jess in the eye who was now staring at her feet. "I don't want you wandering off somewhere on your own. I want you here. With me. I want us to be together."

Jess sniffed. "Fine. But if something bad happens we won't be able to go for help."

"I really don't think there's going to be any more upset," Chloe told her. "We're staying in a cute old cabin surrounded by trees and birds, we just need to refocus on that, stop letting our imaginations – or the memories of too many cheesy horror movies – affect how we see things. It's all good."

And after saying this, she almost believed it herself. Alison gave her a wink of thanks as she guided Jess over to the drinks table.

"Come on, let's get drunk. I don't know why everyone is such a Debbie Downer all of a sudden."

"Hey!" Keren snapped. "That's not how it is. We did see some gross shit today. We are all a little shaken up. That's understandable, isn't it?"

"Excuse me?" Alison hit back. "I know what we saw, Keren, but this was supposed to be a fun weekend. It was supposed to be about us getting away from civilization and enjoying ourselves, away from our problems. Yet you're all acting like I've dragged you here and that this is just some terrible ordeal you need to get through. Jesus!"

She turned her back on them, wiping at her eyes as she did. Keren made to say something else, but Chloe held her hand up, giving her a hard stare at the same time.

"Alison, that's not true. At all," she said, softening her tone. "Is it, girls?"

She eyeballed Keren and Jess who both begrudgingly agreed.

"No. I'm really happy to be here," Keren mumbled. "I'm sorry if I made you think differently, Alison. I am having a good time."

"Yeah, me too!" Jess said. "I guess I just let my nerves get the better of me. I've not been doing so well lately, but I'll try to rise above it. I do want to be here."

Chloe reached out and placed her hand on Alison's shoulder. "What say we all take a break, it's been a weird day, but that doesn't mean we can't turn this around. In fact, we most definitely will! Right?"

Alison had tensed at first but now Chloe felt her relax. She sighed and turned around. "Yeah, cool. I'm sorry too. I've got a lot of shit going on in my head, which doesn't help." She put her hands on her hips and grinned. "Geez, you guys, I don't want to fight with you. You're my besties. My ride or dies."

"Exactly!" Chloe said, checking the clock. "Listen, the food won't be ready for another ninety minutes and none of us slept well last night. Why don't we get some rest for an hour, then reconvene for some proper fun? Plus, I need to put some clothes on." She stepped back indicating she was still only wearing a towel.

"Yeah, good plan," Alison said.

"We will be fine," Chloe told Jess, still sensing her unease. "I promise. We just need to chill out and stop it with all the drama."

Jess nodded. "Yeah, you're right. I am sorry Ali."

"It's fine, hon. It's all forgotten."

"All of it!" Keren agreed.

Chloe gestured toward the bedrooms. "Cool. So, what say we meet back here at three, ready for a good time. Sound good?"

"Sounds awesome," Alison said.

"Sure does," Keren added, nudging Alison playfully. "Party night, baby!"

Yet as Chloe headed for her room and slipped on a pair of jogging pants and a t-shirt, she couldn't help but feel something had shifted between the four of them just now. It wasn't something she could put her finger on exactly. It felt as if they were all play-acting at being friendly. Jess, despite her apparent change of mood just now, had slumped onto her bed without a word and both Alison and Keren's enthusiasm felt a tad forced. But, regardless, they were all here until Sunday and Chloe was keen to rise above all the petty, inter-relationship drama and have a good time. She'd invested a lot in this weekend, both emotionally and financially, and was determined to make the most of it. Even if it killed her.

Chapter 14

Chloe lay on the bed, her head buried into the pillow and willing herself to relax. She rolled onto her back, letting out a deep sigh as she tried to surrender to the solace of sleep. She felt as if she'd done a damn good job back there, convincing the others – along with herself – that all would be well. But maybe not.

Chloe might have been the sensible voice of reason among the others, but that status was only relative, and her mind now spiraled with intrusive thoughts and unresolved memories. The day's disconcerting events – not just the scene in the woods, but the tension within the group – played on her mind, also.

She shifted restlessly for a few moments, tossing and turning in the too-soft bed, before admitting defeat and opening her eyes. Across from her Jess was napping soundly, her breathing slow and steady.

Damn it!

She flung off the covers and climbed out of bed. There was nothing to be gained by staying here listening to Jess's heavy breathing – which was growing more annoying by the second now that she'd noticed it. She took off her loungewear and dressed in a pair of jeans and a heavy knitted sweater. Grabbing her boots and jacket she left her room and walked down the corridor. As she passed Keren and Alison's rooms, she stopped and listened at the doors. Both women sounded like they were asleep.

Well, good for them.

Heading into the kitchen area, she checked the oven, noting the birds would need more time. Leaving them to roast she sat on the couch and put on her boots, lacing them tight before slipping on her jacket. The thought of going out for a walk hadn't been a particularly conscious one until a few seconds ago, but she needed to clear her head. And what better way than a stroll in nature?

She left a brief note for the others; letting them know she'd popped out for a walk and to take the birds out of the oven at three if she wasn't back by then. She ended by writing she'd see them soon for 'PARTY TIME', then folded the note and headed for the front door. With only one key she wondered whether to leave the door open but chose to lock it behind her. She wasn't planning on being gone too long and it was safer this way.

Outside, the forest stretched endlessly in every direction, an ocean of trees and greenery. She stepped off the porch, scrunching up her eyes at the brightness. The sun cast a warm, dappled light through the leaves, tracing a flickering path before her as she wound her way through the towering pines. It felt good to be out in the fresh air. She pulled in deep breaths, holding each one in her lungs for a few seconds, an old trick her therapist had taught her which was supposed to help with anxiety.

Here in the quiet serenity of the forest, it felt ridiculous to think that this place offered anything other than good times and beautiful scenery. Yet, two decades earlier it had been a day very similar to this one. Bright, clear, fresh. A day full of possibility. It was funny how life worked.

But who was laughing?

With every step, Chloe tried to empty her mind of thoughts, focusing only on what was in front of her, the trees, the long grass, the birds in the sky, the small critters scampering unseen through the undergrowth. Her pace was speedy and after a few minutes, she deviated from the main path to take on a more challenging terrain, her aim to get some endorphins pumping around her system. She had no real direction in mind, but she trusted in her homing instincts enough she'd be able to find her way back to the cabin. For now, she just wanted the exercise, to get her blood circulating and get out of her head for a little while. The air was chilly but felt good against her skin.

She'd been walking for about thirty minutes when she noticed something up ahead and as she got nearer, she saw it was another cabin.

Jerry's place.

The realization made her stop, and she glanced back the way she'd come, trying to recall the map Alison had found in the main cabin. Jerry's cabin had looked to be a few miles due north from the one they were staying in. Without the others slowing her down, she'd covered more ground than she'd realized but now she hesitated, wondering if she should turn back.

Her common sense told her, yes, of course she should turn back. Jerry had explicitly warned them he didn't like people prowling around and that they should stick to the main paths. Yet a mix of curiosity and an urge to see what Jerry's home was like drew her closer. He was certainly an odd character and, admittedly, she'd been a little shaken seeing him with a shovel earlier. But she'd already accepted that there was a perfectly innocent explanation for why he was out digging. And he really wasn't as scary as the others made out. To Chloe, he was intriguing more than intimidating.

Moving discreetly, she carried on, winding through the trees towards the old wooden structure. Nestled among the trees, it appeared rather serene. It was smaller than the cabin she was staying in but with its solid log structure and moss-covered roof it was just as charming. In fact, she'd go as far as to say it was rather quaint. Not scary at all. It also looked to be empty as she left the undergrowth and stepped into the clearing surrounding it. Moving around to the side window she peered through into the dim interior. The embers of a fire were smoldering in a stone hearth along one wall and in front of this sat a small table and a solitary armchair. Behind this was another table covered in newspapers and faded documents along with one of those old plastic desk tidies made up of a series of tubes of varying heights – the type Chloe used to have in her bedroom as a kid. In the far corner was an old stove, covered in grease and grime. Next to this was a high, square table with what looked like a large chunk of raw meat lying on top.

Ew!

Opposite this, was an old cot bed with a hunting rifle leaning against it. There was a door on the other side that was hanging ajar revealing the woods out back, but no bathroom, or indeed anywhere to even wash up.

And no Jerry.

Chloe stepped back, eyes scanning the immediate area for any signs of the old man.

"Hello?" she called out. "It's Chloe . . . From the other cabin . . . I was just taking a walk . . ." She waited. Nothing.

Despite the voice in her head screaming at her to walk away, her curiosity was in charge and before she knew what she was doing, she'd moved back around to the front of the cabin and tried the door. It was open.

Shiiit . . .

Was she really doing this?

With her breath tight in her chest, she eased the door open and stepped inside. The cabin held a strange smell – yeasty and meaty, and not pleasant. Her eyes scanned the room, taking in the details: more guns lined up against the adjacent wall, and a noticeboard opposite, full of newspaper clippings that she hadn't noticed while looking through the window. She moved over to get a better look, her eyes widening along with her mouth as she read the headlines.

Hiker goes missing in upstate New York.

Body found on hermit's land.

Chloe swallowed. Or, at least, she tried to. She suddenly had no saliva.

"Jerry . . . Shit . . ." She squinted at the faded newspaper articles. Most of them were from the same period five years ago and covered the same case. A 25-year-old woman called Mary-Beth Andrews had been on a sponsored trek from Pleasant Plains up to Rock City and had gone missing. The skin on Chloe's neck bristled with goosebumps as she read on. There had been search parties and appeals but Mary-Beth's body had turned up two weeks later in a lake near Salt Point, her head bashed in with a blunt instrument.

Woah . . .

A map in one of the articles showed the area in detail. The lake where the body was discovered wasn't far from their cabin – from Jerry's cabin. Chloe continued to scan-read the articles, her heart beating faster as she did so. Jeremiah 'Jerry' Washington was mentioned in two of the pieces. He'd been taken in for questioning, but without enough evidence, the police had released him without charge.

"Fucking hell," Chloe whispered to herself as the implications of what she was reading sank in.

She needed to get out of there. Now. But she couldn't stop staring at the noticeboard.

Had Jerry killed that poor woman?

Finally, she tore herself away, ready to leave when a floorboard creaked behind her.

No!

She spun around to find herself face-to-face with the man himself.

"Jerry!"

He was standing in the doorway with a rifle over his shoulder and holding two dead rabbits by their hind legs. Their eyes met, his bloodshot and watery, an unreadable expression on his face.

"Lost, are we?" he growled.

Chapter 15

Chloe's heart jackhammered against her ribs as Jerry stared at her, his thin lips twisting into a half-smile. Standing in the doorway, silhouetted against the late afternoon sun he looked even creepier than usual. As he stepped inside, the door shut behind him, casting the room in shadows.

"You know this is trespassing," he said, looking her up and down. "You know I don't like trespassers."

"Oh, shoot, yes. I'm so sorry," Chloe yelped, her eyes flickering between Jerry and the door. "I was just taking a walk and I happened upon this place. I didn't mean to intrude. I was just . . ." She trailed off. There really was no good explanation for why she was inside the man's house.

"I told you that it was dangerous straying from the main paths. Didn't I tell you that?"

"Yes. You did."

"Hmm."

The half-smile hung on his lips didn't reach his eyes, creating an expression both friendly and menacing. He stepped closer and Chloe instinctively recoiled, her back pressing against the table containing the slab of raw meat.

"Pretty little thing like you shouldn't be wandering around all alone anyway," Jerry continued, his gaze lingering on her mouth, causing her skin to prickle with unease.

"Yes, you're right," she said. "I'll head back straight away and leave you in peace."

Jerry moved closer, his scent of sweat and something metallic mingling with the mustiness of the cabin. Chloe felt her options dwindling, the window of escape narrowing.

"I didn't realize I'd walked this far," she added.

Jerry sneered. "No one ever realizes a lot of things, Miss."

"I'm sorry," she tried, again, her eyes darting towards the noticeboard as she side-stepped away.

Jerry followed her gaze and sniffed violently. "It wasn't me who did those things. It's all lies. Hearsay."

"No! Of course not!" Chloe replied. If she made a dash for it, she could probably reach the door before he grabbed her. Only her legs didn't want to play.

Perhaps second-guessing her, Jerry moved to block her path. "The people from the town think I'm some kind of monster. They think I killed that girl. But it wasn't me."

"Right. Sure. Then why do you have all those clippings?"

Jerry made a low growling noise and looked at his feet as if considering his answer. "I kept these reports as evidence and for research. I'm still investigating the case. Trying to get to the bottom of things." He moved past Chloe to the table and placed the dead rabbits on top. "There's this money-hungry developer, see. He wants to buy my land to build some sort of luxury resort for rich folk. Only I won't sell to him. This murder was his way of trying to force me out, I'm sure of it. But he won't win. He can try and kill me if he wants. But I'll get to him first. He doesn't know these woods like I do. No one does."

A log in the hearth popped, making Chloe jump. Her mind was whirling. It was clear Jerry was a strange old man and Alison had mentioned he was a paranoid conspiracy theorist to boot. This could be just another of his concocted theories. But it could also be the truth.

Of course, the third option was that he'd actually killed that poor girl and was about to do the same to Chloe. But as she regarded him now, she didn't think so. Up close, in his humble dwelling, the old man appeared more vulnerable than before. He was certainly angry about this would-be developer's plans to take his land but maybe that was justified. Up close, his eyes were tired, and his expression one of world-weariness rather than murderous lust.

"You should go," he muttered, shuffling over to the gun rack, and hanging up his rifle. "And best forget you ever saw any of this. I don't appreciate people sniffing around my business. That's the way I am."

"Yes. I understand. I should go."

"You do that," Jerry whispered, almost sweetly, leaning closer, his breath hot against her cheek. He paused then stepped aside gesturing for the door. "Go on then. Off with you."

Chloe didn't need to be told twice. She headed for the door and practically fell out of the cabin without looking back. The afternoon sun was blinding after the dark interior but her legs, although still shaky, carried her swiftly along through the dense forest as she quickened her pace into a run.

Her breathing came in ragged, anxious bursts as she wove between the trees, branches and leaves scraping against her face. As she ran, her thoughts shifted from panic to pragmatism and back again. Jerry's words, his weary eyes, and the unsettling reality of those newspaper clippings morphed into a confusing mush in her mind.

Was he the victim or the villain?

A strange old man or something much more sinister?

Yet, the further she distanced herself from Jerry's cabin, the more an uneasy calm washed over her. She slowed her pace, heart still pounding in her chest, and cast a wary glance over her shoulder. She was half-expecting to see Jerry in the distance, but the path was empty, the old man nowhere in sight.

By the time the rental cabin came into view, its windows now glowing with a welcoming light from inside, Chloe's frantic sprint had dissolved into a measured walk. Approaching the edge of the clearing, she stopped to catch her breath and ground herself a little more. The sounds of laughter and jovial conversation coming from the cabin buoyed her even further. She decided there and then not to tell the others about her visit to Jerry's cabin. She felt rather foolish all of a sudden and she didn't want to upset them if they were now in a state of fun and relaxation.

As she entered the cabin – making as much noise as possible as she opened the front door, calling out to them so they wouldn't be scared – she was hit by a blast of warm air and the rich, meaty scent of cooked game birds. In the main living area, the others were all sitting around a blazing fire, drinks in hand, laughing and joking.

Ignoring the inquiries about her flushed cheeks and disheveled appearance, she mumbled something about a brisk walk and made a beeline for the bathroom, shutting the door firmly against the sounds of oblivious revelry beyond.

She showered quickly, washing away not only the dirt and grime from her trek through the forest but hopefully the mental residue as well. Steam enveloped her but the images – Jerry's face, the cabin, the newspaper clippings – were still flashing in her mind. She shoved her head under the water.

She didn't need this. Not now. Jerry wasn't a threat. He wasn't. She'd believed him when he said he hadn't had anything to do with that poor woman's death.

Hadn't she?

With her mind wavering, swinging like a pendulum between believing Jerry's haunted warnings and dismissing them as the paranoid delusions of a reclusive man, she twisted off the shower unit and grabbed a towel.

"No more," she told her reflection as she wiped at the steamed-up mirror. "You're here to have fun! You're here for Alison!"

With that, she hurried into her room to get changed.

Chapter 16

Twenty minutes later Chloe was sitting in front of the fire with a cup of white wine spritzer cradled in her lap.

"Great idea to get some rest," Keren told her, with a grin. "I feel like a new girl after that nap. And I'm sorry if I was a bit of a bitch to anyone. I guess I was still in work mode or something." She laughed, everyone else did too.

"It's fine," Alison said. "We get it. I think we're all feeling a lot more chill and ready to party now, right? I know I am."

"Oh, we know you are!" Keren replied, meeting Chloe's gaze. "She's had about three drinks to mine and Jess's one."

Chloe laughed and lifted her cup in salute. "Hey, why not? Let's do this right." But she noticed Jess seemed rather subdued. "Are you okay?" she whispered, leaning in. "Still worried about the car?"

Jess gave a slight shrug. "Yes and no. I still feel a little uneasy that we're stuck here until Sunday. And there are other things, too, but . . . forget about it. I'm fine." She forced a smile. "Let's focus on Alison's weekend. What she wants is more important. Just like always."

This was said so casually Chloe almost missed it. She studied Jess for a few seconds more, trying to get a read on her. There was definitely a hint of malice – of pain, even – in that last comment and she wondered if she should respond. But then Jess lifted her chin and laughed along with something Keren was saying and the moment passed.

"Okay, guys," Alison announced, sitting forward. "I know Truth or Dare went a bit weird yesterday – my fault – but we can still pull this around, right?"

The others nodded and mumbled in agreement. "But no more silly games," Chloe said.

"What about Never Have I Ever?" Keren said.

Chloe groaned, expecting the others to do the same. But they all turned and looked at her expectantly.

"Oh, you're serious?" she asked. "Really? That's the game you want to play?"

"Come on Chloe," Keren said. "Give it a shot."

"Yeah, let's," Alison agreed. "It'll be fun."

"Okay, sorry, I just thought . . ."

"Got something to hide, Chloe?" Keren teased, with a grin.

"Not at all . . ."

I just think it's a dumb game for college students, she wanted to add. But she held her tongue and sipped at her wine.

It's Alison's weekend . . .

"Okay, let me start," Jess said. "Never have I ever . . . kissed a guy – or a girl – on the first date." She looked down, avoiding eye contact with the others. Chloe noticed her cheeks flush slightly, but it could have been the heat from the fire.

"*Lame*," Keren sang, taking a drink along with Alison.

Chloe drank too, thinking of a guy called Martin she'd had a one-night stand with two years previously. It had been a fun evening, but she couldn't imagine even thinking about doing something like that now. Her thoughts drifted briefly to Rob before she shook them away.

"Okay, my turn," Chloe said. "Never have I ever . . . been secretly crushing on a friend."

Eyes flicked towards her. The atmosphere tightened. Keren shifted as if she was thinking hard about something.

"Wait a minute," Alison said, giggling. "Is this about that hot guy who gave you a ride up here, Chloe? Shit, it is, isn't it?"

Chloe grimaced, but laughing now too. "I don't know. *May-be* . . ."

"Ha! I knew it. And yes, you should drink because he was hot! What was his name again?"

Chloe looked away and took a big swig of wine. "Rob. He's called Rob."

"Oh my god, Chloe's in *lurve* . . ." Keren piped up.

"No! He's just a friend."

"A hot friend you want to bone!" Alison hit back.

Chloe drank some more. "All right, I'm done. Move on. Who's next? Keren?"

Keren eyed the others mysteriously as she considered her question. "All right, I've got a good one for you. Never have I ever . . . secretly wanted out of this friendship group."

Chloe gasped as a hush gripped the room, each of the girls' red cups remaining away from their mouths. Eyes darted around the circle, everyone searching everyone else's face for a sign, a tell that might betray agreement with Keren's potentially ruinous statement.

"Come on, Keren," Chloe said. "That's taking things a bit far, don't you think? It could go beyond the realms of harmless fun."

Keren stuck out her bottom lip. "I think it's a valid question."

The tension hung in the air. Chloe looked at Alison, hoping this wasn't what was going to push her over the edge once more. But after a second, she shook her head and laughed.

"Typical Keren, always with the jokes." But her voice wavered, and her gaze lingered a moment too long on her Maid of Honor. "But I guess it is a valid question. Hell, who hasn't wanted out a few times over the years, am I right? That's the nature of friendship groups, especially ones that are so close. So, yeah, I'm going to drink." And she did so, adding, "I'd suggest everyone here should. It's not a problem. Don't we all find other people tricky to deal with every now and again?"

Chloe couldn't help but nod in agreement. Jess did too. They drank in unison.

"Well handled," Chloe whispered to Alison.

"No worries," Alison slurred, wiggling her shoulders in a silly dance of triumph. Yet Chloe sensed the tension in the room hadn't quite shifted.

"Now it's your turn, Ali," Jess said. "Let's have a nice easy one, huh?"

"Where's the fun in that?" Keren scoffed.

Chloe adjusted herself on the couch as Alison considered her question. "Okay, here's one," she said, a sly smile forming, her eyes widening. "Never have I ever . . . had feelings for someone who was in a relationship."

Silence descended, no one seemingly wanting to go first. Seeing no one take a drink, Alison scoffed.

"Liars," she said, taking a big gulp from her cup. "Come on. We've all done it, right? Chloe?"

Chloe hesitated. "Mm. I guess, maybe, back in high school. It's not unusual, right?"

"Well, then – drink."

Chloe did as instructed and, after a moment, Keren joined her.

"Yeah, I suppose I have, too. At college," she said. "But it was innocent. He never knew. No one did. I'd say it's only an issue if you act on those feelings."

"Sure," Alison said. "And have you? Ever?"

Keren fixed her with a hard stare. "You know I haven't. I would have told you. I tell you everything."

Alison laughed, a little drunkenly now. "What about you, Jess?"

"Never." But she looked uncomfortable suddenly and Chloe remembered what she'd told her the night before about Ethan and her recent breakup. All this talk of relationships was no doubt a little triggering.

Chloe cleared her throat. "Maybe . . . maybe we should play something else," she suggested. "Or we could just talk? Or put some music on?"

"I need to pee," Jess said, jumping to her feet. "I've got a Bluetooth speaker in my bag, I'll grab it."

"Awesome, sounds good," Alison said, picking up her phone and flicking through to the music player. "A bit of Taylor or Adele would be cool right about now."

"I'd rather have something a little more upbeat," Keren argued. "Some EDM, something we can properly dance to."

"Well, whatever," Chloe said, patting the air in a pre-emptive gesture. "We don't need to argue about it, we've got all night. We can play everything."

"Totally," Keren said, standing. "I'm going to get a refill. Does anyone else want a drink?"

"I'm good," Alison said.

"Yeah, you probably do need to slow down a little," Keren told her, receiving a derisive but playful snort in return. "Chloe?"

"I'll get myself one in a bit," she said. "Thanks, though."

Loud rap music blared out across the room as Jess reappeared carrying a speaker that seemed too small to be making so much noise.

"It's Drake's new album," she said, beaming. "It's awesome."

Alison raised an eyebrow. "It's not exactly party music though, is it?" she said, immediately going over to Jess and grabbing the speaker from her. "Here, let me connect my phone. I've got just the playlist."

Jess looked crushed for a moment, then she looked angry, then she smiled and seemed to let it go. Chloe, sensing more tension on the horizon, made her way to the drinks table. Maybe she would get that second drink after all.

"Check this out," Alison called over. "Olivia Rodrigo's new track. It's amazing." She hit play and began to dance around as a strutting bassline bounced off the walls. Chloe wasn't particularly a fan, but the tune was undeniably infectious. As she tuned into the lyrics, however – about hooking up with an ex-boyfriend and making bad decisions – she began to wonder if in some way Alison was trying to tell them something. Given her rather inappropriate Never Have I Ever question, and the odd way she'd been acting since they got here, it could be interpreted that Alison wanted to get something off her chest.

Chloe recalled how flirtatious Alison had been with a guy called Blake from their acting class the last time she'd attended. Was it Alison who was making bad decisions? Blake wasn't an ex, but Alison had never mentioned any ex-boyfriends to Chloe. There was Tony, the high-school boyfriend Jess had told her about. But he'd been killed in an accident and was no threat to Noah. But was Blake? Come to think of it, he had reciprocated Alison's flirtatious behavior, and he was super-hot.

Could they have . . . ? Shoot.

If she'd only been with Tony and then Noah, maybe Alison felt like she hadn't had enough experience and wanted more adventure before tying the knot. Was that why she was acting weird whenever the wedding or Noah was mentioned?

No, Chloe!

Stop that!

It was mere speculation, her imagination going into overdrive. She dismissed the idea and put her attention into fixing herself a fresh drink.

"Hey! That's mine!" Chloe looked up to see Alison snatching a red cup out of Jess's hand.

"Woah! Calm it. I didn't know," Jess snapped back. She frowned but it was an expression of confusion rather than anger. "That was your drink?"

"Yes! I only put it down for one second," Alison said, laughing and shaking her head but unable to shake the tension in her voice. "You silly goose, Jess!"

"Right . . . It's just . . ."

"No harm done," Alison said, nudging her. "Come on, let's dance."

Chloe refilled her glass, her gaze drifting over to Jess who was swaying to the music, albeit a bit awkwardly, while Alison and Keren danced around her with abandon. They were in high spirits, their laughter infectious. Chloe poured herself a half cup of white wine but decided to skip the club soda this time around. No point diluting the fun, right? The wine was lukewarm and a little tart for her taste, but it was alcohol, and she was more determined than ever to get into the party spirit.

"Hey, has anyone explored this bureau, yet?" Alison's voice carried over the music. She motioned to the large, weathered piece of furniture next to the refrigerator.

"It's probably just full of dust and old junk," Keren yelled back. "I doubt Jerry's got any treasures stashed away in there. And if he has, I don't want to see what it is."

But Alison didn't reply. She'd opened one of the drawers and was now staring into it. As Chloe watched, she reached down and lifted something out with shaking hands.

"Guys . . ." she called out, not turning around and with all the cheeriness gone from her voice. "I think you need to take a look at this!"

Chapter 17

Chloe wandered over to get a better look, sensing the atmosphere in the room shifting again. Alison stood motionless in front of the bureau cradling an old wooden box.

Keren approached too, her voice heavy with intrigue. "What have you got there?"

"I—I don't know," Alison said, swaying slightly as she carried the box over to the dining table and carefully, almost reverently, placed it down. "But it's creeping me the fuck out."

Everyone gathered around the table, their curiosity drawing them in as Alison stepped back and switched off the music before blowing out a breath as if trying to calm herself.

Chloe's first thought was this was just Alison and her flair for drama, amplified further by too many cocktails. But as she leaned over and peered into the dusty wooden box, she quickly changed her mind.

The box was full of magazine articles and catalog clippings, now yellowed with age, each displaying an image of a woman in bridal wear. There were brides through the ages. Eighties brides, nineties brides, some more modern – their gowns elegant and their expressions serene and happy, ignorant of their inclusion in this bizarre collection. To further add to the weirdness, an old garter lay on top of the pile, its elastic slackened, but its lace still intact. As Chloe reached in and leafed through the papers, she found some postcards displaying bridal wear from the sixties and seventies, along with more folded shiny pages advertising bridal underwear.

"Woah . . ."

"What the hell is going on?" Jess said, going up on her toes to get a better look. "Is this Jerry's stuff? Is he obsessed with . . . brides?" She brought her hand to her mouth, stifling a gasp. "This is so messed up!"

"Wait, it could be innocent enough," Alison said. "But then . . . shit. Now I think about it, I did think it was a bit odd . . ."

"What?" Jess gasped.

"Well, my mom mentioned that Jerry wasn't the best at replying to emails," she continued. "So, I was a little shocked when he got back to me so quickly and agreed to let us rent the place. But maybe this is why. In my email, I told him it was for my bachelorette party. He knows I'm going to be a bride."

"Now, come on," Chloe said. "This box has most likely been left here by some previous renter. Considering the nature of this cabin, I imagine Jerry has a lot of bachelorette parties and bridal showers staying here. He probably doesn't even know this box exists."

But even as she was saying this her mind was racing with images of Jerry's other cabin: the guns, the slab of raw meat, the newspaper cuttings. A detail in one of the articles flashed up in her recall. She'd brushed over it at the time, not believing it to be relevant, but she was almost certain she'd read that the female hiker whose body had been found in the lake was set to marry the year she was found.

Coincidence? Probably.

But the thought still made her feel nauseous.

"Chloe's right," Keren added. "Or maybe it belonged to an ex-wife or girlfriend of Jerry's. Or his sister. We don't know anything about him. He could have been married once."

"No. It's weird." Jess nudged in between Chloe and Keren, jabbing her finger at the box. "Why keep it at all, though? This creepy old garter, the photos and catalogs going back thirty years . . . What if he was jilted at the altar or something and now lures women here who are getting married so he can kill them? He destroys what he couldn't have himself."

"Shit!" Alison exclaimed. "That's terrifying."

"Maybe we're overthinking this," Chloe told them. "We don't know anything for sure and jumping to wild conclusions isn't helpful. But . . . well, there is something I should probably tell you . . ."

Everyone spun around to look at her.

"What is it?" Jess whispered.

"When I was out walking before, I stumbled across Jerry's other cabin," she started, unsure if she was doing the right thing by telling them but unable to stop herself. "He wasn't there but the door was open, and I ended up going inside."

"You did what!?" Jess cried. "Are you crazy? What if he came back?"

Chloe grimaced. "He kind of did."

"What the . . . ?" Keren exclaimed, her expression a mixture of shock and excitement. "What did you do?"

"Not much I could do. He caught me in there," Chloe went on. "I was pretty scared at first, but it wasn't too bad. He wasn't as angry as I was expecting him to be, in fact, he was sort of resigned to it. But before he came back, I saw something on his wall, some old news clippings about a female hiker that had been found dead in these woods a few years back." She swallowed, not wanting to meet anyone's gaze despite sensing the three pairs of eyes all burning into her. "Turns out she was due to get married as well."

"Jesus Christ!" Jess yelped. "We need to get out of here! We're in danger. Jerry . . . He's going to . . . We'll be . . ."

"Hey, hey . . . HEY!" Keren held her hands up. "Stop this! Now! I mean it!"

"She's right," Chloe said. "We're likely getting ourselves all worked up over nothing. This isn't some silly horror movie. I'm sure there's a perfectly reasonable explanation."

"But maybe we should all go and search the other cabin," Alison said, her voice rising excitedly. "See if there are any other . . . clues."

"Don't talk dumb!" Keren snapped. "This is total bullshit. You know, I thought better of you, Chloe. I thought you were sensible."

"I am!" Chloe hit back. "But I know what I saw. Plus, there were a bunch of guns and weapons and a huge piece of raw meat just sitting around on his bench." The second the words were out of her mouth she regretted them. She'd allowed herself to get caught up in the bitchy atmosphere, only making matters worse as Jess let out a whimper.

"Oh, great!" she muttered. "Jerry eats people. He's a cannibal. He's going to eat us. He's going to kill us and eat us."

"Are you just trying to scare us, Chloe?" Alison waved a finger at her. "Is that what this is about? Is this funny for you?" She rounded on Jess before Chloe could reply. "And you're no help, Jess, getting all fucking dramatic at every opportunity!"

"*I'm* getting dramatic?" Jess yelled back. "Are you actually serious right now, Alison? You might want to take a look at yourself if we're talking drama. And also, what is with you and—"

"Go to hell, Jess!" Alison spat. "You're enjoying this, aren't you? Ruining my weekend with all your histrionics and bullshit!"

"Wow! Histrionics? Big word!" Jess screamed back. "I'm just sick of feeling terrified out here in the wilderness. And . . . oh look, we're still stuck here. With no way of calling for help!"

Chloe stepped between the two of them. "Listen, we don't need to call for help because no one's in trouble," she said, focusing on keeping her tone low and calm. "Please, can we all take a step back."

"Maybe this is all a big prank?" Alison said, unrelenting. "Is that it? Is this one of you trying to get at me for some reason? Have I hurt you in some way?"

"Stop it, Alison," Chloe said, lowering her chin to meet her gaze. "Everyone here loves you. We're here for you. Right guys?"

She looked around the group. Everyone was full of adrenaline, their chests rising and falling as their breaths came in short, rapid gasps.

Keren finally broke the silence, her voice steady. "Of course we're here for you," she said, giving Alison's arm a squeeze. "I'm sorry for getting all hyped up. And I'm sorry to you, too, Chloe. I didn't mean anything by it. I guess we all got a bit too caught up in the drama."

Everyone bowed their heads and nodded in agreement. "Sorry, everyone," Jess said. "I don't mean to worry people."

"No. Neither do I," Alison added.

"Okay, cool," Keren said, reaching over and firmly closing the mysterious box. "So, we've agreed – there's no sinister goings on. We're just a group of friends trying to enjoy ourselves. Can we focus on that?"

Chloe nodded. "Absolutely." And she meant it. But as the evening continued, with drinks refilled and the conversation shifting to lighter subjects, she couldn't shake a lingering unease.

They only had two more days here and then she'd be back in New York. But maybe that was the problem and, if so, it wasn't any easier to deal with. If anything, it was scarier. She'd rather spend a night with Jerry in his cabin than have to deal with the crushing pressure of an uncertain future. She still had so much shit to deal with, and so much to consider, but for now, the party was back in full swing and she intended to lose herself in it for a while longer.

And with that thought fresh in her mind, she gulped down her cup of wine and poured herself a new one.

Chapter 18

Chloe sat bolt upright in bed, her heart pounding in her chest at the shock of being wrenched from her sleep. She blinked into the darkness, feeling unsettled, panicked even. Was she experiencing the tail end of a nightmare?

She blinked into the gloom. It felt as if she'd been dreaming about something horrible, the shadow of it still on the cusp of her consciousness, but the details had faded the second she'd opened her eyes.

She glanced around the room. Beside her, heavy-sleeper-Jess was breathing soundly in deep slumber. She listened into the darkness.

Had something woken her?

She leaned forward. It wasn't fair she was feeling like this now. Just a few hours earlier she'd been enjoying what she might describe as the quintessential bachelorette party. Once the group had settled down and agreed to stop scaring each other, they'd danced, made cocktails, ate the roast game birds, and chatted and laughed until well after midnight. Spirits had been lifted and anxieties dissolved in a heady mix of alcohol, camaraderie, and high voices. The highlight had been them taking turns inhaling helium from the party balloons, collapsing in hysterical laughter as their voices transformed into cartoonish pitches. Jess especially sounded like a long-lost Muppet. It had been a perfect distraction; exactly what Chloe had yearned for.

Yet here she was again, with a racing heartbeat, troubled with anxious thoughts. She inhaled deeply, attempting to calm her system so she could get back to sleep. It was just a bad dream, she told herself.

But then it came. A blood-curdling scream that sent a shiver down Chloe's spine.

It was no dream.

It was real.

Chloe thrust the covers aside and leaped out of bed, grabbing up her phone and using the light from the screen to guide her to the light switch. She flicked it on. Nothing happened. She tried again. Same result. The generator was out.

Not good.

Not good at all!

Seizing Jess's sturdy golf umbrella for protection, Chloe hurriedly made her way down the corridor. Keren was exiting her bedroom at the same time using her phone as a flashlight, and they burst into Alison's room together. They found her sitting upright in bed, sheets clutched tightly against her, eyes fixed on the window. Keren tried the light switch to no avail as Chloe moved into the room, the umbrella raised in readiness.

"There was someone there . . ." Alison stammered, her voice rising in panic. "A face . . . right outside!"

A groggy-looking Jess appeared in the doorway "What's going on?" she mumbled. "The lights are all out."

"Yes, we know," Keren said, going to Alison and holding her. "Ali thinks she saw someone at the window. It's alright, you're safe. We're all here with you."

"You sure it wasn't just a bad dream?" Jess asked, echoing what Chloe was thinking.

"NO!" Alison yelled. "I heard a noise. It woke me and when I looked out, there was movement outside."

"A person?" Keren asked.

"It looked like a person!" She started to sob.

Keren shared a look with Chloe, the dim light from her phone revealing a skeptical expression. The unspoken message was clear. Alison had probably been startled by an owl or perhaps a stray tree branch banging against the cabin. Whatever it was, neither of them appeared entirely convinced by Alison's version of events.

"It was probably just an animal," Chloe tried, keeping her voice steady. "Or maybe you just . . ."

But her proclamations died in her throat as Alison shot her a look of pure anger. "Oh yeah, Chloe? And how do you account for the power outage?"

Chloe shifted uncomfortably, her gaze dropping. "The cabin's old. I think it runs on a generator that's probably ancient. I really don't think that—"

"I know what I saw!" Alison snapped. "There was someone out there."

A collective breath hung suspended in the air. Keren got up off the bed and moved over to stand next to Chloe.

"Why don't we go check it out?" Keren suggested, finding Chloe's hand and giving it a squeeze.

"Okay, yeah. Good plan," Chloe agreed.

Wrapping herself tighter in her blanket, Alison shuffled over as Jess climbed onto the bed beside her. "You both be careful out there."

"We will."

Chloe activated the flashlight on her phone and she and Keren made their way through the shadowy cabin.

"I'm pretty sure there's a generator down the side," Keren said. "I noticed it on the first day."

"If so, we should be able to see what the issue is pretty quickly," Chloe replied. "With old places like this, it's likely a single bulb burning out tripped the entire system."

She unlocked the front door, and they stepped out onto the porch, standing shoulder to shoulder as they threw their flashlight beams left and right.

"I don't see anyone," Chloe said.

"Me neither."

The night air was chilly as they stepped down onto the driveway and moved as one around the side of the house.

"Do you know what you're looking at if we find the generator," Keren whispered.

Before Chloe could answer, her flashlight beam landed on their target. Under the side elevation of the cabin, directly in front of them, was an old gasoline generator, the sort she recognized from past vacations with her family.

Rushing over to it, Chloe passed her phone to Keren and used both her hands to wrestle open the weathered casing. Memories of her dad showing her how to use one flashed in her mind. He'd shared many life skills with Chloe over the years. He'd taught her how to fish, how to shoot, how to read a map and compass. How to skin and cook game. How to restart a generator – and attach one to the fuel canister. She was his first-born daughter and he'd made sure she was equipped with as many life skills as possible. He was a good man, and she made a mental note to call him and arrange a visit as soon as she got back to civilization.

Refocusing on the task at hand, she traced the fuel line and found the connection loose. Probably the thread was old or a critter had been trying to chew through it. Either way, it was easily fixed.

"Yay! You did it!" Keren cried as Chloe screwed the line tight and the security lights around the cabin flashed on. Standing up on her toes she peered through the window. "Yep. The inside is lit too. We did it."

For a moment, relief flickered in Keren's eyes as she patted Chloe on the arm. But it was short-lived. As Chloe turned to head back inside Keren froze, her expression suddenly alarmed.

"What is it?" Chloe asked, spinning around to look the way Keren was facing. "What's wrong?"

"There," Keren said, dropping her voice to a whisper. "On the ground at the back of the cabin."

Chloe saw what she was looking at and her heart dropped into her stomach. Footprints. In the dirt. Men's footprints from their size and shape.

"All right,' Chloe whispered urgently, gripping Keren's wrist. "We need to get back inside. Now."

Chapter 19

Chloe kept a hold of Keren until they reached the front of the cabin. Once there she stopped and turned to look her in the eye.

"Listen, Keren, we don't know how long those footprints have been there," she said. "They looked quite worn to me."

"How can you tell?" Keren hissed, eyes darting around her, peering into the dense undergrowth.

"I just can," Chloe lied. "And I don't think it's going to help the situation inside if we tell the others what we've seen. Alison and Jess are already on edge. They don't need any more reasons to freak out tonight."

"But what if Alison's right? What if someone really was watching her? Watching all of us?" Keren's usual husky voice was laced with anxiety.

"There was no one watching us," Chloe snapped. But she was aware she was trying to convince herself just as much. "Those footprints are likely to be Jerry's from days ago, maybe even longer. This is his cabin, remember. Or they could even have been made by whoever stayed here before us. It's not rained for at least a month so it's more than plausible."

Keren wrapped her arms around herself, searching for warmth or comfort. "I suppose you could be right."

"I am right."

But Keren didn't seem convinced. "Don't you think there have been too many weird things happening since we got here? Too many . . . coincidences."

Chloe thought about it. "Maybe. But that's all they are – coincidences. We've all got a little jumpy and now we're perceiving every occurrence through this filter of fear, like we're in some cheesy horror movie. I think as a group we're magnifying situations, allowing our collective anxieties to make neutral, unconnected events seem more sinister than they actually are."

She thought again of Rob's analogy of the shitty glasses. Was it a similar situation here? Were they all just wearing fear-tinted *scary* glasses?

While Chloe hoped that was the case, it didn't diminish the uneasy feeling in the pit of her stomach.

"We should head inside and get some sleep," she said. "I guarantee everything will look better in the morning. It always does."

Keren forced a smile. "I hope so."

They went inside, Keren leading the way and Chloe casting her gaze once more around the clearing. There was no one in sight. No one there watching them.

We're wearing scary glasses. That's all.

She hurried back inside and locked the door behind her, giving it another good shake to check the lock. It held fast and she moved down the corridor back into the living space. Keren was nowhere to be seen but she could hear her voice coming from the hallway leading to the bedrooms. She grabbed herself a glass of water and headed that way, finding Keren leaning against Alison's doorframe.

"I was just asking her if she wanted me to sleep in her bed with her," Keren said, nodding at Alison as Chloe approached. "But she says she's fine."

"She is fine," Chloe said, putting her head around the side and grinning at Alison. "We're all fine. Nothing to worry about."

Keren sighed. "Well, if you're sure." She looked at Chloe, a strange expression on her face as she backed away toward her room. "I guess we should get some rest. Try and salvage what remains of the weekend."

"I'm sorry, guys," Alison called out. "I don't want to ruin everyone's fun."

"You're not, Ali," Keren called back, but her eyes, still fixed on Chloe's, said otherwise. "See you in the morning."

"Goodnight," Chloe added, leaning around and easing Alison's door closed. "We're right here if you need us."

Keren remained in the hallway outside her room and looked as if she wanted to say something else, but Chloe shuffled past her before she had the chance. "I'm wiped out," she said. "Let's speak in the morning."

Keren sniffed and mumbled something inaudible as Chloe proceeded to her room. There, she found Jess sitting up in bed, wide awake.

"I heard you," she whispered. "Just now. Through the window."

"Oh?" Chloe shut the door.

"What was it you saw? I heard Keren say something about 'on the ground.'"

Chloe sat on the edge of her bed, slumping her shoulders as she did. "We saw a few old footprints," she said, unable to think of anything else to say but the truth. "But they were most likely made a while ago. Jerry's probably, or some other person who stayed here. It really is nothing to worry about . . ."

"I want to go home," Jess said, her tone soft but resolute. "I've had enough of this weekend. It sucks. I want to be back in the city, I want . . . I want Ethan . . ." She turned away; her brief moment of resolve wiped away by the tears now rolling down her face. "I hate this. I hate being here. I hate having to think about Alison and Noah and the wedding when I've got . . . When I'm . . . It just sucks . . ."

Chloe massaged her tense neck, hesitating on whether to go over and console Jess. She chose to remain where she was.

"I get it. This must be hard for you," she said. "But it's only two more nights. And we all love Alison, yeah? We want her to have a good time."

"Yeah, but who the hell is having a good time?! She isn't!"

A heavy silence fell between them, punctuated only by Jess's intermittent sobs. Chloe leaned forward, the bed groaning softly under her movement.

"Listen, Jess. We've already paid for this weekend. We're here now. And who knows? Perhaps tomorrow we might see things differently. I admit we've had some odd moments over the last twenty-four hours, but there isn't anything to worry about." She watched Jess for a reaction, and when none came, she continued. "We're safe here, Jess. The doors are locked, and we're all together. No one is outside. I'm certain of it. So, let's get back to sleep. Tomorrow, we'll talk to Alison and Keren about heading into town and getting someone to fix your car, okay? Would that make you feel better?"

Jess sniffed but then nodded. "I guess so." She lay down and rolled over onto her side. "Goodnight."

"Sweet dreams, Jess," Chloe whispered, climbing under the covers and settling herself.

She closed her eyes, but her thoughts revolved around the events of the last two days. The brittle tension in the cabin and the strange goings on outside of it meshed together in her mind.

Was she downplaying the events? Or overthinking them?

Either way, she couldn't help but feel the same as Jess. What she wouldn't give to be going home first thing tomorrow morning, rather than on Sunday evening. Just two more days, then she'd see Rob again. Her Rob . . .

And with the comforting image of his dark wavy hair and heartwarming smile replacing the more unsettling thoughts, she drifted into a sound sleep.

Chapter 20

Saturday

Bright sunshine filtered through the curtainless window, shining onto Chloe's pillow and waking her. She turned over, trying to escape the morning rays but they were too bright, too hot to ignore. Letting out a groan she rolled onto her back and reached for her phone. It was only a few minutes past eight and she didn't feel as if she'd had anything like the requisite amount of rest. She'd woken three times in the night and had struggled to fall back to sleep each time, the experience leaving her feeling hollow and like her skin was made of paper.

Chloe blinked at the ceiling, aware now of a feeling of dread resting on her chest and in her stomach. It was no doubt remnants of another forgotten anxiety dream, but it didn't help matters.

But then she remembered . . .

The last dream she'd had before waking, the one that had probably led to her feeling this way . . .

She'd been dreaming of that day by the lake. Closing her eyes now she could still see the scene in her mind. Her treading water, trying to stay afloat. His face as he gasped for air. Then the sirens, the shouts. The wails.

Damn it.

When she was awake there were endless things she could do to distract herself from painful memories. But not so easy when asleep.

She turned her head, trying to focus on the moment, on what was real, only to discover Jess was already awake and staring at her.

"Oh? How are you doing?" Chloe asked, sitting up. "Did you sleep okay?"

She suspected both questions were rather pointless, but she was still good at the old distraction techniques.

Jess shook her head, loose strands of hair sticking to the sweat on her forehead. "Not really. I kept hearing noises."

"Oh, shit," Chloe said, throwing off the covers and swinging her legs onto the floor. "I mean, we are out in the wilderness, so there will be noises."

"We need to talk to the others," Jess said, propping herself up, "about heading into town today and getting my car fixed."

"We will," Chloe said, giving her the most reassuring smile that she could muster. "It'll be fine, Jess. I swear it. Once we get into town and among people, I think our reactions to the events of the last few days will feel pretty silly. We'll probably be laughing at ourselves come supper time."

"I hope you're right."

Chloe got up off the bed and got dressed, glad the decision had been made. They'd walk into town, arrange for someone to come fix Jess's car, and everyone would feel a whole lot more relaxed. She was also looking forward to being able to use her phone.

Once she had a decent signal, she planned on calling Rob and asking him if he'd pick her up a little earlier than arranged. If he came for her at lunchtime tomorrow, they'd be back in the city by late afternoon. Even if there hadn't been all the other stuff to deal with, being forced into the role of the sensible one of the group was pretty draining. She couldn't wait to get out of here. Plus, if Rob did pick her up earlier, there'd be enough time they could maybe go for some food. Or a movie, even. Maybe she'd suggest it when she called him. It would be good to hear his voice, regardless.

The thought buoyed her as she pulled on a sweater and walked into the main space to grab some breakfast. Jess had dressed also and followed her through.

"Shall I put on a pot of coffee?" Chloe asked.

"God, yes!" Jess sighed. "I need to wake up. I need caffeine!"

Chloe retrieved the French press from the counter and put some water on to boil while she searched the cabinets for coffee. She found it in the one next to the window and was scooping heaped spoonfuls into the press when Alison entered.

"Hey girlies!" she sang. "Hope you both slept well!"

Chloe almost did a double take. Alison's bright eyes and glowing skin were in stark contrast to how Chloe was feeling, but it was Alison's breezy demeanor – as if nothing had happened last night – that was most startling.

"I'm glad you're up and about already," she went on. "I've just knocked on Keren's door to wake her. I was thinking we need to make the absolute most of these last two days."

Chloe met Jess's gaze. "Sure, yeah. Absolutely. It's just we were thinking—"

"It's a glorious day outside," Alison went on, seemingly oblivious to Chloe's interjection. "Sunny for this time of year. We should go for a proper walk, a better one than yesterday. Just four besties enjoying nature and each other's company. Sounds great, right?"

Jess opened her mouth but shut it again. She looked at Chloe, perhaps hoping she'd say something regarding their plan to walk into town. But how could she? Alison seemed so taken with the idea, and this was still her special weekend.

Chloe felt a surge of empathy for Alison. This bachelorette party was supposed to be a time of joy and celebration. But first Hannah didn't show up and now everyone was stressed out and keen to get away as soon as possible. Alison was a good person. She deserved better than this.

Chloe rolled her shoulders back. Maybe with the sun shining it might just be what they needed to shift the mood. They still had the opportunity to make this trip special. She was about to express this to Alison and Jess when Keren stumbled into the room.

"What the hell is going on?" she mumbled, her hair tumbling over her face. "Isn't it a little early for all this noise?" She staggered over to the kitchen area to join them, the dark circles under her eyes a major clue to her foul mood. It appeared she'd had as lousy a night's sleep as Chloe and Jess had.

"We're going out for another walk!" Alison announced. "We've got two whole days left and I want to make the most of it. Plus, the exercise will help lift our spirits."

Keren opened her mouth, no doubt ready to unleash a torrent of reasons why this was a bad idea when Chloe placed a hand on her arm. She moved in front of her, urging her silently to not say whatever it was she was planning on saying.

"The fresh air will do us good, Keren."

"Will it?" she muttered. "You said that yesterday, you keep saying it. You're all positivity and light, aren't you, Chloe? But it doesn't seem to do any good."

Chloe leaned in, whispering so only Keren could hear. "Let's just give it a shot. It might help clear our heads. And remember, this is Alison's weekend. You're her Maid of Honor."

Keren glared at Chloe. "Fine," she sneered. "Then I suppose I'd better get dressed."

Chapter 21

The air wasn't as warm as the bright sunshine suggested but it was still a nicer day than the previous one and Chloe felt a lightness in her step as they began their journey from the cabin, heading eastward. A revitalizing freshness hung in the air. The sharp scent of pine mingled with the earthiness of the forest floor and the occasional aroma of wildflowers.

It was a good day, Chloe thought. It was going to be a good day.

"I'm so sorry about last night," Alison said as they made their way through a sea of large ferns that came up to waist height. "I definitely saw something, but it might have just been a trick of the light."

"We've all been a tad on edge," Chloe replied, casting a fleeting glance towards Keren and Jess. "It's understandable, but we need to be careful of getting too overexcited from now on. Let's focus on what we know to be true, not what our imaginations are telling us."

"You were just as bad, Chloe," Jess cut in. "I could see it in your face last night. You were shitting it."

Chloe coughed. This felt rather harsh coming from Jess, but she chose to rise above it. "Maybe I was a little scared. But I'm happy to admit that. And today's a new day. I feel like we made the right choice staying put."

"Why? Who wanted to leave?" Alison said, suddenly stopping and spinning around.

Shit!

Chloe blew out her cheeks, mentally cursing herself for the slip.

"No one wanted to leave," she said. "Jess and I were . . . umm . . . wondering about maybe walking into town to see if we could find a mechanic. But that was last night. Today, we're fine here. Right, Jess?"

Jess snorted. "Whatever."

"Don't worry, Rob will be able to fix your car when he gets here tomorrow, I'm sure of it," Chloe continued. "And look – we're outside in such glorious surroundings. Where else would we want to be?"

"Exactly!" Alison said. "By my reckoning, if we continue along this path we'll get to the lake soon enough. I was thinking of some skinny dipping to reconnect with nature."

"Oh . . . ? Sure." But on hearing the word 'lake', Chloe's spirits plummeted.

It was going to be a good day.

Famous last words, huh?

"Is something wrong?" Keren asked, nudging Chloe as they set off walking once more.

"What do you mean?"

"You just don't look so happy all of a sudden."

"It's fine. I'm just not a big swimmer, that's all."

"I see. It's just you were the one who so desperately wanted Alison to have her own way. Yet now it seems you aren't too keen."

Chloe raised her head, trying to ignore the bitchy comment. “I’m fine.”

But as they pressed on, Chloe could sense Keren’s scrutiny. Her gut churned.

“You don’t seem fine,” Keren said, after a little while.

Chloe glanced at her, and all at once she felt a surge of vulnerability. Maybe sharing her story would help. Maybe it was time.

It couldn’t make her feel any worse.

“I had a bad experience at a lake like this one,” Chloe began, her voice croaky. “Like I told you already, I used to go camping with my family when I was little. Me, my mom and dad, my kid sister, Blair. It was awesome. I loved it. I learned a lot.”

She sucked in a deep breath. Was she really going to tell Keren what had happened?

Could she? Should she?

But the genie was almost out of the bottle now. And it wasn’t as if she hadn’t talked about this before because she had. Many, many times and with multiple therapists.

“My uncle and his kids often came with us on these trips. I was a year older than my cousin, Sam, but we got on well. Always competing, always laughing. We had a great time on those vacations. It was a week or so out in the country, filled with camping, hiking, and bonding. Sometimes we stayed in log cabins just like Jerry’s place. But that one summer – the summer when it happened – was centered around water activities. My dad and uncle had planned river crossings, fishing, lake swimming, that sort of thing. I remember Sam and I were having the best time. I think I was twelve and he was eleven and I'd beaten him in most of the events. On our last day, Sam decided he wanted to race me across this lake. It seemed calm enough, but what we didn't know was that it was the source of a river and had a heavy undercurrent in places."

Chloe paused as they navigated through a dense cluster of trees. Up ahead, Alison turned around and walked backward for a few steps, urging them to keep up with a big grin on her face. Chloe waved back, her pulse echoing in her ears.

"What happened?" Keren asked.

"Everything was fine initially," Chloe continued. "Sam and I were both strong swimmers. I remember he was a little way in front of me. I think I was letting him win after all the fuss he'd made about losing the other events. He was laughing and splashing me but then out of nowhere the current got stronger. It caught us both off guard, but I was able to swim back to calmer waters in time. Not Sam. He was in too deep, and it pulled him under. I watched, frozen, as he struggled to right himself. I tried to reach out, to pull him back, but the current was too strong. By the time our parents had realized what was going on and dived in after us, Sam had disappeared beneath the surface. He never came back up. They think maybe he got his leg wrapped in some river weeds, or something. His body was found a few hours later once the police and medics arrived."

"Fuck," Keren whispered. "I had no idea, Chloe. I'm so sorry."

"It's okay. I think maybe it's good I'm talking about it. It's been in the back of my mind since I knew I was coming away this weekend. You see, I've not stayed in a cabin or been near a forest since. We didn't see much of my uncle and aunt after that, either.

Sam was their only child and although no one ever said it to me, I think they held me responsible. As I was the oldest, they thought I'd instigated the race. They blamed me. I blamed me, too. For a long time."

"That sucks. And listen, if you don't want to go to this lake, I think Alison will understand . . ."

"No. It's fine. I want to go. For Alison."

She smiled. A real, genuine, demon-killer of a smile. It felt surprisingly good to have spoken these things out loud. She felt lighter. But Keren seemed to be struggling to know what to say. To save her awkwardness, Chloe quickened her pace to try to catch up with Alison and Jess.

As she got closer, she caught the tail end of their conversation and heard Alison telling Jess, "It's not what you think."

Worried the jovial mood had descended back into bitchiness and back-biting she was ready to jump in with words of placation – *what a great day it is to be outside*, that sort of thing – but then they stumbled into a wide clearing and all talk ceased.

Chloe's heart lurched into her throat as Alison stifled a gasp, her hand instinctively flying to her mouth.

In front of them, hanging from a tall tree and swaying gently in the breeze was an old wedding dress.

"What the hell is this?" Jess gasped. The dress looked to be vintage, from a bygone era. Its once white bodice was now dirty and torn, its intricate lace and appliqued stitching ripped in places.

"Jesus . . ." Keren muttered in Chloe's ear. "This is . . . messed up."

Chloe nodded, her eyes transfixed on the fluttering hem of the dress. She felt as if she should say something, to ease the tension and fear now clinging to the four of them. But there were no words. She had nothing to add. Any way that she looked at this it was creepy as hell.

Chapter 22

Jess spoke first, her usually wavering voice now stern and resolute. "That's it!" she said, finding her legs at the same time, and backing out of the clearing. "We need to get out of here."

"Wait!" Chloe called after her. "We should stay together."

But Jess was already on the move. Leaving the macabre wedding dress hanging in the clearing the others chased after her, pushing through the tangled undergrowth as it lashed at their legs and low branches scratched at their cheeks and foreheads.

It was Alison who reached her first, grabbing her friend's arm to halt her frantic escape. "Jessica! Wait!" she snapped. "Where the hell do you think you're going?"

"I'm walking into town," Jess replied, her eyes wild with emotion as she took in all three women. "Or at least until I find a main road and get a signal on my cell."

"And who are you planning to call?" Keren asked.

The question seemed to faze Jess momentarily. She stepped back and shook her head. "Well . . . the cops."

"The cops!" Alison repeated, a faint smirk playing across her face now as she looked at Chloe. "And tell them . . . what, exactly?"

"That we just saw . . . That there's a . . ." Jess pointed back the way they'd come, into the clearing, at the hanging dress. "It's not normal . . . . It's . . . ." She trailed off and wiped at her eyes with the heel of her hand, leaving dirty smears on her cheeks. "Fuck! I just want to go home!"

Alison pulled Jess into a comforting embrace. "I get it, hon. It's terrifying. I have no idea why that dress was placed there but I do not like it – at all." She held Jess at arm's length to look her in the face. "But you can't go marching off on your own like that. You could've gotten lost."

"She's right," Chloe patted the trembling Jess on the shoulder. "We're all shaken up by what we just saw, but we need to stick together while we work out what to do. It also doesn't mean Jerry is going to harm any of us. He's a strange old man with even stranger . . . *interests*, but that doesn't mean he's going to hurt any of us." She thought of the newspaper clippings in Jerry's cabin, of what he'd said to her about the poor dead hiker and the land developer. He was certainly a paranoid person, perhaps with an axe to grind against those who'd tried to ruin him, but that didn't make him a deranged killer.

Did it?

"We need to call a mechanic, at least," Jess said, her tone leveling out as the adrenaline subsided.

"I'd say we need to get out of these damned woods first," Keren sneered, stepping past them. "Get back to the cabin and lock ourselves inside until Chloe's boyfriend arrives."

"Hey, he's not my . . ." Chloe started but stopped herself as Keren strode off through the trees.

And didn't we just stress the importance of staying together?

The earlier buoyant mood of the group was now fracturing into fear and bitchiness once again. Paranoia and self-preservation taking over. It was understandable, perhaps, but it certainly wasn't helpful.

"Keren! Slow down." Chloe set off after her. They'd walked in a circle and, recalling the map, she knew there was a steep ravine nearby leading down to the old quarry Jerry had mentioned. The last thing they needed was for one of them to slip and fall while not looking where they were going. "Let's talk about this. All of us!"

"We can do that," Keren called back. "But only once we're safely back inside the cabin with the doors locked."

She wasn't stopping. That was clear. Chloe turned back, gesturing for Alison and Jess to follow them. Jess shook her head. Alison gave a resigned smile.

"Come on, please," Chloe pleaded. "We need to stick together. We'll get inside, regroup, and plan our next steps. Calmly. Okay? We're not ruling anything out, Jess. But let's keep moving. We can't stay out here."

Jess looked at Alison, then back at Chloe. Then with a shrug, she set off, with Alison following behind her. Chloe managed a small smile, relieved. It was something at least. She had no clue what they should do for the best but staying out in the elements wouldn't be top of her list, nor would continuing their journey to the lake.

"I hate it out here," Keren muttered as Chloe got closer. "The bugs, the wet, the vastness of it all. I'm a city girl. I'm someone who likes the nicer things in life. I make no apology for that."

Chloe patted her on the back. "I get it. This isn't what any of us expected."

"I knew we should have gone to Montauk," Keren continued. "Or even the Hamptons. My father's client has a summer house there. We could have rented it for good money. I should have put my foot down. I am the fucking Maid of Honor after all! But oh no, Princess Alison has to have her own way as usual. I mean, sure, it's her bachelorette party but it's supposed to be my job to organize it, right?"

"Usually, yeah, I think so," Chloe said, unsure if agreeing with Keren was helpful or not. Chloe might have been thrust into the role of the 'sensible older one' but that didn't mean she was any good at it.

"She's such a control freak," Keren muttered. "She has to have everything exactly the way she wants it. And perish the day if it's not like that."

"She's great though too, right?" Chloe added. "She's fun, loyal, kind . . ."

"When she wants to be. When it benefits her." Keren shook her head and made a sound halfway between a sigh and a groan. "Shit, I know I'm being a bitch and I shouldn't be so negative. I'm just on edge after getting zero sleep. I'm exhausted and miserable and I just want to go home."

Chloe could empathize with everything Keren was saying but kept silent. As they moved closer to the quarry, the dense forest gave way to a breathtaking view over the ravine. Tendrils of vibrant green ivy crept over the rugged stone. The once industrious quarry, reclaimed by the relentless growth of nature.

But this was what nature was all about, Chloe thought. Both beautiful and dangerous, teetering between serene and macabre. The quarry presented a calm setting but right now it was a little too quiet for Chloe's liking, especially given all that had happened over the last few days. Exposed here on the cliff-side the air was much cooler than in the forest. A chill breeze whipped through the trees that clung precariously to the edge of the ravine. If Chloe strained her neck, she could see the edge of the lake over to the west.

Yep. Time to go.

She hurried after Keren, who had set off down one of the well-beaten paths that would take them back to the cabin.

"Hey, Keren. Wait up," Chloe called out. Glancing over her shoulder she saw Alison and Jess making their way alongside the quarry deep in conversation. The thought of waiting for them crossed her mind, but they seemed engrossed, so she pressed on.

Keren was wading through a boggy area as Chloe caught up with her, a look of sheer disgust crinkling her pristine features. "This is not what I signed up for," she grumbled.

"We're not far from the cabin now," Chloe reassured her. "Once there, we can get showers, and warm ourselves. Who knows, we might still be able to salvage some semblance of fun and—"

"Enough!" Keren snapped, holding her hand up. "I do not want to hear your positive spin on this, Chloe."

"Okay. Fine."

They negotiated the rest of the bog in silence, both focusing on where they were putting their feet, trying to stay upright. Keren got to the other side and waited for Chloe to join her.

"Listen, I'm sorry," she murmured, not making eye contact. "I didn't mean to sound so harsh. I know this hasn't been easy for you either, especially after what happened with your cousin. I can't imagine how that felt."

Chloe smiled. "It was a tough time. But it's in the past. I try not to think about it too much. It's important to keep facing forward, right? Look to the future!"

Keren nodded with a smile. "Let's keep moving."

They set off walking, but as Chloe looked back, she saw Alison and Jess had now stopped and their deep conversation appeared to have descended into an argument. Alison was stabbing a finger into her temple as if informing Jess that she was crazy. In turn, Jess was flapping her arms, pointing back the way they'd come, toward the wedding dress, or the direction of the town. Chloe sucked in a deep breath.

Geez.

Maybe it was time to admit it.

This weekend was a total disaster.

She felt so bad for Alison but maybe if she'd discussed her plans with the group beforehand, they could have come up with a location they could all enjoy. She even wondered what Alison was getting out of being here. Sure, her mom had recommended Jerry's place, but it wasn't Alison's style. She was a party girl, favoring glitter and cocktails over rustic cabins in the wilderness. Maybe she wanted something different but how was that working out for her?

Chloe watched as Alison and Jess argued for a few moments longer before turning around and following on behind Keren.

Damn it.

Why hadn't she taken more notice of her gut instinct? She'd not wanted to come here in the first place. Four girls, all cooped up together with no phones for the weekend – it was bound to end in disaster. There were too many egos at play, too many princesses, and not enough distractions.

Right now, all she wanted to do was get back to the cabin and rest. The lack of decent sleep last night was taking its toll on all of them. Judging by the sky, it was nearing midday. She mentally calculated the hours left before Rob would arrive. Twenty-eight hours to go. The sooner he could get Jess's car running, the sooner they could all say their goodbyes and forget this ill-fated weekend ever happened.

Twenty-eight hours.

She could get through it. But it'd be a lot easier if she slept for a good amount of that time.

She trudged on, keeping her head down and allowing Keren to stride on ahead. She was happier walking alone. It was unclear what Alison and Jess were arguing about, but she decided it best to leave them to sort it themselves. As she walked, she sucked in deep breaths to try to calm her nerves. It almost worked.

Keren was sitting on the steps of the cabin as Chloe entered the clearing a short while later. Her expression was one of frustration and as Chloe raised her chin quizzically, she gestured angrily into the forest.

"Alison has the only key," she said.

"Ah, balls." Chloe wandered over and joined her on the steps. "She and Jess were having a heated discussion about something. I walked on ahead."

They waited, both staring forward into the trees without further comment. Five minutes ticked by but there was no sign of them.

"Where the hell are they?" Keren asked.

It was a reasonable question. Chloe stood and walked to the edge of the clearing, squinting into the forest. "Jess? Alison?" she called out. "Are you there?"

There was no response. She turned back to Keren who was also on her feet. She moved over to stand next to Chloe. "You don't think something . . . bad has happened to them?"

Chloe bit her lip. "Like what?"

"I don't know. Jerry could have jumped out at them or something."

"Jerry doesn't seem the sort of guy who jumps anywhere," Chloe replied. "Besides, we need to stop always thinking that Jerry—"

Woah.

The sharp crack of a distant gunshot echoed through the trees.

Keren yelped. "Shit. He's shooting at them!"

"No. It was too far away," Chloe said, trying to convince herself just as much. "And if it was Jerry, he was probably shooting rabbits or birds. Or it could be a poacher, he said he had trouble with them and . . . listen!" She held her hand up at the sound of rustling leaves.

Chloe held her ground as Keren made a groaning noise and stepped back. A second later the branches of a bushy group of pines parted and Alison appeared.

"Oh, thank God!" Chloe gasped. "We were getting worried."

But Alison just barged past them, heading straight for the cabin.

"Hey, Ali. What's wrong?" Keren called after her. "Where's Jess?"

"Screw Jess," Alison snarled, spinning around. Her cheeks were red, and it looked as if she'd been crying.

"Is she okay?" Chloe asked, staring into the gap in the pines. "Where is she?"

"Jess is gone, Chloe," Alison said, pulling the cabin key out of her pocket. "She's left us!"

Chapter 23

Chloe joined the others by the front door of the cabin as Alison struggled to turn the large brass key in the lock. Her hands were shaking, making it difficult.

"What do you mean, Jess has left us?" Keren's voice was incredulous. "Are you serious?"

"Yes, I'm serious!" Alison replied. "She stormed off. Said she was sick of being scared. She's heading into town, happy to ruin my special weekend. So, good riddance to her. Argh! Jesus!" She stepped away, flinging her arms in the air in frustration at the lock. "Can someone help me with this damned thing?"

"Here, let me." Chloe gently took the key from Alison. The lock was old and stiff but by holding the door handle at the same time and giving it a shake, she managed to unlock it.

Keren bundled Alison inside, placing her arm around her as they made their way into the living room. Chloe shut the door and locked it then followed them through.

Alison was on the couch, tears rolling down her face. Keren sat beside her, patting her friend's knee in an attempt to soothe her. She looked up at Chloe as she entered the room and pulled a worried face.

"So is Jess really walking all the way into town?" Chloe asked, trying her best to keep her tone calm. "Does she know the way?"

Alison's voice was shaky. "I don't know. She was horrible to me. She said she was having the worst time and wanted to get away from here as soon as possible. She's going to find a mechanic to fix her car and then drive back to the city."

Chloe tried for a reassuring smile. "Well . . . that might not be a bad thing, all things considered . . ." She widened her eyes at Keren, hoping for back-up, but she just carried on pulling that stupid face and didn't speak.

Great. Thanks. Some help you are.

"It doesn't mean we have to leave, right away?" Chloe added. "But with the car fixed, it'll put our minds at ease knowing we can get out of here. When the party's over, I mean."

But her words only seemed to be making Alison more upset. She bawled out a cry and buried her head in Keren's shoulder.

"It's okay, Ali," Keren cooed. "Let it all out. I know . . . I know . . . It's not cool."

What the . . . ? Seriously!?

Taking a deep breath, Chloe moved over and sat on the edge of the couch beside the other two. She took a moment to gather her thoughts as Alison's sobs filled the room. Chloe felt bad for her friend, of course she did. But she also knew Jess had been struggling emotionally, and finding someone to fix the car wasn't the worst idea in the world.

"Do you think I should go after Jess?" Chloe asked, hoping – somehow – that only Keren would hear her. "She's all alone out there. Does she even know the way?"

"Oh, yeah, sure!" Alison yelled, sitting up and turning to Chloe, red-eyed and with snot pouring from her nose. "Why don't you get lost, too, Chloe? Hell, why don't you all go and leave me? It's only my fucking bachelorette party, after all. Go on, go! Abandon me! You too, Keren. At least now I know who my friends are."

"Hey, what did I do?" Keren asked.

Alison scoffed bitterly and pulled away from her. "Oh, don't get me started on that . . ."

"Woah! You need to calm down, Ali."

"Don't you dare tell me to calm down. I am calm."

Keren sat back, open-mouthed as Alison got to her feet and marched over to the drinks table. Chloe met her gaze and held her hands up, patting the air as she did. "She's upset," she whispered. "She didn't mean it."

The last thing they needed right now was more tension and conflict. "Alison. Ali . . ." Chloe called over. "Do you think drinking is a good idea right now?"

Alison didn't turn around, but her shoulders slumped. "I don't know. I'm so tired and sad and I don't know what to do. I just wanted everyone to have the best time here, and it's all gone to shit. Everything always goes to shit!" She burst out crying and Chloe rushed to her side holding her as she wailed. "This was supposed to be my big weekend. The start of my new life. We were going to have such a good time. How can this be happening?"

Chloe pulled her close but felt something wet on her arm. Looking down she saw a streak of dark crimson across her wrist.

"Alison, I think you're bleeding!" She stepped back to examine her.

"Oh, yeah," Alison sniffed. "I cut my arm on something, maybe a branch. I was too angry and upset to take much notice." She turned back to the drinks but made no move to pick up any of the bottles. "This is not how this was supposed to go."

"I know," Chloe said. "*We* know," she added as Keren walked over.

Chloe gritted her teeth. It hurt to see her friend so upset – so unlike the usual breezy, fun-time Alison – but she didn't have a clue how to help her.

"We'll stay here with you," she offered, for want of anything better to say. "I'm sure Jess will be fine."

"Maybe we should get some rest while we wait for her?" Alison said, yawning to further emphasize the point. "We're all exhausted, and after some sleep, things might feel different."

"Yeah. Sounds like a good plan," Chloe said. "We can still enjoy the evening. Have some fun. Jess should be back by then."

Keren snickered bitterly. "She might not be." She looked like she wanted to say more, but catching the hopeful look in Alison's eyes, she stopped herself. "You're right, Ali. I'm exhausted. Some rest would be good."

"And we can still have fun later, right?" Alison said, clearly not wanting to admit defeat regarding her bachelorette party.

"Sure." Chloe rubbed at her back. "And I think we'll all benefit from some downtime." The door was locked, and it would take

Jess at least two hours to get back from the town, even if she found a mechanic straight away. They'd be awake in time to let her in when she returned.

As she and Keren guided Alison towards the bedroom Chloe glanced at the clock above the hearth. It was almost 2 p.m. A full twenty-six hours to go before she could get the hell out of here. In the grand scheme of things, it wasn't that long a time.

But right now, it sure did feel like it.

Chapter 24

The twisted branches overhead reached down at her like gnarled fingers, eager to snatch at her, and pull her into the darkness beyond. With her breath hitched, her feet pounding on the forest floor, Chloe sprinted away, her lungs burning with the cool night air. A primal fear gnawed at her insides. She was running as fast as she could but didn't seem to be getting anywhere. It was as if she was running on a treadmill with the scenery painted on a piece of canvas being winched past her, like in a cartoon. The same trees, the same rocks and birds, going past her over and over again. But she couldn't stop. To do that would be even worse. Looking over her shoulder, shadows flickered and danced into the shape of men and beasts. The fear they brought was a sensation that rippled the skin on her arms. Whispers, indecipherable, yet familiar, trailed in the wind.

Was this a memory? Or a premonition?

Suddenly, she was submerged, engulfed once again in the icy lake, the black waters pulling her under, enveloping her, her screams stuck, a silent bubble in her throat.

An intense pressure bore down upon her chest and the scene shifted. Now she was in a cabin. Jerry's cabin. He wasn't there, but he was everywhere, his presence suffocating, his joyless chuckle the soundtrack to her terror. Her heart played a staccato beat against her ribcage. A shadow lingered just out of view.

"What the fuck . . . !"

With a strangled gasp, Chloe woke up, the nightmare clinging to her like a second skin as her eyes darted around the room.

It was just another bad dream . . .

That's all it was . . .

She grabbed her phone from the nightstand. She'd switched it off to preserve the battery and as she booted up, the familiar glow rooted her back into reality. Cell phones, social media, being glued to a screen twenty-four-seven – these things might be the scourge of Chloe's generation, but they sure felt comforting in the eerie stillness of the cabin. There was a moment when she held her breath, hoping beyond hope that the period spent switched off might have shocked her phone into finding a signal once revived. But no. No bars. No wi-fi. No contact with the outside world.

After checking the time, she switched off her cell once more and then got out of bed, stretching her arms as wide as they'd go. After she and Keren had settled Alison, Chloe had collapsed onto the top of the covers, fully clothed, but now she felt stifled. Pulling at the front of her sweater to fan her torso she walked to the door and stepped out into the hallway. Both Alison's and Keren's doors were slightly ajar and as she passed Keren's room, she heard the bed springs creak.

"Keren," she whispered. "Are you awake?"

"Barely," came the reply. "Come in."

Chloe eased the door open to find Keren sitting up in bed, rubbing at her eyes. "It's a little after four," Chloe told her. "We've been asleep almost two hours, but I feel a lot better for it. I think."

"Yeah, me too," Keren agreed, throwing off her covers and getting up. "Is Ali awake?"

"Not sure."

Keren sighed. "What a weekend, huh? Could it have gone any worse?"

"Maybe not," Chloe said, leaning against the doorframe. "Poor Alison. I feel bad for her. And like you said – she didn't seem herself even before all this crazy stuff happened."

Keren began tying her hair up. "She gets like this sometimes when she's super stressed. She goes into manic mode, and won't listen to reason. She used to do it all the time at Brown, especially during our finals. But I've not seen her like this for a while. Maybe the pressure of the wedding is taking its toll."

Chloe straightened up, suddenly realizing something. "Has she said anything to you about her and Noah?"

Keren scowled, letting the ponytail she'd been gathering drop around her shoulders. "How do you mean?"

"Well, for someone who's getting married to the man of her dreams in two months, she hasn't really mentioned him much. I came here expecting it to be all *wedding-wedding-wedding-Noah-Noah-Noah*, but she's been kind of . . . reserved."

Keren looked away. "I think she just wanted it to be about the four of us, you know? That suits me. I've heard enough about the damn wedding to last a lifetime." She scoffed.

"Maybe she just tired herself out talking to me so much about it beforehand."

Chloe watched as Keren went back to tying her hair up. She was probably correct, but there was something about the way she spoke that bothered Chloe. She sensed a bitterness suddenly.

"Do you think Jess is okay?" she asked, attempting to change the subject.

"Yeah, Jess will be fine. She makes out she's this quiet little mouse but she's a tough one is that girl. She and I didn't used to get on so well, but I have a lot of respect for her."

Chloe tilted her head to regard Keren, rather surprised by this comment, also. They didn't *used* to get on? She'd have hated to have been around when that was the case.

"What do you want to do when Jess gets back with help?" she asked.

Keren turned around, her expression serious. "We support Alison, of course. If she decides to stay until tomorrow evening, then we do, too."

"Agreed." Chloe said. "Why don't we see if she's awake and go make some food?"

"Add 'drink wine' to that list and it sounds like a good plan."

"Cool. I'll go check on her."

Alison had fallen asleep almost immediately when they'd put her to bed and had been snoring softly before Chloe had even left the room. Clearly, she'd needed the rest more than any of them and Chloe's hope was they could now spend a few unflustered hours while they waited for Jess to return. She'd make a fire, fix them some drinks, they'd have some girly talk, some laughs. It would be nice.

But as she eased Alison's door open, she was met with an empty bed and no sign of her friend.

"Alison?" She stepped into the room, checking every corner. No sign of her. She stepped out in the hallway and over to the bathroom. "Alison, you in there?" she asked, rapping her knuckles on the wood.

"What's going on?" Keren asked, coming out of her room.

"Alison's not in her room."

"Jesus," Keren sighed, rolling her eyes. "She probably woke up all hyper again and started making plans for the evening. Typical of her when she's in this state of mind. I thought we were supposed to be resting?"

"Me too," Chloe said, unable to ignore the sinking feeling in her stomach. She moved down the hallway and into the main space, calling out as she went. "Alison – are you in here?"

But the living room was empty.

What the hell . . . ?

Chloe walked through the kitchen area, past the dining table, past the couches and the hearth. Everything looked the same as it had when they'd returned to the cabin two hours earlier, but there was no sign of her.

"Alison?"

In the entrance hall, Chloe halted, staring at the disheveled rug that snaked its way toward the front door. It was gathered up and ruffled, as if something heavy had been dragged across it. A piece of furniture, or . . .

"Alison?" Keren appeared beside Chloe, her voice edged with panic. "Where is she?"

Chloe ran back into the living room and grabbed the large brass key from off the table. Rushing to the front door, she unlocked it and stepped outside onto the porch. The evening chill nipped at her skin, making her shiver. She scanned the immediate area. There was no movement in the trees, no signs of life. She walked down the cabin steps and over to Jess's car, going up on her toes to get a better view of the clearing.

"Alison!" she called out, louder now. "Come out! Where are you?"

Keren approached. "You see anything?"

"Nothing."

"What the hell is going on? Has she taken any of her stuff?"

It was a good question. Chloe had been looking for Alison back in the cabin, not clues to where she'd gone, or what else might be missing. Racing back inside, she and Keren returned to Alison's room and began opening drawers and rifling through her things.

"Her ID is still here," Keren said, holding it up. "Plus, her make-up, her hair products. She wouldn't have gone far without them . . ."

Inspecting the closet, Chloe found a collection of outfits. Knowing Alison there were less clothes than she'd imagined, but more than anyone needed for a weekend away in the wilderness. It was hard to determine if anything telling was gone.

"Are her boots here?" Chloe asked, crouching to peer under the bed. There were two pairs here, but she didn't know how many Alison had brought. Her heart pounded in her chest as she got to her feet.

"Maybe she went for a walk?" Keren said, slumping on the bed. "We were sleeping, and she didn't want to wake us."

"It's a theory but her coat's still here," Chloe said, pointing to the jacket hanging on the back of the door. "And she was pretty adamant she wanted us to stay together this weekend. But where is she? It's going to be dark out soon enough."

Keren sighed, almost resigned. "I'm sure she'll be back when she realizes the time."

Chloe stared at her.

How could she be so calm?

It was like she didn't care about her friend. Was this the extent of these poor little rich girls' relationships – it was all sweetness and roses until it was inconvenient for them, and then their friends could go to hell? It certainly felt that way and Chloe wanted no part of it. She'd been right not to want to come away on this lousy weekend.

"Wait!" she gasped, heart dropping into her mouth as she realized something. "The key . . ."

Keren's eyebrows knitted in confusion. "Which key?"

"It was still here . . ." Chloe muttered, holding a hand up to stop Keren interrupting her thoughts. "Inside. On the table. The front door key. But the door was still locked. That was the only key, so how did Alison leave?"

Keren didn't respond. The unpleasant feeling in Chloe's stomach blossomed from a faint quiver of agitation to full-on dread.

"He said it himself," Chloe went on, her tone almost robotic. "Jerry. He's the only other person with a key. It must have been . . ."

Keren sat up. "Shit! You mean."

Chloe nodded. "Yeah. Jerry's got Alison."

Chapter 25

Keren was off the bed and pacing up and down, the old floorboards groaning beneath her. "We need to call the police."

"We can't," Chloe replied. When Keren glared at her she threw her arms up. "I mean we physically can't. There's no signal, remember?"

"Balls. What do we do?"

"We need to find her – we need to find *them*."

All the weird goings on that Chloe had dismissed for the last few days rushed back to hit her in the guts – the figure in the trees, the blood and guts in the forest, the box of wedding clippings, the wedding dress, the footsteps. She thought of the newspapers in Jerry's cabin, the way he'd ogled each of them, Alison especially, when he came round that first night.

How the hell had she missed this?

She'd been so bothered about giving the old bastard the benefit of the doubt, she'd overlooked the truth.

And what was that?

That he was a . . .

That he'd . . .

Chloe shook the thoughts away, too horrible to even think about. But maybe that had been the problem, too. She was too skilled at burying her head in the sand, not facing up to her problems. She'd done it her entire life – rationalizing horrific situations to avoid having to deal with them.

And now this.

That grizzly wildman with the cruel smile and harsh, penetrating eyes had taken their friend. If they didn't find them soon then he was going to . . . Alison was going to . . .

"Chloe!" Keren's sharp tone jolted her back to the moment. She looked up to see her standing in the doorway dressed in outdoor gear. "We need to get out there and look for her."

"Yes! You're right."

Chloe rushed to her room and put on her hiking boots and jacket before grabbing her cell and joining Keren at the front door. They headed out, calling Alison's name, casting their gaze around as they made their way through the undergrowth.

Keren was leading the way but after a few minutes Chloe found her bearings and grabbed her arm. "We're heading west, but we need to go north," she said, pointing down a narrow trail between rows of pine trees. "I'm pretty sure if we follow this path for thirty minutes or so we'll get to the other cabin."

Keren stared in the direction she was pointing. "You think that's where he's taken her?"

"I don't know. But we need to find out."

Chloe set off walking but was dragged back as Keren grabbed the hood of her jacket. "Wait. You can't be serious?"

Chloe faced her. "If he's taken her—"

"He's got a gun, Chloe! *Guns.* Plural. He's a murdering, cannibalistic weirdo!"

"We don't know that."

"We know what we saw! We know he's the only one who could have got into our cabin. We know Alison is gone. What if he shoots us? We're no good to her dead."

Chloe spun around, eyes darting through the trees, her mind spinning just as fast. She had no idea how far they'd have to walk until they reached a point where their cells would work.

"Okay, you walk back that way to the main road," she told Keren. "As soon as you get a signal, call the cops. I'm going to carry on this way looking for Alison."

"What?!" Keren shrieked. "No fucking way. I'm not going off on my own. What if Jerry's expecting us to go for help? What if he's lying in wait? What if he's . . . What if this is exactly what he wants." She gasped for air. Her words were coming out fast and garbled. "He's going to kill us! We're all going to die!"

"Keren, calm down!" Chloe grabbed her by the upper arms and shook her. "We can't freak out now. Alison needs us."

"What good are we going to be? This is his land. He's got a gun."

"Yes, but he's not some huge ogre of a man. He's tough and wiry, sure, but the two of us would be able to overpower him – in the right circumstances." The words were coming out as fast as she could think them, and she was a little shocked at how rational she sounded given the situation. She looked deep into Keren's eyes, a plan forming. "We should spread out. Just far enough we can still hear other each if we get into trouble. That way he won't realize there are two of us. One of us can distract him while the other grabs his gun – or something."

"*Or something*?" Keren cried. "You make it sound simple. What if he hears us? What if Alison's already . . . dead!"

"Then we have to take the bastard down!" Chloe said, her voice sounding much firmer and more resolute than she was feeling. Maybe she was a better actress than she realized. "Trust me. I think with a bit of luck this could work. You take that path; I'll head a little further into the undergrowth. Tread carefully, keep your eyes open and don't do anything reckless. I'll be able to see you. If we find Jerry and Alison play it cool, keep him talking, whatever you need to do. I'll sneak around the back of him and . . . you know."

She didn't want to think that far ahead, it would only freak her out. When the time came, she trusted she'd know what to do. She just hoped to God she'd have the courage to do it.

"Listen, Keren," Chloe said, holding eye contact. "I know this is scary but as far as I can see it's our only choice. Alison needs us. So – are we doing this?"

Keren looked at the ground and nodded. "Fine."

Chapter 26

Chloe moved stealthily through the dense forest, hunching down, and lumbering from tree to tree to remain concealed from view. Every now and then she glanced over to her left, catching glimpses of Keren through the leaves. The poor girl looked terrified, her face was pale and her eyes wide with worry, as if she was heading for her own execution. She was walking fast, her head darting left and right. She yelped at every rustle of leaves, every scampering critter.

Come on, Keren. Keep it together.

They were almost fifteen minutes into their search for Alison, with Keren heading due north and Chloe moving in a wider arc, staying hidden from the path. She was sweating, her muscles burned with effort, and her stomach groaned with hunger, but she pressed on. The scenery was starting to look familiar to her now, the bushy pines that surrounded their cabin giving way to American beech and sycamore trees. If they continued this trajectory, at this pace, she estimated they'd reach the second cabin in less than ten minutes. But there was still no sign of Jerry or Alison.

What have you done, Jerry?

"Chloe!" She looked over as Keren hissed through the trees. "Are you still there?"

"I'm here," she replied, whispering. "But this isn't going to work if you keep yelling out to me and giving away my location. Trust that I'm here, okay? We're going to be fine."

Keren made a loud scoffing noise but said nothing more. Chloe carried on. Both her hands were balled into fists and the adrenaline in her system was making her teeth grind together. Could she actually do this? If they found Jerry holding Alison, did she have the strength and courage to apprehend him? What if he heard her coming? What if he swung around and blew a hole in her chest with the shotgun that he carried with him?

No! Push those thoughts away.

Thinking that way wasn't helping anyone. She'd come this far, and she was determined not to let history repeat itself. Alison was not going to die like Sam had done. Chloe had always believed she could've done more to save her cousin. This was her chance to redeem herself.

As the density of the trees lessened, Chloe adjusted her course, diving deeper into the forest to remain unseen. Though the distance meant she could no longer hear Keren's footsteps or labored breathing she still caught fleeting glimpses of her through the trees. It was all good. If, or rather when, they encountered Jerry, Chloe was ready with her plan to circle around the back of him and take him by surprise. She could do this.

Large oak and maple trees towered above her as she pressed on, navigating through a dense cluster of trees, and ducking under overhanging branches. A sharp cry, possibly that of a hawk, caused her to halt. She shot a glance over at Keren who had heard it too, her eyes drawn to the treetops.

"It's okay," Chloe whispered to herself, blowing out a long breath to calm her thundering heartbeat. "It's only a bird. Nothing to worry about."

She continued on, squinting through the dense foliage in front of her for signs of the cabin. The air was rich with the earthy scent of moss and decay, but also something else now. Something she couldn't quite place. A few more steps and the trees parted once more, and she found herself in a small clearing. In front of her was a sea of tall ferns and thick vines draped down on both sides, obscuring her view of Keren and the path.

She was startled by a scuffling sound to her right, and stepped back, instinctively lifting her hands in a defensive stance. A moment later a small rodent type thing emerged from the long grass. It was around ten inches long, covered in short grayish fur and with a white, pointed face and round ears. Its tail was long and pink, like that of a giant rat. Chloe recognized the creature as an opossum, a youngster from the size of it. She'd encountered them a lot on family vacations. Back when she was also a youngster.

"Hey," she whispered, glad of the momentary distraction. "You made me jump." The opossum snuffled past her, making for the other side of the clearing but then stopped and looked up at Chloe, snuffling its little nose at her. She noticed there was blood on the tip of it.

"Oh, no, are you hurt?" she asked, leaning down to get a better look. But she saw no cuts or gashes and the blood didn't look to be coming from the critter's nostrils. She gasped and straightened up, scaring the little thing which scampered off into the ferns.

Driven by a heightened sense of urgency, and with every pulse point throbbing, Chloe left the clearing and retraced the creature's steps deeper into the forest. The long grass made swishing noises against her jeans as she walked.

"Alison," she whispered into the trees. "Are you there? Can you hear me?"

That same undefinable scent wafted on the air. It was stronger now. The tang of metal. Chloe froze as her eyes settled on a smear of blood, wet and vivid against the pale bark of a tree. Her stomach churned and she grabbed at her mouth, desperate to stop any cries from forming that might give her away.

No! Please . . . no!

She glanced back over her shoulder, bouncing from one foot to try to see Keren through the trees. But the forest was too dense.

"Keren," she whispered, as loud as she dared. "I need you."

Chloe stumbled forward, her heart hammering a frenetic rhythm in her chest. It felt as if the entire forest was closing in on her.

"Alison? Are you here?"

Another step and her foot nudged something soft, but solid. She stopped, hardly daring to look down. But she had to. She had to know. She had to see for herself. With trepidation, she forced herself to gaze downwards.

Oh, shit!

Chloe recoiled, a scream strangling in her throat as she eyed the the bloody, lifeless body at her feet. The sight was undeniably grim. Yet as her eyes, wide and unblinking, traced the contours of the corpse, recognition, mingled with shock, cascaded through her.

Cold, vacant eyes stared up at her. But it wasn't Alison. It was Jerry.

Chapter 27

Chloe recoiled, her thoughts spiraling into chaos. Jerry was dead. Shot in the chest. The man they'd feared. The man they'd assumed had abducted their friend.

But if he was dead, where was Alison?

Chloe stared down at the grisly scene. Beneath his bushy beard, Jerry's mouth was twisted in a rictus sneer, half-surprised, half-angry, displaying two rows of yellow teeth. His rifle lay discarded beside him, indicating he had been caught off guard. Chloe shook her head, not able to take her eyes off the body. But there were no answers to be found here, only terrible, terrible questions.

She shivered, suddenly feeling very vulnerable and alone.

Who did this?

And were they still out there, watching her?

Her mind raced. Alison? If Jerry had kidnapped her, she might have managed to fight him off and turned his rifle on him. But if so, where was she now? She would have undoubtedly made her way back to the cabin, screaming for help. They'd have at least heard her.

Could the land dispute be the reason? She thought of the press cuttings in Jerry's cabin. Had they gotten themselves unwittingly caught up in a deadly power struggle? Jerry had told her the land developer had tried to frame him for that poor hiker's death. If that was true and this person had been willing to murder an innocent woman to get his hands on Jerry's land, it wasn't a massive leap that his next step was to kill Jerry, and maybe Alison too. Had he come with a motive to settle old scores, and then, realizing there were witnesses, decided to eliminate them all?

She thought of the animal remains they'd found, the torn wedding dress. Could that have been him trying to scare them away? And then, when that didn't work, he'd decided to take matters a step further.

Chloe stifled a cry. Was this how it ended for her, entangled in a stupid vendetta that had nothing to do with her, far away from her home, from her family, from Rob?

She looked around. She had to get away from Jerry's body. Putting one foot in front of the other she managed to mobilize herself, back towards the path.

"Alison? Keren?" she called out, her voice hoarse with stress. "Where are you?" She sprinted through the grass, leaping over fallen trees and piles of leaves. She was frantic, desperate. She was also terrified.

Up ahead she saw the path, the last spot where she remembered seeing Keren. But now, there was no sign of her.

"Keren! No!" She stopped and spun around, shouting some more.

Where was she?

Where the hell was she?

Her breath came in shallow gasps as fear and panic constricted her chest. Tracing Keren's steps she ran down the path, calling out her name. Her best guess – *her supreme hope* – was that something had spooked Keren and she'd retreated to the safety of the cabin.

That had to be what happened.

Please let that be what happened!

Chloe quickened her pace, cursing herself as sharp branches scraped at her arms and pine needles prickled her cheeks. It had been a dumb idea to venture into the forest so unprepared. This was on her. It was her fault. Just like it was with Sam . . .

Minutes stretched on, every second feeling like an eternity. Chloe's sides ached and the muscles in her thighs burned but she didn't slow down. Tears, mingled with sweat and grit, blurring her vision. She prayed to any God who would listen for a safe return to the cabin alive. She prayed, too, that Keren and Alison would be there waiting for her. They'd get inside, lock the door, and wait for Jess to return with help. That was the sensible thing to do. It was what they should have done in the first place.

She carried on running until, finally, the claustrophobic canopy of trees opened out into a clearing and she saw the cabin in front of her, standing like a beacon of hope in the early evening dusk.

Thank you! Thank you so much!

But the place looked deserted, with none of the lights on. She cried out, hoping against hope to hear her friend's voice in response. She got nothing. Although she hadn't wanted to tempt fate, deep down she'd been desperately clutching onto the possibility they'd be here waiting for her. It had been the one thing driving her on these last few miles. But now, confronted with their absence, the weight of her situation crashed down on her. She was here and they weren't. No Alison, no Keren, and no Jess, either.

Just Chloe. Alone. Scared. Lost.

"Why is this happening?" she wailed.

Her aching limbs, propelled by adrenalin, barely registered the pain as she stumbled towards the cabin, pulling the key from her jacket as she reached the front door. She got inside and locked the door behind her before collapsing against the rough wood and sobbing unreservedly.

This was not supposed to happen.

She should never have come here.

Collecting herself, Chloe moved through the cabin, rubbing away her tears as she scanned her surroundings. She wasn't sure exactly what she was searching for but the act itself gave her a semblance of control. Progressing down the corridor she entered her room, grabbing Jess's golfing umbrella once more. It would be little help against an armed land developer with a blood lust, but it was all she had. She was about to go back into the living room and take refuge by the fire when she saw something glinting in the light – Jess's car keys.

She scooped them up and hurried through the cabin, unlocking the front door and running down the steps to Jess's car. It was a long shot, but she remembered her dad had once called a mechanic out to fix their broken-down Ford Taurus, only for the car to start just fine the second the repair guy arrived and tried the ignition. So, yes, it was a long shot, but long shots were all she had. And it wasn't beyond the realms of possibility.

Pressing the key fob to unlock the car, she slid behind the wheel and locked the doors. The air in the car felt a few degrees colder than outside but the confines of the vehicle made Chloe feel a little less vulnerable.

"Come on now. Let's do this . . ."

She inserted the key into the ignition, turned it, and . . . nothing.

"Damn it!"

She tried again, her frustration mounting. But the engine was completely dead. It didn't even offer her a teasing flash of dashboard lights like sometimes happened.

"Shit! Shit! Shit!" She slammed her open palms on the wheel a few times before slumping back in her seat and closing her eyes.

It wasn't fair. None of this was fair.

She thought of Alison and Keren. She thought of her dad, of her cousin Sam. She thought of Rob. What was he doing now? Probably enjoying a nice homecooked meal with his mom, all cozy and warm in his family home.

A pang of regret washed over her – she could have joined him this weekend. She knew he was sort of joking when he'd invited her, but she was sure if she'd accepted he'd have been happy about it.

Why the hell hadn't she?

Things could be so different right now. In every way. She opened her eyes, sensing more sobs bubbling up in her chest before a blinding light outside the car refocused her attention.

Sitting up and narrowing her eyes she saw another car pulling into the driveway. Thank God! She even blurted out a relieved laugh, which quickly turned into a hysterical cackle. It had to be Jess, returning with help. She was saved.

Everything was going to be okay.

But as the car screeched to a stop a few feet away from her she realized it was far too small to be the vehicle of a car mechanic. The pale pastel blue color also gave it away. As did the fact there was just a solitary woman with dark hair sitting behind the wheel.

"Hannah?" Chloe gripped the wheel, leaning forward to wipe her hand against the fogged-up windshield. "What the . . . ?"

It was indeed Hannah. Chloe opened the car door and stepped out as Hannah did the same. It was only then that Chloe saw her injuries. Hannah's left eye was swollen shut and she had a deep gash across her forehead.

"Chloe, thank God," she gasped.

"What happened to your face?" Chloe asked, her mind spiraling with dark thoughts. "I thought you were working this weekend?"

Hannah glanced around, eyes wide, jaw rigid. "Where's Alison?"

"I don't know," Chloe replied. "There's been a lot of weird shit going down. We think maybe the owner of the cabin is caught up in some—"

"We have to find her!" Hannah cut in, eyes still darting around. "And Keren?"

"I don't know!" Chloe cried. Standing here now, trying to explain to a third party what had happened, she felt overwhelmed and foolish.

They should have done something sooner, walked to the town the moment they felt unsafe. Their decision to stay here, spurring each other on, it had led to a situation spinning out of their control. And now Keren and Alison were gone.

Chloe knew, deep down, that this wasn't her fault, the same way it wasn't her fault that Sam had drowned – but it sure did feel like it was. "I think they might be hurt," she whimpered. "Or worse."

"We have to find them," Hannah said, heading for the cabin. "We have to stop her."

"What?" Chloe followed on behind. "Stop who?"

"Alison," Hannah replied, spinning around. "She did this."

"Did what?"

"This!" Hannah gestured to her damaged face before pulling back her coat sleeves to reveal angry red abrasions around each wrist. "You need to understand, Chloe. Alison . . . she's dangerous. And if Keren's with her then we need to find them. Fast. Otherwise, Alison is going to kill her."

PART 2

Chapter 28

3 weeks before the bachelorette party

A low hum of ambient chatter settled over the room, punctuated only by the occasional high-pitched laugh or the clinking of wine glasses. Tucked away in a quiet corner of Manhattan, The Marlowe had only opened a few months earlier but was already well known to those who appreciated the finer things in life. The décor was a fusion of sleek design and understated luxury. High ceilings lined with intricate chrome patterns lent an airy openness to the space. The walls, which looked to be made of raw plaster but were painted to appear that way, emphasized the relaxed atmosphere, as couples and friends drank and conversed around the circular mahogany tables. The menu, boasting a range of small plates as expensive as larger ones sold elsewhere, was to die for. As was the wine list, boasting organic, vegan wines from all around the world.

The Marlowe was Alison's sort of place. Exclusive and expensive but not too in your face about it. She sipped at her glass of South African straw wine – trendy, refreshing, recommended to her by the over-friendly sommelier – as she took in her environment.

There was a lot of greenery on show, she realized. In each of the four corners of the small but perfectly formed establishment stood tall potted ferns, their delicate fronds reaching upwards. Hanging from planters above the tables, smaller plants with thick, succulent leaves added splashes of green, breaking the monotony of wood and metal. Along the large panoramic windows that looked out into the city streets, a series of planters spilled over with cascading vines, offering patrons a touch of nature amid urban luxury. It all looked great and was about as much greenery as Alison could take. She'd been a city girl her entire life and she planned to keep it that way. She never understood why people would want to go roughing it in the wilderness, away from modern appliances and luxury. It was all just too . . . earthy. Not her thing. At all.

"I was thinking maybe Montauk for my bachelorette," she told Noah, who was sitting across from her, staring out the window.

"Sorry? What?"

Alison rolled her eyes at him. "What's wrong with you tonight, sweetie? You seem distracted."

"I guess I am, a little. Listen, Ali I—"

"I was talking about my bachelorette party," she continued. "I think I want to do it in Montauk and Keren agrees. It'll be nice in late spring and there are some gorgeous boutique hotels up there. I'm thinking hot tubs, pampering sessions – plus, plenty of cocktails of course."

"Right. Sure."

"Don't worry," she giggled. "It'll be all very classy and above-board, of course, just me and my besties. No strippers or anything seedy. I'm hoping your bachelor party will be the same!"

Noah smiled at this, but it seemed to Alison to be a little forced. "I haven't given it much thought," he said.

She giggled again. Men, what are they like? No imagination.

"You'd better decide soon," she told him. "The wedding will be here before we know it." She grinned, baring her teeth in an eager grimace. It was all super exciting.

So, why did Noah look as if he was carrying the weight of the world on his shoulders?

Alison narrowed her eyes, watching him as his fingers drummed rhythmically on the stem of his wine glass. She could sense the heaviness in his gaze, the way it seemed to avoid hers. But he was probably just stressed after a long day at work.

Noah Glaser.

Her hard-working financier fiancé. It was quite the tongue twister.

And he looked so handsome tonight she could get over him acting a little distant. Fresh from his job in the city, he was wearing a dark navy suit with a crimson tie and a stark white shirt. As usual, his hair, skin, and smile were all impeccable.

Alison picked at one of the black paper napkins. "We need to let the caterers know our final selections for the canapes before Monday," she told him.

Noah didn't look at her. "Oh, yes. I remember."

"I was thinking of the salmon parcels rather than the smoked salmon for the second fish option. Is that okay with you?"

"Mmm." He sipped his wine. He still wouldn't look at her.

A sense of dread began to form in the pit of Alison's stomach. It was a feeling she recognized but one she'd hoped would never have to experience again.

"What is it?" she heard herself say.

Noah cleared his throat, his eyes still dancing around the room.

"Nothing."

"Come off it, Noah. Say it. Whatever it is."

"Alison," he sighed as if saying her name itself was a chore. "I didn't want to do this here . . . But, well . . ." He trailed off, taking a deep breath as he finally met her gaze. His eyes were full of remorse, maybe fear, too.

"What is it?" she asked, her voice wavering. She grabbed for her wine, gripping the stem for dear life as she gulped down most of the contents. She knew what was coming.

Please, not Noah.

He was different. He was her rock. Her soulmate. She thought she'd found her person.

"What is it?" Alison asked again.

Noah hesitated, running a hand through his dark hair. "Alison . . . This isn't easy for me." He looked sheepish. How dare he?

"Just say it . . ."

He blew out a breath, shaking his head. "Shit. I had all this worked out in my head, but now we're here . . . I'm so sorry, Alison . . ."

The alarm bells that had been quietly sounding in the background of Alison's mind started ringing louder. She swallowed hard, still trying to keep her voice steady. There had to be an explanation for why he was acting this way. He couldn't be doing – *it*. Not now. He wouldn't. He couldn't!

"What's going on?"

"I think . . . God, this is hard." He paused, drawing in another breath as if steeling himself for battle. "I can't do this anymore."

His words hit her like a freight train. She felt as if all the air had been sucked out of the room.

"You can't do what, Noah?"

"The wedding. Us. Any of this. I think we need to end things."

"You think?"

Noah frowned. "I *know*. I have to end things. I am ending things." He reached for her hand, but she yanked it away, bringing it to her mouth to try and stifle the sobs bubbling up in her chest. "I don't want to hurt you, Alison."

Excuse me?

It's a bit fucking late for that, Noah!

But all she could come out with was, "Why?"

He paused, eyes rising as if searching for the right words. "I'm sorry," he said. Again. "It's just as the wedding gets closer, I realize more and more that I'm not ready. Not for marriage, not for settling down."

"We've been together for three years!" Alison spat, her voice rising. "We are settled. I thought we were!"

Noah gritted his teeth. "All right, Ali, don't yell."

"Don't you fucking tell me what to do!" She felt the weight of every eye in the room on her, but she didn't care. Tears formed, but she held them back. "You brought me to this place to dump me?!"

"No! I just told you I didn't want to do it here. But I've been carrying this decision around with me for so long and when you asked just now it felt right. I couldn't wait any longer."

"Oh, you've been carrying it around? How awful for you!" Tears were streaming down her cheeks, and she made no move to wipe them away. "I'm so sorry if I'm embarrassing you, darling."

"Alison, please. Don't make a scene."

"Do you love me?"

He swallowed, holding eye contact now, perhaps scared to look away. "I do. But . . . not enough I guess."

"Not enough." She laughed bitterly as she leaned back and folded her arms. "So that's it? You just decide it's over, and I'm supposed to accept it?"

"Keep your voice down." Noah leaned forward. "People are staring Alison."

"Let them!" she snapped, her voice rising even more. "You owe me an explanation!"

Noah sighed, rubbing the bridge of his nose. "You know, when you get like this, it just confirms my decision. I'm sorry. I really am."

Alison felt the rage boiling within her, overtaking the shame that threatened to crush her.

It was happening again.

It was actually happening again . . .

She lifted her glass and, without thinking, threw the drink at him. It was a rather pathetic gesture as there was only a tiny amount of wine left but, regardless, the act elicited gasps from the nearby tables.

"You bastard," she hissed, jumping to her feet, her chair scraping loudly against the floor.

Noah, wiping his face, looked up at her, his expression one of embarrassment rather than sadness. "Let me at least take you home."

Alison scoffed, "Go to hell. I'd rather walk."

She grabbed her bag and coat and stormed out of the bar, not managing to make it to the door before she burst into tears. Loud sobs, from deep inside of her, bringing with them the ghosts of her past.

Pushing out onto the street she hailed a cab, barking her address to the driver as she climbed into the back. All she could think of as they drove away was how stupid she was to have allowed herself to get to this point. No one should be made to feel this way, least of all her.

She didn't deserve this.

It wasn't fair.

Chapter 29

Twenty minutes later, the cab pulled up in front of Alison's apartment building – a typical brownstone with iron railings lining the front steps, situated between East Williamsburg and Bushwick.

"That'll be $44," the driver told her, not turning around.

Alison had caught his gaze in the rearview mirror a few times on the journey, but he'd made no effort to ask how she was. She'd been crying her heart out for God's sake. Did no one care?

She reached into her bag for her wallet, eyes blurred from a haze of tears as she eyed the meter.

Screw it.

She handed over three crumpled twenties, telling the driver to keep the change. It was Noah who always took care of these sorts of things, and she chided herself for over-tipping considering how unpleasant the guy had been. But the last thing she wanted was to wait around for him to find change. As she exited the cab, the chilly evening air bit at the exposed skin on her face and legs. It felt as if even nature was mocking her this evening. The whole world, conspiring against her.

Shuffling up the steps of her building, she unlocked the front door. A familiar aroma enveloped her as she entered – a blend of cleaning supplies, and the cuisines of many different cultures. The smell was often comforting to her but tonight, it was anything but.

She walked over to the table where the mail for the building was placed, leafing through a stack of envelopes and flyers advertising local pizza joints and bars. There were two letters addressed to her. Both looked like replies to the wedding invite she'd sent out three months earlier. With the wedding only two months away, the tardiness of whoever these were from would have annoyed her on any previous day. But now the sight of the crisp white envelopes with her and Noah's names on the front triggered a fresh wave of tears.

How could he do this to her?

It was the worst pain she'd ever felt, worse than her dad leaving, worse than Tony's betrayal. Yet, at the same time, it also didn't feel real.

Alison felt herself spiraling, felt herself going back to the dark place. But she couldn't. Not now. She'd come too far. Had done too much work on herself.

She had to stay strong.

Blinking her tears away, she walked up the stairs to her apartment, leaving the letters, unopened on the table.

She could hear the muffled sound of the TV as she unlocked the door to her apartment. Hannah was lounging on the couch, watching some lame-looking sci-fi series. She lifted her head as Alison entered, her eyes widening no doubt at the sight of her roommate's red, swollen face.

"Woah. What happened?" she asked, lowering her legs onto the hardwood floor, and sitting up. "Is everything okay?"

Alison headed into the kitchen.

No, of course everything isn't okay!

Do I look okay?

"Ali?"

"I'm fine," she insisted.

She'd have to tell people what had happened eventually, but not just yet. To say it out loud would only make what Noah had done to her feel more real. For now, she needed solitude and the safety of her room. Retrieving a bottle of mineral water from the fridge and a large packet of cheese puffs from the cupboard, she shuffled back into the living room.

As she passed by, Hannah was sitting upright, watching her. "Ali, you don't look fine," she said. "What's wrong?"

Pausing, Alison took a moment to compose herself and a sense of resolve washed over her. "My mom just called with bad news," she said. "My aunt passed away last night. We were really close when I was younger. But I'm fine. I just want an early night and to pig out."

Hannah eyed the cheese puffs with a slight smirk playing on her lips. Perhaps to the mature, perfect little Hannah, indulging in a packet of maize snacks wasn't the epitome of pigging out. But if that was what she was thinking, she didn't say it.

"I'm very sorry for your loss," she offered. "Let me know if you need anything."

Alison nodded. "Thanks. I'll be okay."

Continuing her journey, she entered her bedroom and closed the door behind her. She threw her bag onto the bed but, even in her distressed state, resisted the urge to fling her jacket on the floor. It was a Yves Salomon jacket after all – this season's puffer jacket in white with fur trim. It had been a birthday present from her father – or, rather, she'd bought it using the credit card he still paid for her and informed him it was for her birthday. Instead, she neatly hung the jacket on the back of her door before peeling off her Levi jeans and Ralph Lauren sweater and depositing them in the laundry hamper.

Moving over to her dresser she caught sight of her reflection in the full-length mirror standing beside it. Having anticipated spending the night at Noah's apartment, she was wearing her new, red Victoria's Secret lingerie set.

What a waste.

She removed the underwear and opened the bottom drawer of the dresser, rummaging around in the back until she found what she was looking for – her pale blue pajamas with a smiley face on the front. She'd had these pajamas since she was fourteen years old, almost a full decade. They were threadbare, soft from countless washes, but felt like home. However, this evening, as she slipped into them, the soft, thin material against her skin offered scant comfort.

She examined herself in the mirror. Being about the same size as when she was fourteen, the pajamas still fit okay, but so much had happened since then. What she wouldn't give now to be that naïve young girl. That version of Alison was full of wonder and hope. She believed life was carefree and that love came easy. But then her dad ran off with a woman from his gym and she realized for the first time the crushing pain of loss.

Alison could remember it like it was yesterday. Her mom, slumped in a chair in front of the kitchen table, her usually neat brown hair sticking out in odd places from where she'd been tugging at it in frustration. And her dad sitting opposite; his face creased into an expression of pity but also of impatience.

They hadn't seen Alison right away and she stayed back, hidden in the darkness of the hallway as her mom pleaded with her dad to stay. She remembered how her voice, usually so full of spirit and warmth, sounded like that of a child.

She kept saying the same thing. "Please, don't do this."

Please don't do this . . .

The sight of her mother, usually so strong and resilient, reduced to this raw, shattered person, was an image Alison would never forget.

And her mother's words, the pleading, it did no good. Soon after, her father left to be with his new girlfriend and that was that.

It was in the following months that Alison learned to put on a brave face and a breezy smile. It was her first step into acting, into becoming someone else. Because she needed to be strong for her mom. She thought if she presented herself as a happy person then her mom might follow her lead. Unfortunately, things didn't turn out that way.

Even today, ten years later, her mom was still trapped in the past, unable to get over her dad leaving. She was broken, bitter, weakened from grief and unrequited hope. She had boyfriends but they never lasted long, and she only had to have a couple of wines before the talk would drift to Alison's father. He was on his third marriage now and Alison had made her peace with him to a degree. But she'd never forgive him for what he did to her mom. And she'd vowed long ago never to end up the same way.

It was the shame that really ruined a person. The shame of being the one left behind. The wronged partner. The loser.

It was why, when Alison had discovered Tony was cheating on her with that bitch, Willow Anderson, she'd taken matters into her own hands. After researching it online she'd sawn through his brake cables – not completely, so he wouldn't notice right away, but enough they'd fail at a critical moment. Tony was an eighteen-year-old boy with his first car and liked to drive as fast as most other eighteen-year-old boys with their first cars. He was speeding along Route 80 with his friend, Josh, when he lost control and drove into a tree. The cops said both men were killed instantly, but a part of Alison hoped that in those last seconds – as Tony hit the brakes but felt no resistance underfoot – he realized she was behind it.

Hell hath no fury . . . and all that jazz.

Being highly skilled at compartmentalizing her life by this point, Alison was able to play the part of the grieving girlfriend with aplomb. She told herself it wasn't her fault, it was his. Tony's car was old and had been fixed up for him by his older brother who was far from being a qualified mechanic. The accident was confirmed by the authorities to be the result of a worn-out brake cable. A tragedy, but nothing more.

And Alison, while still being seen as the heartbroken girlfriend, walked away with her freedom and reputation intact. Her greatest fear had always been to end up like her mom: shamed, embarrassed, broken by her loss. That wasn't going to happen to her. People felt sorry for Alison, but they didn't pity her in the same way they would have if Tony's cheating had come to light.

She was no loser.

She climbed into bed, hugging her legs to her chest as she considered her options. Noah wasn't cheating on her, at least she didn't think so. But if he left her now, with the wedding planned and the invitations sent, it would make her look foolish and pathetic. She couldn't bear to see the sympathetic looks on her friend's faces. She'd rather die before that.

With the events of the last few hours swirling in her mind, she pulled the blankets over her and opened the bag of cheese puffs. She had to talk to Noah properly. Clearly, he was confused and not thinking straight. If she only knew the reason behind him calling off the wedding, she could work out how to talk him around.

Did he want space? Fine. She'd give him space. However long he needed. She'd show him what his life would be like without her. Or maybe he needed more love, more affection.

Maybe he just needed a reminder of what he stood to lose.

She had to show him how great a person she really was, and how amazing a wife she would be. Because one thing was certain – she would not end up broken and alone like her mom. She would not be shamed.

Stuffing her hand into the bag, she pulled out a handful of bright orange cheese puffs and shoved the whole lot into her mouth.

She had to fix this.

She was *going* to fix this.

Chapter 30

Alison paced the length of her living room, her head full of dark schemes and intrusive thoughts. Despite having next to no sleep the previous night, she felt wired and couldn't sit still. Her nerves sizzled; her skin hummed. It was always the same when she was having 'one of her episodes.'

She moved to the window. The lurid glow from the streetlamp outside bled through the slats of her blinds, casting the room in an orange haze. It had gotten dark without her realizing it and she guessed it must be nearing six.

Almost time.

Parting the blinds with two of her fingers, she peered out. She was only on the second floor, but she felt so disconnected from the people going about their lives on the street below. A young couple strolled by, their closeness sending feelings of jealousy and regret spiking through her heart, which she promptly shrugged away. It wasn't the time to be feeling sorry for herself.

She had important work to do.

Leaning her forehead against the glass, Alison cast her attention up and down the street. There was no sign of him. But he'd told her he was coming straight from the office, and they always kept him working late. Impatience tightened her jaw. She was ready for him now. If she waited longer her prickly focus might tip over into rage, or worse.

Alison returned to pacing, the hardwood floor creaking underfoot as she moved. She'd persuaded Hannah to go out for the night, explaining that Noah was coming over to go through wedding plans and that they needed privacy. Being a good friend, she'd relented easily enough and had bought Alison's story completely. But why wouldn't she have? Alison was a great actress.

"Come on, Noah," she whispered to the ceiling. "Where are you?"

Three days had gone by since she'd left him in The Marlowe with a wet shirt and a face colored with anger. That first night she'd cried until she fell asleep, and the next day she'd called him over and over, only to be met with his voicemail every time. By the second night, her sadness turned into determination. She wasn't going to get Noah back by showing weakness. She needed a plan, a smarter approach.

Since then, communication had been reduced to the occasional, necessary text. Noah clearly needed space, and Alison's tearful begging wasn't going to change his mind. That wasn't to say Alison hadn't wanted more contact. There were so many things she wanted to say to Noah, so many questions she needed answers to. But one thing was certain – she wasn't going to beg him to stay like her mom had done with her father.

Despite the pain and torment of the last thirty-six hours, Alison had clung to the hope that some time spent apart would bring Noah back to his senses and that he'd come rushing back to her, apologizing for how silly he'd been. Yet, his text that morning shattered those illusions. She'd seen his name flash up on her phone and felt a rush of eager anticipation, only for her hope to be dashed on the rocks of grim reality.

Noah's text was the same as all the others, stark and business-like, asking if he could drop by after work and pick up some important items he'd left at her apartment – one of his good suits, a client file he needed. Alison's first reaction had been to tell him to go to hell but her desire to see him had trumped her resolve and she'd agreed.

But she wasn't a doormat, she reminded herself firmly. Far from it.

She moved down the hallway into the kitchen to check the clock on the oven. It showed 7:15. Noah should have been here fifteen minutes ago. Frustration bubbled up inside her. She was hungry, having eaten very little in the last few days, but she couldn't even contemplate cooking or even making a sandwich. If she lost a few pounds, it wouldn't be the worst thing in the world. Noah had often expressed a preference for skinny girls.

Heading back into the living room she stopped by the mirror in the hallway, sucking in her cheeks as she took in her reflection. There was a restlessness in her eyes, the same kind of wild desperation she'd seen before. She blinked a few times to try and shake it off, smiling as she did so. Back into her role as Little Miss Perfect.

When the intercom buzzed a second later it startled her. Out here in the hallway, it was louder than she realized. She glared at her reflection, still smiling at herself to settle her racing heart.

This was it! He was here.

Tucking a strand of hair over one ear she went to the door.

"Hey, come up," she spoke into the intercom, hitting the buzzer and opening her apartment door an inch.

She settled onto the couch, exhaled a long sigh, and dropped her expression, getting into character. She could hear Noah's footsteps on the stairs.

Showtime.

Alison had always had a knack for manipulation and was well-versed in setting situations up to get her own way. She often played friends off each other, feigned tears with her family – and Noah – so they'd bow to her whims. And of course, there was the Tony situation, which couldn't have gone better. Not only had she saved face and paid the bastard back for his infidelity, but she'd managed to get her final exam marks raised because of the 'trauma' of losing her boyfriend.

Yet despite this not being her first rodeo, Alison was still unsure how best to handle Noah. Getting rid of him would be simple – like it had been with Tony – but how did she make him stay? She needed his love, his sympathy, she needed to make him understand how bleak life would be without her.

She'd considered staging a bad fall, or even a failed suicide attempt, but felt these options were too risky. Plus, they reeked of desperation in her eyes and Alison was not weak. She was not like her mom.

Another option was to tell Noah she was pregnant. That would have been a real doozy. She knew he couldn't wait to have kids and it would make him think twice about leaving.

She'd have to pretend she'd miscarried at some stage, of course, get sympathy that way. Yet she couldn't deal with the idea of Noah and his mom cooing and fawning over her even for one second – touching her belly, viewing her as a vessel for new life rather than her being the prize. Having children was always going to be a sticking point for her and Noah, as Alison secretly hated the idea. But she planned to continue taking birth control while they tried to conceive, hoping that, eventually, he'd accept it wasn't going to happen for them.

So, no babies. Not even fake ones. She wanted Noah to stay for her, not for some stupid kid.

But she was now out of ideas and could hear his footsteps on the landing. He was sheepishly knocking at the door of the apartment. He was easing the door open.

"Ali? Are you home?"

"Through here," she called out in a small voice.

She shifted around on the couch as Noah appeared in the doorway. He stood there for a moment, taking her in, perhaps assessing what sort of mood she was in. She smiled.

"How are you doing?" he asked. "You look . . ." He trailed off, thinking better of whatever he was going to say next.

They stared at each other for what felt like minutes, nodding and smiling politely.

Like fucking strangers, Alison thought.

She wanted to scream. She wanted to leap on Noah and scratch his eyes out. She also wanted to hug him tight and never let him go.

Damn him.

Damn him for doing this to her.

"Do you want to sit?" she asked, shuffling up the couch to give him some room.

"Ah, no. I—"

"Please. Just for a minute. I've missed you."

Noah looked at the floor and shook his head. "I've missed you, too, Alison. I have. But nothing's changed."

"Excuse me?! What?" She sat upright, her voice rising. "*Everything* has changed, Noah! You've changed *everything*."

Noah sighed. "Listen, I didn't come here for an argument. We can talk about this properly later, how we go about telling people . . . you know . . . But not now. I've had a bastard of a day at the firm. I just need to get my stuff and—"

"Oh, I'm so sorry!" Alison snapped. "Of course. This is all about you, isn't it? I'm just the poor girl who believed you when you told her this was forever."

"Alison . . ."

"Is there someone else? Is that it?" The words were out of her mouth before she realized what she was saying. They brought with them a ripple of nervous energy that lifted the hairs on the back of her neck. She glared at Noah. These were questions that had been hovering in the shadows of her psyche since The Marlowe, but she'd not had the courage to acknowledge them until now.

Noah looked away. "No. Of course not. It's not that."

"What is it then?"

Another sigh. "It's complicated."

"Is it? Is that what it is?"

Noah glanced down the hallway toward Alison's room. "I don't want to do this now. I'm going to get my things and I'm going to go. Okay? I think the best thing I can do for you now is give you space and—"

"I'm sick!"

Noah faltered, whatever he was about to say dying on his lips. "What are you talking about?" he asked, but the sternness had left his voice. "You mean . . . ?"

Alison nodded, getting more into character as tears formed in her eyes. "I'm sorry to have to do this now, Noah. I know you're confused and so am I. But it's true. I wasn't going to worry you so close to the wedding, but I've not felt good for a few months. I went to the doctor's last week and they took my blood, and did some tests." She shook her head, the tears spilling down her cheeks. "It's bad, Noah. I'm sick. Really sick."

"Oh, Alison." Noah moved around the side of the couch and sat beside her. "What is it . . . Cancer?"

She turned to look at him. "Brain cancer. The doctors say it's advanced. I might only have a year left. If I'm lucky . . ."

"Oh, Ali."

She didn't take her eyes off him as he leaned forward with his head in his hands processing the devastating news. He didn't look to be coping too well but that made two of them. She was making Noah appreciate what he stood to lose. But at the same time, a voice in her head was screaming at her to pull back.

Pretending she was pregnant was a better plan than this.

Because what happened when she wasn't sick? When she didn't die? Did she pretend there'd been some sort of miracle?

How was this going to play out?

But, right now, Alison didn't care about any of that. All she cared about was the compassion on her fiancé's face as his defenses crumbled – and his strong arms around her as he pulled her close.

"Baby girl," he whispered in her ear. "I'm so sorry."

"Yeah. Me too."

Alison let herself revel in the closeness, the scent of the Tom Ford cologne she'd bought him on his last birthday filling her senses. He smelled good. She never wanted to let him go.

"We can fight this," he told her. "Together."

That was all she needed to hear. She smiled to herself. "So, you'll stay? We'll get married?"

Noah tensed for a moment, then nodded. Good enough.

"Thank you," Alison sobbed. "I love you."

"Wait. I just thought . . ." Noah pulled away, holding onto her arms as he regarded her with a grave expression. "A client of mine is a brain specialist. They say he's one of the best on the East Coast. I'll give him a call, and ask him if he'll take you on. He's expensive but I'll pay. Whatever it takes."

Alison held her breath. Noah was already pulling his phone out of his pocket and scrolling through his extensive contacts list.

"No, don't do that. I've got a doctor, already. He's very good. But he's been very clear. There's nothing they can do. Nothing *anyone* can do."

Noah was still scrolling, a deep scowl creasing his forehead. "Sanderson is the best, Ali. We need to get a second opinion on this. Ah, here he is, I'm going to call him now."

"No!" Her hand shot out instinctively, knocking the phone out of Noah's hand before he could hit the call button. "I don't want you to."

"What do you mean? This is your life we're talking ab . . ." He trailed off and raised his head to stare at Alison, the realization there in his piercing blue eyes.

"Noah . . . Please . . ."

She reached for him, but he leaned back. "You're not actually sick. Are you?" He shook his head as he looked at her, his mouth twisted in disgust. "Alison?"

She looked away. Could she turn this around? Did she have it in her?

"I just wanted you to remember how much I meant to you," she said. "How much you love me. How much you don't want to lose me."

"You're a fucking psychopath," Noah growled, jumping up off the couch as she grabbed for him again. "This is why we can't get married, Alison. You're crazy. But thank you. Thank you very much for making this easy for me!"

"Noah, please . . . ! I'm sorry!" she cried out as he marched down the hallway toward her bedroom. "I love you! I need you!" She hated herself for sounding so weak, but she couldn't stop herself.

Noah wasn't even listening.

She'd totally screwed this up.

What the hell did she do now?

A fresh wave of frustration washed over her, tinged with just a bit of self-disgust. Her gaze flitted around the room, looking for something to throw against the wall. Her eyes landed on something on the floor, under the coffee table. Noah's phone. He must have knocked it off the couch just now when he stormed off.

She snatched it up, her reflection staring back at her in the darkened screen. What secrets were held within, she wondered. Leaning over the back of the sofa she peered down the hallway. Noah was in her room, yanking open drawers and pulling out items of clothing. He'd be a few minutes at least. Positioning herself with her back to the hallway, she hunched over the phone and swiped at the screen.

Chapter 31

Alison closed her eyes, picturing the quick rhythm of Noah's fingers as he tapped his passcode into his phone. He'd done it often enough in her presence, always assuming she wasn't paying attention. But Alison always observed. She always noticed.

1-9-9-8. The year of Noah's birth.

Holding her breath, praying he hadn't changed it, she tapped in the numbers, puffing out a sigh as the screen opened up.

Well, shit.

Noah used to have a photo of Alison as his wallpaper – her posing in a tiny bikini on Miami Beach last year (and looking mighty fine she might add!) – but he'd already swapped it out. The wallpaper that greeted her was just a series of geometric shapes in differing shades of blue, one of the default images supplied by Apple.

It was another kick to the guts. Only two days since Noah had turned Alison's world upside down and he'd already removed her from his life.

Listening for his footsteps in the hallway she began scouring his messages for evidence there was someone else involved. Because if there was, if Noah was cheating on her, then that changed things and she'd act accordingly. But most of the messages revolved around work, interspersed with mundane exchanges between family and friends. There was nothing to indicate deceit.

Undeterred, Alison turned to Noah's photo reel, but here too there was nothing of note. She did, however, find the photo of her on Miami Beach, and the fact he hadn't deleted it completely brought her a moment of respite. But it was short-lived. Because none of this made sense. She was about to place the phone back on the floor when she remembered something.

Flicking back to the messages app she clicked on 'Filters' at the top of the screen which brought up the main menu. She scanned the options: 'All messages', 'Known Senders', 'Unknown Senders', 'Unread Messages'.

And then, there at the bottom, 'Recently Deleted'.

Alison tapped on this last selection, which opened the list of message threads that Noah had deleted in the past forty days. Most of them were messages from his online bank, sending two-step verification codes, but there were a couple from delivery companies too. And then, there at the bottom of the list – a deleted thread from someone saved in Noah's phone as 'K'.

Alison gasped, her hand shaking as she restored these deleted messages to the main inbox. Her heart thudded but she had to know.

K?

God, no. Please no.

The tension in her jaw mirrored the tightness gripping her shoulders as she navigated back to the main message screen.

There it was, the thread from 'K' reinstated, three from the top. Meaning it had been active recently. Most likely in the last few days. She opened the thread, scrolling up to the top of the page as deep feelings of shame and confusion gnawed at her insides.

Noah, how could you?

Her breath hitched as she saw that the thread went back six months to last September. What was she doing back then? What had Noah told her he was doing? Chewing on her lip, she began to read, not able to take her eyes off the screen.

Jesus . . .

To say the messages – especially the early ones – were intimate would be an understatement. Alison had never gone in for sexting, believing it was a rather unclassy and juvenile way of flirting. Yet it was clear to her now that Noah enjoyed it. She'd never thought herself to be prissy, but even she found herself wincing at some of these messages. Talk of excessive bodily fluids, and what they wanted to do to each other. It made her want to throw up. It also made her want to throw the phone out of the window. But maybe that was because these messages were between her fiancé and a woman with the initial K.

Keren.

No!

It couldn't be. But there was something about the way this woman wrote her texts that seemed familiar. Then she read on.

I'm feeling guilty about Alison, but not enough to stop. Xxx

I want you so much, my naughty secret . . .

Can't wait to see you tomorrow xxx

Each word was like a dagger to Alison's heart. That last message had been sent on her birthday, last November. She remembered she'd wanted to go for afternoon tea with Noah at the Mandarin Oriental overlooking Central Park but at the last minute, he'd had to work. Or that's what he'd told her. Clearly, the only work he was doing was on her friend. *Her best friend.*

She wiped at her eyes.

"Keren," she gasped, her voice barely above a whisper. "You fucking bitch."

How could she do this to Alison, after everything they'd been through together? She wanted to scream. She wanted to burn down the entire city. How had this happened without her even noticing? Her best friend and Noah.

Darkness began to envelop her thoughts, pushing away logic and reason. She would not be the wronged woman. She would not let the same thing happen to her as it had to her mom. She would fight this with all she had and . . .

Oh! Shit!

Her heart somersaulted as she got to the last few messages in the thread and read how things had turned sour between the two love birds. It appeared Noah had broken things off – with him texting her that it was getting 'too complicated' and that he 'needed space'. Keren had begged him to carry on, but to no avail. It was over. That was last week. There'd been no messages since then.

Alison lowered the phone, a wave of conflicting emotions fighting for supremacy in her system. What did she do with this information?

She realized in that moment that she loved Noah too much to do to him what she'd done to Tony. But she needed to get Keren away from him. It was she who was to blame for this betrayal. Clearly, she'd thrown herself at Noah, and being a typical man, he'd been unable to resist. Keren was the problem. That evil witch. She was Alison's Maid of Honor for God's sake.

Not cool. Not cool at all.

Footsteps from the bedroom jolted Alison from the dark pit of her thoughts. In one swift motion, she deleted the thread, locked the phone, and slid it back under the coffee table as Noah emerged from the bedroom.

"I'm done," he told her.

Alison, who had resumed her role of the broken woman turned away from him and stifled a sob. "Okay." She watched Noah out of the corner of her eye as he glanced around the room, tapping at his pockets as he did.

"Have you seen my phone—? Ah, there it is. Must have dropped it." He scooped it up and slipped it into his trouser pocket. "So . . . that's it, I guess."

Alison swallowed and shifted around to look at him. "Fine."

"I've got some time off so I'm going to my parents' for a few weeks," he muttered, not meeting her eyes. "Will you be okay?"

Alison scoffed and turned away. It was all she could do.

Noah sighed. "Fine. I've got to go."

Without another word, he marched down the corridor and was gone. Easy as that. Alison wiped at her cheeks, her gaze lingering on the door as he closed it behind him.

The room was still, the only sound coming from Noah's footsteps as they echoed up the stairwell. But a smile slowly formed on Alison's lips as she sat back on the couch.

"Will I be fine, Noah?" she whispered after him. "Yes, actually, I think I will be fine. But Keren . . . ? I'm not so sure about her."

Chapter 32

2 weeks before the bachelorette party

Alison sat cross-legged on her bedroom floor, her acting journal open in front of her, its pages filled with scribbled notes, torn pictures, and old sketches. It was in this journal where she'd plotted her past acting roles, given her characters backgrounds, desires, motives. It was all part of the process, the journal an essential part of her actor's toolbox. But now it would serve a more sinister purpose.

Turning to a blank page, she reached for her pen, pulling the cap off with her teeth and rolling it across her lips. At the top of the page she wrote, 'Keren's death = Accident?'

She had to be clever about this. It had to be planned out to the last detail. Anything less and it could backfire on her. Not only did she need to remove Keren from the picture, but she also had to do it in a way that was both believable and relevant. If she could also come out of the situation looking like a heroine, all the better.

But how to do it . . .

She stretched her arms, feeling the tendons strain and pop. She'd hardly slept or eaten in the past week, existing purely on nervous energy but she couldn't stop now. Seeking inspiration, she flicked back through her journal. She read through her notes on 'affective memory' and 'emotional preparation', on how to harness past trauma for a role . . .

She'd probably be able to add to that last one soon enough but for now it was no help. Turning the page, she found the notes from a character study workshop she'd attended last year. There were pages of writing, all relating to an improvised piece done by her friend, Blake, who had based his character on an old woodsman he'd met on a hunting trip in upstate New York – a man called Jerry Washington. Reading back over the notes she recalled the session vividly. Blake had been brilliant. Funny in places, super creepy in others. It was hard to believe that this paranoid weirdo who lived alone in the woods was a real person, but Blake had assured them he was real. Then she remembered something. Blake had stayed in the guy's cabin. He rented it out now and again for hunting trips and the like.

And a plan began to form . . .

Alison read back through everything she'd written on Blake's improvisation. With him being her closest friend in the class she'd taken real notice and had captured all the essential elements of the piece. Jerry was a character drawn from local rumor and hearsay, but the facts were that he owned two cabins in the woods, where he lived, isolated from civilization. And best of all, his name had been linked to a suspicious death a few years earlier.

With newfound enthusiasm, Alison spent the rest of the day diving into research. On the local town's Facebook page, she discovered posts mentioning the old man in the woods. Some warned he should be avoided, that he was an old kook who shot at those he found on his land. Others said they'd heard he was a cannibal and was responsible for the death of a female hiker. It could be gossip; it could be true. Either way, Alison was sold. A weekend in a secluded cabin, probably with no WI-FI or cell reception, while a paranoid, gun-wielding freak roamed the woods – it sounded perfect.

Alison located Jerry's property on Airbnb easily enough and sent him a message asking if she could book the place for her bachelorette weekend. She offered to pay the full rate in advance, too, if it helped sway his decision. Almost a week went by before she received a curt message back explaining that the cabin was indeed available on the weekend she wanted. She grabbed her purse and booked it on her father's credit card immediately.

Done. Now she had her backdrop and her foil.

The only problem was she and Keren had already discussed the bachelorette party in detail and had all but decided on a long weekend in Montauk. It would take some good acting on Alison's part to convince Keren and the others she'd changed her mind and that she now really, *really* wanted a weekend in the wilderness. But if anyone could do it, Alison could. She'd tell them her mom had stayed in the old cabin and had recommended it to her, something like that. She began drafting a text to the girls about an exciting venue change, but paused, opting instead to deliver the news face-to-face, capitalizing on her acting chops.

But the date was set. Two weeks from now, she and Keren along with three more of her closest friends would be traveling up north to Salt Point. Five would set out, but only four would return. With Noah laying low at his parents' house in Vermont, it was the perfect time for Alison to act. For her to do what was needed. Once his flirty little K was out of the way, he'd have to realize how much he loved Alison. Just as it should be. Now all she had to do was make it look as if Jerry had killed Keren, and she'd be home free.

Easy as pie . . .

Chapter 33

1 week before the bachelorette party

Everything was falling into place. Keren was going to pay for her betrayal and Alison was convinced that using Jerry to achieve that aim was a stroke of genius. The old man was paranoid, volatile, and with a past that was already tainted with suspicion. She could hardly wait to get out to the cabin and put her plan into action.

But for now, patience was crucial.

Her immediate task was scouring through the many thrift stores in the East Village. It was a bright early spring day, almost too nice a day to backdrop what Alison was doing. But as she kept telling herself – none of this was her fault. Despite being somewhat concerned over how her chaotic mind had been working since Noah stared into her eyes and told her it was over, she accepted it as part of her journey. She'd been driven to be this way. This was on Noah. And it was on Keren most of all.

The gentle hum of the city surrounded her as she walked alongside Tompkins Square Park. She'd already visited three thrift stores this morning but hadn't found what she was looking for. Now, standing outside a place called *Thriftastic!* she peered through the window. The large store was packed full of vintage clothes and ancient knick-knacks, yet nothing immediately caught her eye.

Stepping inside, she was greeted by the musty signature scent of 'vintage.' Each store so far had smelled the same, a potent blend of mothballs and mildew with a musty undertone of leather. A girl with severe bangs and wearing a black turtleneck sweater sat behind the counter. She looked up from her magazine and regarded Alison with a suspicious glance as she moved down the first aisle.

"Just browsing," Alison told her, with a breezy smile. "It's such an awesome place."

The girl threw up her eyebrows and returned to her magazine. She was probably thinking Alison looked too well-dressed and pristine to be in a store like this. If so, that made two of them. Alison had never gone for the whole boho chic look, even when it was fashionable a few years back. She enjoyed the nicer things in life, designer clothes, expensive shoes, bags that probably cost as much as the entire contents of this store.

But she was here for a reason.

She surveyed the racks with determination, her gaze flicking from one garment to the next, her hand grazing a worn leather jacket as she moved deeper into the store. After having no luck in the previous three stores, she wasn't holding out much hope of finding what she needed here, but as she entered a smaller room at the back of the store she stopped and let out an excited yelp.

There it was, hung in the corner in front of a row of real fur coats – a vintage wedding dress. The white fabric had yellowed slightly with age but that was perfect. The neckline was detailed all around with fine lace, and small white pearls adorned the bodice.

Alison walked over and lifted it from the rack, feeling a twinge of sadness as she did so. Meanwhile, a stunning wedding dress awaited her final fitting at Kleinfeld – a blend of modern style and timeless elegance, with an off-the-shoulder neckline complemented by a modest plunge. It was perfect.

And she *would* get to wear it.

"That's a pretty unique piece, right?"

Alison spun around to see the girl from the desk leaning against the doorframe. She looked Alison up and down and frowned.

"I think it might be a little large for you, though."

"No. It's ideal," Alison told her, holding it up against herself, her eyes glinting with mischief. "It's exactly what I'm looking for."

The tag read $150 but after batting her eyelashes at the girl, she managed to get the price down to $140 and even convinced her to throw in an old wooden box she'd spotted by the counter. It, too, was exactly what she was looking for.

Later, back at her apartment, Alison surrounded herself with her newfound props. Her acting journal lay open in front of her, its pages now filled with ideas and schemes relating to her new mission. She glanced at the old wedding dress draped over her chair, imagining the eerie scene it would create once she'd set Jerry up as a deranged old man with a bridal obsession.

But that was for later. Her focus currently was on a collection of old bridal magazines and trade posters she'd bought off eBay. Sitting cross-legged on the floor, she set about aging the more recent ones, scrunching them up and staining them with strong coffee. Once done she placed the photos into the old wooden box she'd got with the wedding dress. With its worn leather and rusty clasps, it sure looked the part. Gathering everything together, she stuffed the box, along with the wedding dress, under the bed.

Her plot was now taking shape, but she wasn't done yet. Every step had to be perfect, every detail executed flawlessly. Once Keren was out of the picture and Alison heralded a heroine, Noah would surely come around. She imagined their reunion, the tears, the apologies, her dressed in her real wedding dress, and a triumphant smile spread across her face.

Keren had no idea what was coming.

Chapter 34

3 days before the bachelorette party

The heels of Alison's Isabel Marant ankle boots clicked against the sidewalk of the Upper East Side as she strode purposefully along 86th Street. With every step, she attempted to focus on the task ahead, going over what she was going to say, and how she was going to say it, but her mind was racing and she felt dizzy.

A gust of wind tousled her blonde locks as she approached 'Gallagher's Meat and Produce.' The store, nestled between a modern juice bar and a boutique pet spa, looked out of place like a relic from another era. Its window display was a bloody celebration of raw meat, steaks and cutlets laid out on silver trays, with larger pieces hanging from hooks at the back. She hesitated, her heart racing, but out of apprehension rather than excitement. Alison would never consider herself a vegan, or even a flexitarian, but the sight of raw meat had always made her stomach churn.

Taking a deep breath and adjusting the silk scarf around her neck, she pushed open the door. A bell tinkled softly, announcing her arrival. The metallic scent of blood and flesh assaulted her senses, making her eyes water. The sight of more meat, so visceral and raw behind the glass counter, threatened to overwhelm her. She tried not to breathe too deeply, but the stench was inescapable. She felt out of place and far too well dressed for this place.

The butcher, a burly man with a hipster mustache and tattoos peeking out from beneath the sleeves of his white butcher's coat, glanced up from his chopping. Interest sparkled in his dark eyes as he met Alison's gaze.

"Good morning," he said, with a nod.

"Hey there," Alison replied, working through some of the relaxation techniques she'd picked up in acting class. Her hands were clasped tightly around her designer purse, manicured nails digging into the soft leather.

The butcher wiped his hands on his apron, leaving a smear. "How can I help you?"

Alison cleared her throat. "Do you have . . . I mean, the thing is . . . I need some off-cuts. Intestines, guts, that sort of thing. And blood . . ." Her voice trailed off towards the end. She felt stupid, thinking he was going to laugh in her face and tell her to get out of his store. But she had to see this through.

The butcher raised an eyebrow, giving her a once-over. "And what's a nice girl like you need with all that nasty stuff?"

Alison lowered her chin, regarding him through her false lashes. Was this guy seriously hitting on her?

She paused, going for the rehearsed answer rather than improvising. "It's for my dog," she said, firmly.

The butcher smiled, still flirting with her. "Fair enough. I've just finished butchering a prized pig out back as it happens. I've got the entrails saved in a couple of buckets. Though I was going to use some of them for sausages. So, I'll have to charge you for them."

"That's no problem," Alison replied. "Whatever it costs. My little pooch is worth it."

"Well, all right then," the butcher said, reaching under the counter and producing a plastic bag. "What breed is it?"

Alison winced internally. She'd not considered being asked this question. It was an oversight on her part and that was bad. She couldn't afford to make mistakes. Not now.

"She's a . . . Malamute," she said, picking the name out of the air but confident with her selection. Her mom's friend Lola had an Alaskan Malamute. They were big dogs. They looked like wolves. "So, give me everything you've got. Please. She's a hungry girl."

"Ah, nice," the butcher said, chuckling to himself. "Okay. Give me a moment and I'll sort you out some good stuff." He disappeared through a door into the back room and soon returned with two bulging plastic bags. As he placed the bags on the counter Alison could hear the squelch and slosh of the organs and could make out a morbid collection of entrails inside. It made her want to throw up there and then. But, suppressing her revulsion, she thanked the butcher, offering him a grateful, albeit strained smile. Oddly, she was starting to find him rather attractive. Maybe it was the knife he was carrying, the power he wielded.

"And you wanted some blood as well? You sure about that?"

Alison swallowed, steeling herself with a grin. "Please. She loves that stuff."

"Wow. You certain you've not got yourself a werewolf?" he asked, with a wink. "Or a vampire?"

Alison giggled, twirling a strand of hair around her finger. "Sometimes I wonder. But she's a good dog. It's her birthday, you see. She deserves a special treat."

"That's sweet. Coming right up."

Grabbing up a paper container – familiar to Alison as the kind used for takeout noodles or chicken soup – he moved down the counter and funneled a ladle of dark, viscous liquid from a large vat into the container. Alison's stomach turned over once more, yet she maintained a grateful demeanor as he placed the sealed container into another plastic bag to avoid any leaks.

"Let me grab something to make carrying this easier for you," he said, placing the blood next to the bags of offal and retrieving a cardboard box from the back counter. "Have you got far to go?"

"Sort of. But I'll get a taxi," Alison said, eyes widening as the butcher hoisted the sloppy bags of grossness into the box in front of her. She was going to have to store them in her closet or under her bed for the next day or so. She hoped they didn't stink too bad.

"That'll be thirty bucks," the butcher said, watching her with an odd gleam in his eyes.

Alison quickly handed him the cash and hoisted the box into her arms. "Thank you so much for all your help."

"Hey, listen," he said, as she started to move away, prompting her to stop. "Apologies if this isn't appreciated – but I don't suppose you want to grab a drink with me sometime?"

"Of blood?" Alison asked.

He smiled. It was a nice smile. He was a lot hotter than she'd first realized. "No. Not blood. That's not my thing, I assure you."

Alison tilted her head to one side and pouted her lips. "That's sweet," she told him. "But I have a fiancé."

"Ah, shoot, my bad. No worries then. You have a good day anyway."

"Thanks, you too." She turned and headed for the exit.

"Whoever he is," the butcher called after her, "he's a lucky guy."

Alison hesitated for a moment, a smirk spreading across her face.

Yes, she thought to herself. He was a lucky guy.

Damn lucky.

Chapter 35

2 days before the bachelorette party

Alison sat in the passenger seat of her father's Ford Bronco, her head resting against the window as they drove. She could sense his questioning gaze now and then but remained facing away from him, watching out the window as the trees flanking the narrow roads grew taller and the vegetation more dense.

"Why out here, Ali?" he asked finally, his voice laced with a mixture of concern and disbelief. "I can't imagine you staying somewhere so rustic. I mean, it's not very . . . you, is it?"

Alison let out a derisive snort.

Like you'd know, Daddy dearest.

She sat upright and turned to look at him. "I just wanted a change of scenery. Somewhere where me and my besties can chill out without interruptions." He met her gaze, and she gave him her sweetest smile. His was doing her a big favor driving her all this way on his day off, but it was also crucial she uphold the pretense that this was what she wanted.

"I suppose I get where you're coming from," he said, clicking his teeth. "But it's pretty isolated out here, and lacking any kind of luxury, I'd assume. Are you sure you don't want me to pay for you and your friends to go to the Hamptons or Montauk? Hell, even Florida."

"Really?"

"It's your big weekend, princess. You're about to get married. Nothing but the best for my little girl."

She sighed. This was what he always did – trying to buy her affection. His futile attempt to somehow make up for the years he'd been absent from her life.

"I like it up here," she lied. "It's unique. Besides, I've got everything planned out just how I want it."

Her dad shook his head but didn't say anything else on the matter. His eyes momentarily flicked to the rear-view mirror, taking in the two gym bags on the back seat. "What's in those, anyway?"

Alison giggled. "Oh, you know, stuff for the weekend. Party games, balloons, decorations, that sort of thing. I just want the cabin to look amazing when everyone gets here."

"Why do you have to do all this?" he asked. "Shouldn't Keren be decorating the place in her role as maid of honor? Or helping you out, at least."

Alison's gaze returned to the window. But it was a fair question and the fact she was here alone had been somewhat of a stumbling block for her in instigating this plan. Keren herself had been understandably confused and a little upset when she'd found out that – at almost zero hour – Alison had changed all the plans and was now organizing the weekend herself.

Well, good, let her be confused and upset. The malicious bitch.

Yet the last thing Alison wanted was for Keren to know her true feelings. She needed to remain oblivious to the fact Alison knew about her affair with Noah – and it was just as important their friends believed everything was fine between the two of them. Fortunately, except perhaps for Chloe – her friend from acting class – they all knew Alison well enough to believe this was just her having one of her manic episodes. The control freak in her taking over and wanting every single detail to be just so.

But her father was still waiting for a response. "Why do you have to handle everything?" he added.

"Keren's got so much going on with work," she replied with a feigned carelessness. "And you know how I am – always wanting things done a certain way."

"Oh, yes. I know how that goes," he chuckled, narrowing his eyes at the road ahead. "Anyway, we should be arriving soon enough."

He reached over and turned the volume up on the radio, no doubt having exhausted his conversation. Interactions between Alison and her father were like that these days. They got on okay but in small doses.

Ten minutes later the dirt tracks they'd been driving on ended and they rolled into a clearing surrounding a large cabin.

"I think this is it," her dad said, bringing the Bronco to a stop.

"Right, yeah. Sure." Alison peered through the windshield at the wooden structure in front of her. It looked bigger than it did in the photos on the website but also a lot more rustic. She forced a grin. "Looks awesome!"

Her father looked as if he was about to say something, maybe another attempt to get her to change her mind about the venue. But before he had a chance, she unbuckled her seat belt and climbed out.

"I'm going to be a while here," she told him, opening the rear door and hauling the two heavy bags out onto the driveway. "Why don't you head into the next town and grab a bite to eat."

"You sure? I mean . . . I haven't got your eye for design or decoration, but I can carry things."

"I can manage."

He glanced around. "It's pretty quiet around here. Will you be okay on your own?"

"Daddy, I'm fine!" She fixed him with a big grin. "The owner has left me a key, and I just want to get on with it."

He seemed unconvinced, but as usual, chose not to confront her about it. "All right, you be careful. I'll be back to pick you up in . . . what? Two hours?"

"Perfect."

Alison carried the bags up the steps onto the porch as her father started the engine. Once there she knelt, pretending to retrieve a key from next to the door. Jerry had told her in his emails that he'd leave the door open for them on the day of their arrival, with a key inside. But he had no idea she was coming up here a few days earlier.

Standing, she waved at her dad as he pulled the Bronco around and rejoined the dirt track. But then the car stopped.

What the hell was he doing?

Alison kept waving. "Go on, drive away," she muttered to herself, gritting her teeth beneath a smile. "Get lost."

The car waited another few seconds before finally pulling away. Alison carried on waving until the Bronco disappeared around a bank of trees and let out a deep sigh. Then she picked up the bags containing the animal entrails and vintage wedding dress and headed into the woods.

The stage was being set, and she was ready to play her part to perfection.

Chapter 36

Friday (Day 1 of the bachelorette party)

The apartment buzzed with activity and excitement as Alison and Hannah packed for their weekend away in the wilderness. In the living room, the large speaker that Alison had linked to her laptop pulsed with a selection of upbeat songs – her 'getting ready to go out' playlist.

She felt good.

She felt ready.

Despite the fact she was still not sleeping well, and her thoughts came at her in a chaotic and overly frequent manner, she was confident she'd done all she could. And for now, the anxiety that had plagued her sleep was temporarily at bay, replaced by a chilling determination. The cabin and its surrounding area were ready for their arrival. Her bachelorette party was about to begin.

She'd be having another party, of course. Once everyone had got over the terrible tragedy that was about to transpire – and Noah had learned the error of his ways. In fact, she'd realized, to her delight, that none of her friends or family would ever have to know she and Noah had even split up. After this weekend, she'd tell them they'd decided to put the wedding on hold while she grieved for her dear friend. Not only would she get all the kudos and respect for putting her friend first, but she then had time to implement phase two of her plan – ensuring Noah changed his mind about marrying her. But that wouldn't be too difficult. He still loved her, she knew that. He'd just had his head turned by that trampy little whore who Alison had thought was her friend. But once Keren was out of the picture and Noah heard how brave and brilliant Alison had been, he'd want her back.

Of course he would!

And then, six months down the line – once she and Noah were back together and stronger than ever – Alison would rearrange the wedding and ask Jess to plan her a proper bachelorette weekend. Somewhere classy and luxurious – Montauk or The Hamptons, maybe even the Caribbean.

Returning to getting ready, she walked into the front room, weaving around Hannah who was heading back to her room from the bathroom.

"Are you almost ready?" Alison asked her, grabbing her phone charger from next to the TV.

"Just about," Hannah called back. "I can't wait to get there. I don't remember the last time I kicked back and had a weekend away."

"I know, right? It's going to be awesome!"

Alison headed back into her room. Her suitcase was open on top of the bed but only half full. Piles of make-up, clothes and underwear were strewn all around and she needed to hurry up.

Jess was picking them up in her crappy little red Ford in less than thirty minutes.

Alison swayed to the music, a half-smile playing on her lips as she gathered up a stack of panties and stuffed them into the suitcase. She was usually such a neat person, organized, too, but not when she was in this sort of mood. Then, her outer world often mirrored her inner world – tumbled, disordered, frenetic. But she'd laid the groundwork, she'd done her preparation. She just had to trust herself. She could do this.

A new song came on the speaker, Dua Lipa's 'Don't Start Now'. It was one of her and Keren's favorite songs from their time at Brown. They'd play it loud before going out, dancing carefree around their dorm room as they chugged shots and talked about boys. Today, however, the lyrics – about moving on from an ex that didn't deserve you – felt especially apt. Yet it wasn't her relationship with Noah that Alison was getting over. It was her relationship with Keren. And permanently . . .

Hannah's voice from the other room pierced her thoughts. "Alison, you remember that top you borrowed last week? Mind if I pack it?"

"Yeah, it's on a hanger behind my door. Take it," Alison called back, not pausing in her task.

She selected three pairs of jeans and placed them into her suitcase before taking a deep breath. She felt thirsty all of a sudden and headed into the kitchen.

"Hey, Hannah, you are bringing sunscreen?" she called out as she grabbed a glass off the side and opened the fridge. "Do you think we'll need it?"

There was a slight pause, followed by a distracted, "What?" from the other room.

"Never mind. One second." Alison took the jug of water from the lower shelf of the fridge and poured herself a large glass, drinking it down in one go. "I said, do you think we'll need sunscreen?"

She placed the glass in the sink, listening for Hannah's reply.

None came.

"Hannah, did you hear me?" she called out, walking back to her bedroom. "I said do you think we need . . ." She trailed off. Her heart felt like it had stopped.

Hannah was standing in front of Alison's bed. She had her back to the door, but even from this angle, it was clear what she was holding in front of her. And, more importantly, what she was reading.

"It's not what it looks like."

Hannah spun around, her eyes wide with shock. She opened her mouth and closed it again. She slowly shook her head. She didn't blink. The acting journal in her hands was open on an entry Alison recognized all too well – a seven-point plan to dispose of Keren while framing Jerry for her murder.

Shit.

Shit, shit, shit.

She'd left the journal next to her case. She was in such a whirlwind she hadn't noticed it lying open when she went to get a drink of water.

She licked her lips. Her mouth was already dry as a bone. She tried to speak, to explain, but no words would come. She wondered if she might be able to swing this, use her charm and improv skills to explain it away as a short film idea or something equally innocuous. But from the horrified expression on Hannah's face, she knew it would be too hard a sell.

"Alison?" Hannah said, her voice shaking. "What is this?"

Chapter 37

Alison stared at Hannah. Hannah stared back. Time seemed to slow down, to stop. Alison tensed. What the hell did she do now?

"I can explain," she said.

Hannah frowned. "Really? You can?" She flipped through a few pages, shaking her head and her eyes widening further as they took in the entries.

"It's my acting journal," Alison told her. "Just ideas . . . Thoughts . . . None of it is real. None of it is going to happen . . ."

But it was going to happen. And if she came on this trip, she'd know that.

This was bad.

This was really bad.

"And what are these?" Hannah asked, lifting out receipts for the butcher's shop, for Thriftastic! and waving them at her. "Are these just ideas too?"

"Yes."

There was genuine fear in Hannah's voice, laced with disdain. "What have you done, Alison?"

"Give it back!"

Panic surged through Alison like wildfire, driving her to lunge at Hannah in a desperate attempt to reclaim the journal.

Hannah twisted away, clutching the journal out of reach, but Alison, powered by her frantic state, came at her again, her fingernails clawing at Hannah's hand.

"Give it to me!" she spat.

The two of them spun around, like two dancers trying to lead, neither willing to follow. As they grappled, a side table tipped over, spilling its contents onto the floor – a magazine, Alison's phone. In the background Dua Lipa reached the coda of the song, the intense beat providing a suitable backdrop to the tussle. Alison's focus was razor-sharp on the journal, but as Hannah tried to pivot away, their feet got tangled. In the struggle, Hannah swung the journal like a weapon, striking Alison on the side of her face. Stinging pain radiated from the blow, and for a brief second, the room went hazy. Yet she retaliated quickly, driving her shoulder into Hannah and pushing her backward.

The sudden blow caught Hannah off guard. She staggered, trying to regain her balance. But it was too late. She stumbled over and smashed her head into the sharp edge of Alison's desk.

Oof! Shit!

There was a sickening thud and Hannah slumped lifelessly to the floor, the journal falling open beside her.

For a moment, everything was still. Then Alison stepped forward, panting heavily.

"Hannah?" she whispered, her voice cracking. "Oh, God!" She knelt beside her friend's limp form, her mind racing, her heart thumping wildly against her ribs.

Was Hannah dead?

Was that a good thing?

What did she do now?

Alison reached out and grabbed Hannah's shoulder. She shook her hard.

"Hannah! Wake up! You stupid girl! Look what you made me do!" She ground her teeth together, glancing around for inspiration. "Hannah? Are you dead?!"

This was not what she needed right now. She scratched at her head, fighting the strong urge to rip a clump of her hair out. The pain would help focus her. Maybe she should. She got to her feet, her breath coming in short, ragged bursts.

This wasn't cool. She hadn't planned for this.

"All right, calm it down, Ali," she told herself as a prickly heat blossomed across her chest and up the back of her neck. "You've got this. Just think . . . Think!"

If Hannah was dead, could she dissolve her body in the bathtub? Alison had seen it done in the movies and she could probably find out what chemicals she'd need, and how to do it, after a quick internet search. But then Hannah groaned, and her eyelids flickered.

"Shit! Shit . . . shit . . . shit!"

Alison realized all at once that Hannah being alive didn't help matters. In fact, it made everything ten times worse.

She knew too much.

She'd seen too much.

Alison had to do something. And fast.

With adrenaline coursing through her veins, trying to avoid Hannah's vacant eyes, she hoisted her friend into a sitting position. Wrapping an arm around her chest, and grunting and gasping with the exertion, she dragged Hannah's limp body from the bedroom, through the hall, and into the living room.

Once there she laid Hannah on the floor next to the radiator, pausing to catch her breath and wipe the sweat from her brow. She needed to secure Hannah before she regained consciousness. Her eyes darted around the room, searching for a belt or some rope, something she could use to tie her up. But then she had a better idea. With Hannah still groaning weakly Alison raced back to her room, rummaging through her dresser until she found what she was looking for – a pair of steel handcuffs. She'd bought them for her and Noah to try out, but he'd not been into the idea – yet they were proper police-issue cuffs – strong, secure, almost impossible to remove without the right key. She also found an old silk scarf that had belonged to her mom and returned to the living room with both items.

With trembling hands, she clasped one metal cuff around Hannah's slender wrist. Then threading the loose cuff around the sturdy pipe of the old-fashioned radiator she pulled Hannah's other wrist up and clamped the handcuffs shut.

Hannah's groans were growing louder now. She was starting to sir. With a decisiveness that surprised even her, Alison gathered up the silk scarf and wrapped it around her roommate's mouth, tying it securely at the back of her head.

And . . . what now?

Alison shifted away as Hannah's eyes fluttered open, confusion giving way to terror as she realized her predicament. She tried to move, she tried to scream, but the scarf muffled her cries and the handcuffs held her firmly in place.

Alison got to her feet, her pulse pounding in her ears. She watched Hannah a few moments more. She wasn't going anywhere but they were supposed to be leaving for Salt Point any minute. Jess was already on her way over. Alison bounced from foot to foot. She had to figure out her next move. Leaving Hannah handcuffed to the radiator seemed her only option, but what then?

She knew too much.

She'd seen too much.

The sharp trill of Alison's phone ringing cut through the chaos of her thoughts. Heading back to her room she scooped it up off the floor and saw Jess's name on the Caller ID. After closing her bedroom door and taking the deepest of breaths, she answered, stepping back into the role of excitable bachelorette.

"Hey, hey! It's party time baby!"

"Yep. It sure is." Jess's tone was brusque and functional. It always was on the phone. "We're outside. Are you ready?"

No! Of course she wasn't ready! She had her roommate bound and gagged in the living room and had no idea what she was going to do with her.

"Hannah can't make it," Alison said, speaking fast. "I'll tell you about it later. But it's all fine. Don't worry about it. Just give me five minutes, okay?"

"Ah, Ali. Shall we come up?"

"NO!" Alison cleared her throat and laughed. "I'm totally fine. I'll be done as quickly as I can. Wait down there. Bye!"

She hung off before stuffing her phone in her purse and then finishing packing her suitcase. It was even more of a frenzied job now, as Alison pulled sweaters and jackets out of her closet and stuffed them into the case.

Her thoughts swirled with the Hannah problem. She'd have to leave her tied up and gagged, she couldn't risk her shouts alerting a neighbor. Yet with the scarf around her mouth, she couldn't eat or drink. Alison would be gone for four days. Could Hannah survive that long without fluids?

But maybe that was the point.

A plan formed. She'd leave Hannah here, restrained and gagged. When she returned, she'd stage a break-in gone wrong. Someone had entered their apartment, taken any valuables, and tied Hannah up. Left her here to rot. The idea of her friend succumbing to dehydration played out in Alison's mind. She could feign shock, horror, grief. She could do all the emotions. She'd tell them Hannah hadn't come on the bachelorette weekend and had stayed home alone. What a shame, she'd say, through her tears. If only she hadn't had to work . . .

But would people believe another tragedy so close to Keren's mysterious circumstances?

Well, they'd have to. Alison had the perfect alibi. She'd be miles away in a cabin when Hannah died, surrounded by friends. Losing two close friends so close to her wedding would be seen as a terrible, terrible coincidence, that was all. Poor Alison, they'd think. What a strong woman she was to deal with such heartbreak.

Her phone buzzed again, this time with a message:

Ali hurry up! We're waiting!

"Hold on, Jess!" she whispered to herself, her fingers trembling as she typed out a hurried response.

Be down in a sec.

She zipped up the suitcase and dragged it off the bed, wheeling it into the front room. Hannah was now weakly struggling against her restraints, her muffled cries exacerbated by the tears running down her face. Her left eye was swollen shut, and she had a deep gash on her forehead. Maybe she'd succumb to her injuries, Alison wondered, bleed to death. Either way worked for her.

"I'm sorry, Hannah," she whispered. "But you should've never looked at my journal."

Stepping over her she switched on the TV, raising the volume to a typical 'watching TV' level, but loud enough it would disguise Hannah's muffled cries if anyone came to the front door of the apartment.

Down on the street, she heard the beep, beep of a car horn. Probably Jess urging her on.

"I'm coming!" she called out.

Giving Hannah one final glance, she headed for the door, her thoughts shifting from the messy scene behind her to the bachelorette party. This morning had been the perfect dress-rehearsal for the opening night this weekend.

She smiled to herself as she locked the door behind her. She was getting good at this. And she was more than ready for what came next.

Bring it on!

Chapter 38

Thursday, afternoon

Jess's constant whining was really getting on Alison's nerves. A city girl at heart, her oldest friend was clearly feeling out of her comfort zone venturing into the wilderness for a weekend. But hell, didn't she want them all to know it? She hadn't shut up for the entire journey.

Keren was worse. Every word that came out of her mouth, no matter how banal, triggered a fierce loathing inside of Alison. The trip had already begun on the wrong foot with Keren claiming shotgun and refusing to give it up even when Alison reminded her whose bachelorette weekend it was.

But wasn't that just Keren all over? Mean. Selfish.

Disloyal.

Alison despised the duplicitous bitch, but she couldn't let it show. Not yet. So, she smiled and laughed along through gritted teeth, dug her fingernails into her palms, and watched out the window as she tried to block her out.

Upon arrival at the cabin, they unloaded the car and made their way inside. The place was awful, worse than Alison had expected – rustic, cold, lacking any modern touches – but it was also perfect for her needs. She allocated the rooms, deliberately placing herself next to Keren while suggesting Jess and Chloe share the large room across the hall, lessening the likelihood of them overhearing anything.

With their bags unpacked and the initial exploration complete, they set about decorating the cabin, blowing up the pink and white balloons Keren had brought and hanging a colorful but lame banner across the rafters.

While Keren and Jess were occupied unloading two boxes of liquor bottles from Jess's trunk and setting up a makeshift bar area on one of the side tables, Alison crept back to her room and retrieved the vintage wooden box from the side compartment of her suitcase. She had already found a hiding spot for her father's old boots – stashed at the back of the closet under a throw – ready for when she needed them later.

She carried the wooden box through into the main space, concealing it behind her back as she moved over to the bureau. Once there, she slid open a drawer and placed the box inside but looking up she noticed Jess watching her. Alison froze, her heart skipping a beat, but then Jess beckoned her over with a cheerful grin.

Thank God.

She hadn't seen it.

Once the decorations were done, they gathered for drinks. Alison played bartender, generously pouring out large measures of vodka for the others while skillfully pretending to add it to her own cup. She longed for the sweet tang of a strong Cosmopolitan right now, but she needed to remain sober.

Chloe's arrival kicked the party into high gear. With the drinks flowing as fast as the conversation Alison settled into her role, expertly steering the talk and party games in the direction she wanted them to go. Typically, Jess and Keren were still cranky about their less-than-luxurious surroundings, but Alison ignored them, playing the cheery host as always.

To most people, even her friends, this is who Alison was – sweet, charming, fun to be around, definitely not a vindictive murderer. She had to make Chloe believe that most of all. Being so smart and sensible, she was Alison's point of reference. If Chloe fell for her plan, then everyone else would. Plus, when the time came, she needed Chloe around to provide the authorities with the right narrative. The one Alison was about to create.

With the gang all together, the atmosphere in the cabin was electric. As the girls interacted, Alison realized how easily she could manipulate the situation. Guiding the conversation to Jerry, she planted seeds of suspicion with carefully chosen comments, setting the stage for later. When the old man turned up unannounced, acting as creepy and unsettling as she'd implied, it couldn't have gone better if she'd planned it.

It was Keren who'd suggested they play Truth Or Dare but this wasn't unexpected. In fact, Alison was counting on it. Keren was naturally nosy and liked to make people feel uncomfortable. This often led her to initiate Truth or Dare or Never Have I Ever after a few rounds of drinks. To further make sure of it, that morning Alison had messaged Keren, asking her specifically not to suggest playing either game that weekend, almost certain she would do just the opposite out of spite. And being the bitch she was, that's exactly what happened.

Alison had also predicted Jess would be too scared to venture outside alone at night. She aimed the dare at her, counting on the fact she'd throw it right back at her.

And . . . what do you know?

Her two supposed best friends were as predictable as each other.

Alison had relished playing the part of the terrified girl who'd seen something in the woods. She'd always been able to cry on demand, but she felt her frantic, rattled performance – as she stared into the trees and shook with fright – was practically Oscar-worthy. If only her acting teacher, Andre, could have seen it.

The time outside on her own was also strategic, allowing her to discreetly locate the cabin's generator and disconnect the gasoline supply. She'd done her research and was relieved to find a relatively modern set-up. There was a clear line out from generator to canister that would make it easy for her to disconnect the fuel later when needed.

It was all coming together, and Alison realized she was actually enjoying herself. It was a welcome diversion after the stresses, strains and heartbreak of the past few weeks. She was back in control, back doing what she was good at, and delighting in her scheme's devilish details. She still wanted to claw Keren's eyes out whenever she opened her mouth, of course. But she was playing it cool, biding her time and pretending all was well. Because there'd be plenty of time for revenge. Plenty of time to make the bitch suffer.

Yes, it was all coming together exactly as Alison had planned, and tomorrow was going to be even more fun.

Chapter 39

Saturday, morning

Alison stifled a smile as she trailed through the woods behind the others, all the girls now visibly shaken by the recent discoveries. They might have been able to overlook the box of old bridal magazines Alison had 'discovered' but not the torn wedding dress hanging in the middle of the forest.

She had been worried she'd not be able to find her way back to the place where she'd hung it a few days earlier, but her sense of direction was better than she'd given herself credit for. And what a scene it had been when they got there. Being trained to act in the moment, she was able to buy into the situation whole-heartedly, and even she was disturbed to see it hanging there. It was sinister and weird and creepy as hell. It could not be dismissed.

Now her heart was racing, but not out of fear. As the others ambled forward, the excited chatter turned to hushed whispers as they discussed what they'd just seen, what it meant, and what they should do about it. Jess seemed especially shaken, jumping at every rustle and movement in the undergrowth. Alison would usually find such behavior annoying, but today her friend's nervousness added to the tension. It would also make her a good witness later.

As the others whispered, Alison allowed herself a brief moment of pride. Everything was unfolding just as she'd planned it. Next came the final act. The denouement. The climax.

The reckoning.

"What do you think, Ali?" Jess's question snapped her from her thoughts. She'd stopped to wait for Alison next to a tall oak tree and was huddled over with her arms folded. "Pretty fucking scary, huh?"

Alison nodded. "Sure is."

They carried on walking.

"I think we need to leave," Jess continued. "I'm sorry, Ali, I know this is supposed to be your special weekend, but things have gone far too weird and I think we're in danger. We need to walk into town and get help."

"I don't know, Jess. I'd say the safest place for us to be is back at the cabin. We don't want to be trekking through the forest if someone is out there."

Jess didn't look convinced, but she didn't argue. That worked for Alison; she just needed Jess worried enough to stay on script, not panicked enough to disrupt everything.

They pressed on, the late afternoon sun filtering weakly through the dense tree canopy above and casting hazy shadows on the earth. Alison could sense Jess wanted to say something and as they walked alongside the side of a deep quarry she turned to Alison and lowered her voice.

"I thought you'd be keen to get back to civilization," she said. "Given . . . you know . . . your condition."

Alison turned to her. "What are you talking about?"

"Last night, I drank from your cup by mistake," Jess went on, lowering her voice even more. "There was no liquor in it. So, are you . . . pregnant?"

Shit!

Alison's heart skipped a beat. She knew Jess had picked up her cup, but she thought she'd snatched it back off her before she had a chance to drink. Apparently not.

"No. I'm not pregnant," she said, her mind spinning as she worked out how this affected her plans. "There was liquor in there."

"There was not. And if you aren't pregnant, what's going on, Ali? It's not like you . . ."

Alison chewed on her lip. This was bad. An unexpected eventuality. She'd known Jess for most of her life and she could be a real pain in the ass when she got an idea in her head. She wasn't going to drop this without a proper explanation as to why Alison was only pretending to drink.

Only she didn't know what to tell her.

"All right, I am pregnant," she whispered. "But don't tell the others, okay?"

"Really? You're pregnant?" Jess didn't sound so happy about it. But she was rather puritanical. She probably thought Alison should wait until marriage before conceiving.

Well don't worry, Jessica! There is no baby.

And there won't be a wedding if you mess this up for me.

Alison sighed. "But just between us, remember."

"But all the more reason for us to get out of here," Jess urged, halting to confront Alison. "We can walk to town, and get a room for the night. You look exhausted, and . . ." She reached out to Alison, who quickly brushed her hand away. "Please, Alison!"

"No, we're staying here. We have to."

"But, why though?" Jess implored, reaching out once more and grabbing Alison's wrist. "Please. I want to leave."

"Let go of me!" Alison snarled.

But Jess wouldn't let up or let go. "We need to find help. You need to rest!"

"I said I'm fine!"

"Alison! What's going on?"

Goddamn it Jess.

She was too eager, too nervy. She wasn't going to let this go. And here, on the edge of the quarry, Alison's instincts screamed out an idea. A quick glance confirmed Chloe and Keren were out of earshot, having pressed on ahead. With a sudden, forceful move, Alison lunged at Jess, shoving her back and sending her toppling over the side of the ravine. She yelled out but her cries were quickly swallowed by the dense foliage and the quarry's echoing depths.

Oh, man . . .

For a moment, Alison stood frozen, her breaths shallow. Then, after what seemed like minutes but was probably a few seconds, she tentatively approached the edge. Below her, Jess was motionless, her body splayed out next to a pile of rocks.

But rather than remorse, a rush of wild exhilaration overcame Alison, a sense of power and control she'd never felt before.

She even smirked. "Sorry about that, Jess," she whispered, owning her new role as a movie villain. "But you shouldn't have been such a Debbie downer."

The joke was weak, but it made her smile anyway.

Alison lingered for a moment longer and then set off after the others, pulling more emotion from her actor's toolbox and slipping into her next role. The one she'd need to pull this off.

By the time she reached the cabin, Alison had already crafted her story. Jess had stormed off after a heated argument, claiming she was heading to town for help. If anyone suggested going after her, Alison would turn on the tears and guilt trip them into staying.

It was believable. It was perfect. So, screw Jess, her death would only add to the narrative. Jerry had found her and pushed her off the cliff. It was fine. It would all be fine.

And she had work to do.

Chapter 40

Saturday, evening

With Jess out of the way it had been easy to persuade Keren and Chloe they should get some rest. They were all exhausted and the two of them had shuffled to their rooms and without argument.

Alison waited for another twenty minutes and then, when she was certain they were both asleep, got up and got busy. She was now ready to tackle the final, most risky parts of her plan. These steps were going to be tricky as hell and she'd need some luck on her side, but she could do this. She was ready.

With a fire in her belly and adrenaline surging through her system, she pulled on her hiking boots, grabbed her coat and headed out, locking the front door of the cabin behind her and taking the key.

She had to first make it look as if Jerry had snatched her from the cabin while Keren and Chloe were asleep. But to do that, she needed Jerry's spare key.

She was heading for the second cabin but took a detour past the quarry. She expected to see Jess's body where she'd left it and was shocked and a little worried to discover it was gone.

"What . . . Jess . . . ?"

Alison squinted into the early evening light, scanning the area for any sign of her friend. There was no sign of her, but Alison had read that there were wolves in the forest – bears, too. Most likely, Jess had been dragged away to provide food for some beast and its young. It was a sobering thought, but Alison quickly refocused. Jess had brought this on herself and like they said, all was fair in love and war.

This weekend was about both.

Casting one last glance around the quarry Alison rolled her shoulders back and set off. Keren and Chloe were exhausted, but they wouldn't sleep forever. And she had work to do.

With Jerry being an outdoorsy soul, she'd counted on him not being home when she got to his cabin. She was relieved to find that, not only was this the case, but he'd also left both the front and back door unlocked. Slipping inside, she found the spare key for the main cabin in a drawer and swiftly pocketed it before grabbing one of the many rifles Jerry had hanging on the wall.

Alison had been shooting a few times at her grandfather's house over in Harrisburg, so she knew how to handle a rifle. She found a box of ammo and loaded ten rounds into the magazine. She wouldn't need all of them. With any luck, she'd only need two. The action was a lot stiffer than on any rifle she'd used before, but she managed to pull it back and chamber a round. Once done, she clicked back the safety pivot and held the rifle at waist height. Ready.

Focusing on her breathing, trying to remain calm she stepped back out of the cabin and stood in its shadow for a few moments, listening. Over to her left she could hear a distant *thwack-thwack-thwack* and then the sound of wood splintering. It had to be Jerry. She followed the sound, her fingers whitening as she gripped the rifle. She only had one go at this.

She found him chopping wood in a clearing about thirty yards away from the cabin. He had his back to her and didn't hear as she approached. As she got closer, she raised the rifle and aimed down the barrel. It would be so easy to take him down this way, but she knew the authorities would be able to tell she'd shot him in the back and that didn't fit her narrative.

Swallowing – or attempting to, at least – she relaxed her shoulders the way her dad had shown her and exhaled.

"Hey . . . Jerry!"

He spun around, his face a mask of lines and confusion. "What are you—?"

He never finished his sentence. Alison pulled the trigger and shot him in the chest, right through the heart. He jerked back and tried to speak before slumping forward onto his knees and then dropping face-first onto the ground.

"Well, would you look at that?" Alison muttered to herself. "Still got it."

Slinging the rifle strap over her shoulder she hurried over to the old man's fallen body. Her original plan had been to drag him back to the cabin before dealing with Keren, but time was now against her. Nevertheless, she hoisted him up and was surprised by how light he was. Despite being of similar height to her, he was nothing more than a shell, his clothes hanging over a frame of sinew and bone. He was probably not long for this earth, anyway. Just some old weirdo living on borrowed time.

She let his lifeless body drop to the ground. Once Keren was dead, she'd come back for him. It wouldn't be too difficult to drag his slight frame back to the cabin and haul him inside. Once there she'd position him in a chair and shoot him again, aligning the rifle's barrel with the existing chest wound to simulate a second, fatal shot. The resulting blood pattern would splatter against the cabin wall, placing him there at the moment of death. She was also planning on unbuckling his belt and pants to add another layer to the sinister narrative. This was no game for Alison, she'd done her homework.

Stepping back, she stared into Jerry's cold, lifeless eyes. The creepy old bastard. He probably would have kidnapped and raped them all given half the chance. She was doing the world a favor.

She'd inform the cops that Jerry had taken both her and Keren, tying them up in his cabin while preparing to do horrible things to the two of them. Only, before he could do so, they'd freed themselves and attempted an escape. But not without tragedy. In the ensuing chaos, Jerry would fatally shoot Keren before Alison managed to overpower him, wrestling the rifle away and killing him in self-defense.

Alison surveyed Jerry's body with a self-satisfied smirk, proud of her foresight and attention to detail. As far as she was concerned, she'd set it up so no one could deny her version of events. Keren would be gone, and Alison would be hailed as not just a survivor, but a tragic heroine. Someone with a tale to tell.

Hell, the closer it came to zero hour she'd started to think even bigger. She was now picturing a book deal, maybe even a movie – with herself in the starring role, naturally. Wouldn't that be awesome . . . ?

No! Focus, Alison.

You're not there yet.

But it was time for the final act.

Heading back to the cabin, she grabbed one of Jerry's spare rifles from off the rack and, after checking it for ammo, propped it up behind the door. Then she raced back the way she'd come. Her lungs ached and the muscles in her legs burned with effort, but she didn't stop until she reached the clearing and the main cabin. Tiptoeing up the steps, she unlocked the door and let herself in before creeping down the hallway toward the main living space. She left one of the keys on the coffee table in front of the large orange couch and then swiftly retraced her steps, ruffling up the hallway rug to make it look as if a struggle had taken place. Once done, she left the cabin and locked the door behind her.

Another task crossed off her 'to do' list.

Alison then took refuge in the woods, concealing herself behind a row of spruce trees until Chloe and Keren emerged from the cabin, their worried eyes scouring their surroundings for their missing friend.

Come on, you know what happened – Jerry's taken me.

Better get searching . . .

She waited, the muscles in her jaw and across her chest tightening, not daring to breathe. But, as she'd hoped, they'd set off down the track towards the second cabin and she'd followed them, staying out of sight but within earshot.

At one point she heard Keren whining. "He's got a gun, Chloe! *Guns.* Plural. He's a murdering, cannibalistic weirdo."

She couldn't help but smile at that. It was exactly what she'd hoped for, as was Chloe's suggestion a few minutes later.

"We should spread out," she heard her say. "Just far enough we can still hear each other if we get into trouble. That way he won't realize there are two of us. One of us can distract him while the other grabs his gun – or something."

Alison fist-pumped the air in silent triumph, almost shrieking with delight. Good old Chloe. Ever the clever, sensible one. She was playing her part impeccably, as Alison had hoped.

Biding her time, Alison trailed Keren until she'd moved far enough down her path that Chloe was out of earshot. Then sneaking up on her from behind, she grabbed her, clamping a hand over her mouth to mute any cries.

"Hey! It's me," she hissed, releasing her grip but holding a finger up to signal for silence. "I need you to come with me. Now!"

"But . . ." Keren whispered, glancing around. "What about Chloe? We need to—"

"No! She'll be fine. We'll come back for her in like a minute." Alison grabbed Keren's arm, yanking her forward and into a fast walk. "I've found Jess. She's in trouble. I need your help."

"But—"

"Don't worry. Chloe's fine. But Jess is hurt. She needs us. Quickly!" Alison spoke fast and kept moving, dragging Keren along with her. She was relying on the fact that in her confusion and panic, she'd be more pliable. It seemed to be working.

"Where are we going?" Keren gasped as they moved into a small clearing encircled by a ring of tall cedar trees.

"You'll see,"

Alison propelled Keren through the forest, still gripping her arm and putting more distance between them and Chloe, heading for Jerry's cabin. Whenever Keren's alarm threatened to bubble over, Alison quelled it with urgent whispers.

"We're almost there, just a bit further."

Arriving breathless at Jerry's cabin Alison released Keren, gesturing urgently at the open door. "Inside, Jess is in trouble," she told her. "We have to help her now!"

Keren, propelled by concern, stumbled into the dim interior. But the room was silent, and there was no Jess to be seen. She spun around to face Alison, a question forming on her lips.

But Alison was ready. With one fluid motion, she grabbed the rifle from behind the door and swung. The stock of the gun connected with Keren's temple with a dull thud and she crumpled, unconscious before she hit the floor.

A surge of dark satisfaction rushed through Alison as she stepped forward and stared down at Keren's limp form.

Yeah, that felt good.

It felt really good.

Chapter 41

Alison gripped Jerry's rifle, the stock pressed hard against her shoulder, her finger poised on the trigger. In front of her, Keren, who was now securely bound to the chair in Jerry's cabin, the torn sleeve of one of the old man's shirts wrapped around her mouth. She regarded Alison with wide, terrified eyes as she reached out and yanked the gag from over her mouth.

"Scream and I'll shoot you," she snarled.

"What . . . the . . . fuck . . . is going on?" Keren gasped, finding it hard to speak over the convulsive breaths quaking her chest. The side of her head was bleeding from where Alison had knocked her out a few minutes earlier. "Wh . . . wh . . . . why?"

Alison sneered at her. "You know why."

"No! I don't! Please I just—" Keren's attempt at protest was cut short as Alison replaced the gag. She couldn't bear to hear her bullshit right now. It was best for everyone that she stayed bound and gagged.

Alison stepped back, her thoughts wandering briefly to how Hannah was doing, having been bound and gagged back in New York. It had been almost thirty-six hours since she'd left her there. Would she be dead by now? From somewhere in her memory Alison recalled a person being able to survive for three days without water, so maybe not. But soon.

As Keren squirmed and groaned and tried to scream Alison busied herself with the rope, wincing as she drew it tight around her own wrists. The fibers bit into her skin but she grimaced through the pain and yanked it tighter. She considered herself a method actor, and she needed these marks to prove she too had been tied up. Once the deed was done, she'd untie Keren and arrange the setting to match her narrative. She shivered, her breath catching as she rehearsed the scenario in her head.

"We . . . we managed to free ourselves, officer . . . . We nearly made it out of there . . . but then he . . . Jerry, he . . . he grabbed a gun from off the rack. The next thing I heard was a loud bang and . . . Keren . . . she was . . . He'd . . .

Cue tears.

Cue another Oscar-worthy performance as Alison broke down and was comforted.

With her wrists now red and sore, bleeding in some places she picked up the rifle and moved back over to Keren.

"How long was it going on for?" she asked, suddenly needing to know. "You and Noah?"

Keren scowled, tears running down her face. She mumbled something but it was indecipherable with the gag around her mouth. Alison yanked the material down under her chin once more.

"I mean it. If you scream, I'll kill you."

Keren gulped back large gasps of air. "Why are you doing this?" she wailed. "Please let me go. I've done nothing . . . !"

"Don't play dumb with me, bitch," Alison spat. "I saw the messages on his phone. I know, Keren. I know everything."

"Please, Ali, I don't . . . I haven't . . ." She burst into tears, snot pouring from her nose. "Please don't hurt me."

"Oh go to hell." She lifted the gag back over Keren's mouth. "You're pathetic. Do you know that? You deserve everything you get."

Keren tried to respond, her wide eyes locked with Alison's as sweat dripped from her brow, mixing with the tears, snot and blood on her face.

She was terrified.

Well, good!

There would be no quick, painless death for Keren. No sudden realization before total oblivion like Tony had gotten away with. Alison intended to make her old friend suffer before she died. But she couldn't begin the final act just yet. There was one more obstacle she had to deal with.

Chloe.

Alison couldn't enjoy what she was about to do with the knowledge she might burst in on them at any second. She hoped that Chloe had retreated to the safety of the cabin, but she needed to know for certain. Ideally, Alison wanted Chloe alive at the end of this to back up her version of events, but if she had to kill her as well, so be it.

"Don't go anywhere," she told Keren, with a sly grin, before heading out of the cabin, rifle in hand, and moving to the edge of the clearing. She could hear something scampering through the long grass over to her right but it sounded too small to be a person. Moving into the trees she raised the rifle to her shoulder, pressing her finger on the trigger.

"Chloe?" she whispered.

There was no reply.

She traversed a row of bushy spruce trees until she came across one of the paths that led here from the main cabin. Jerry's body lay not far away and through the trees in front of her, she could see Chloe running in the other direction.

"That's it, hon," Alison muttered. "You keep going."

Chloe was heading toward the main cabin. Maybe she'd lock herself inside and wait for Jess to return with help. She might even run to the next town herself. But either way, she'd clearly given up on the idea of searching the woods alone.

Good girl.

It was the sensible thing to do after all and she was still playing to type. Chloe would be the perfect witness when the authorities came sniffing around. She was mature and rational, and she only knew the version of events Alison had meticulously stage-managed.

And now it was time for the last act.

Slinging the rifle over her shoulder she trudged back to Jerry's cabin, her mind a whirlwind of dark creativity as she plotted her final scenes. Killing Tony had been easy – she hadn't been involved in the actual details of his demise – and she had worried she might not be able to pull the trigger and shoot someone when the time called for it. Yet, killing Jerry had come easy to her. In fact, she'd found it extremely exciting. Not sexually, of course, but not far off. Having that much power at her fingertips had made her feel alive, vital, strong. Alison liked feeling all those things, they were emotions far removed from the shame and weakness that had destroyed her mom. Alison would never be like her.

As she entered the cabin Keren looked up, her eyes red and bloodshot. She glared at Alison, pleading, with her eyes, for her to have mercy. Her expression told Alison she was scared, that she was sorry, that she didn't mean to hurt her.

Bullshit.

Alison's lips twisted with contempt as she regarded Keren. Here she was – her supposed best friend, her maid of honor. The sadness and regret that had threatened to crush her upon learning of Keren's betrayal were now gone, replaced with hatred and fury.

She was going to enjoy this.

"You brought this on yourself," Alison hissed at her. "You couldn't let me have him, could you? You had to open your legs and tempt him in. This is what you always do."

Keren groaned, shaking her head from side to side. "Mmmmimimnt! Meease!" Alison moved closer, pressing the muzzle of the rifle against Keren's cheek, delighting at the sobs emanating from behind the gag. "Meeease!! I Momt. Mam Mot!"

Alison chuckled to herself. Maybe she should tweak the narrative a little. Maybe Jerry *had* subjected Keren to some horrible shit before he killed her. She scanned the cabin for something that could serve as a prop for her cruel theatrics. Nothing showed itself but she was good at improvising. And this evil bitch, this so-called best friend of hers, had to be taught a lesson. She'd tried to shame Alison. She'd tried to take her man and destroy her.

She'd tried to turn her into her mother for God's sake!

That was unforgivable.

So let her whine and cry and beg for forgiveness. It wouldn't work. Keren was going to die today. She was going to pay for what she did.

PART 3

Chapter 42

Saturday, early evening

Chloe rubbed the back of her neck, trying to process everything that Hannah was telling her.

"And by the time you'd regained consciousness she was gone?" she asked.

"She just left me there to rot." Hannah stopped pacing for a moment and glared at Chloe. She had a weird look in her eyes, wild and a little unsettling, like she was on drugs or hadn't slept in weeks.

"But Alison? She's the last person I'd suspect of doing anything like this . . ."

"Like I say, heartbreak can have that effect on a person. And it's all there in her journal," Hannah replied, punctuating her words with a sharp slap of her hand into her other palm. "I only read snippets before she caught me, but it's clear she's planning some horrible, fucked up shit this weekend. There's some weird old guy who she's going to pin everything on and then take the credit for saving the day. It's totally twisted. At first, I thought it was just a wild story, but then she attacked me and handcuffed me to a radiator. And thinking about it now, what I read . . . it wasn't just ramblings, it was a plan of action, a blueprint on how to get away with murder. She's doing this, Chloe. And if she and Keren are gone, then Keren's in serious trouble."

"Wait a minute. Stop!" Chloe cut in, squeezing her eyes shut and pinching the bridge of her nose. "So all this weird shit that's been going down these last two days – the blood and guts, the wedding dress in the woods – that was all Alison's doing?"

"Yes. Noah's broken up with her and it's her sick way of trying to win him back. I swear, she's ready to kill for love. She could have killed me."

Chloe regarded Hannah. Her face was swollen and bruised. She had a scab on her forehead and streaks of dry blood crusted into her eyebrows. Someone had given her a good beating.

But . . . Alison? Really?

"She's lost it, Chloe," Hannah added, as if reading her thoughts. "I was chained to that radiator for a whole day and night. I've hardly slept. I had to pee in my pants, it was horrible. I was banging my feet against the floor, knocking things over to try and get someone's attention. I thought I was going to die there. But then a few hours ago I heard the people downstairs returning home and I started stomping my feet as loud as I could. They heard me and broke into the apartment. I don't even know them, but the guy had a hacksaw and he cut me free."

"Jesus!" Chloe scrunched her face up, trying to focus her thoughts. "I can't believe it. How did she think she was going to pull this off?"

"She's snapped. I could see it in her eyes. I know it's hard to associate the Alison we know with someone who can do this but something's not right with her." Hannah puffed out her cheeks. "I think she's been struggling lately with stress and anxiety and possibly there are deep-rooted issues we aren't aware of. I should have seen it. I mean . . . I sort of did. But I ignored it. I've got my own shit going on, you know? But she's not in her right mind, Chloe, and she's going to do something terrible if we don't stop her."

"We need to call the police," Chloe said. "If she's as dangerous as you say they need to be involved."

"I called them as soon as I was free," Hannah said holding her hands out. "But they wanted to come to the apartment and take a statement first. You know what they're like. It was all 'now calm down, miss' and 'we have to follow procedure'. I couldn't wait around for them to take action. There was no time for statements and interviews or trying to get them to take me seriously. I knew I had to get up here and warn everyone. But it looks as if I'm too late." She shook her head. "I feel wired as shit, but I had to do something. Luckily my car had just got back from the shop so I could drive up here. I even rang the local PD on the way up before my cell signal went."

"Okay, great," Chloe said. "And they're going to help us?"

Hannah made a face. "Who knows? It was just one old cop manning the phones. He said he'd send a patrol car up here, but he was pretty vague about when that would be. Could be in the next hour. Could be tomorrow. I don't think we can wait that long."

"So, what should we do?" Chloe asked, her stomach churning as she already knew the answer.

"Got any idea about this old guy Alison's planning to pin this on?" Hannah asked.

"Jerry," Chloe sighed. "He owns this cabin and a smaller one north of here. But I found his body thirty minutes ago in the woods. Someone shot him."

"Alison."

Chloe nodded. She didn't want to admit it, but it was looking more and more that way.

How had she not seen any of this coming? Had there been signs? Was she so absorbed thinking about Sam, and her own problems that she'd missed vital clues to something being very wrong here?

"If Jerry is dead," she muttered, "then that means . . ."

"It means Alison's plan is almost complete," Hannah finished. "It means, if the situation is playing out like in her journal – and from what you've told me it is – then Keren's life is in danger. Alison is going to make it appear as if this Jerry guy killed Keren before she gets the better of him and kills him in self-defense. She wants to be the heroine of the piece so Noah will fall in love with her again. She wrote pretty much those exact words in the journal. 'Alison, the beautiful heroine wins back Noah's love forever.' It was written in block capitals with about five exclamation marks. She needs help. But Keren needs it first. We need to stop Alison before she kills her."

The two women stared at each other. It felt as if the air between them was suddenly full of static electricity.

"Come with me," Chloe said, marching towards the door. "I think I know where they are."

Chapter 43

Chloe led the charge with Hannah following close behind, as they bolted from the cabin and headed down the forest path toward Jerry's other property. Their breaths came sharp and ragged, cutting through the cool air, as they stumbled on the uneven terrain. Branches whipped at their faces, spiny pines reaching out like fingers, scratching at their arms and faces, yet Chloe barely noticed any pain. Her mind was focused on one thing: stopping Alison from doing the unthinkable.

She couldn't let it happen again.

She wouldn't.

No one else was going to die on her watch.

They pressed on, leaping over fallen trees and ducking under low branches, Chloe's mind moving as fast as her feet. She thought back to when she first met Alison at acting class, how friendly and welcoming she'd been, offering to run lines with her in her spare time. When Chloe had told Alison she could no longer afford the classes she'd been so sweet about it, insisting they remain friends, offering to share her notes. Was she that good an actress, or had something seriously snapped inside of her? It didn't seem possible that Alison, of all people, would be capable of murder. Yet, the evidence was there. It was undeniable.

As if to further highlight this point, Hannah let out a horrified scream, stopping Chloe in her tracks. She followed Hannah's horrified stare through a bank of trees to a clearing, where Jerry's lifeless body was propped up against a tree.

"So he's the . . . ?" Hannah gasped, fighting for air. "And Alison . . . ?"

"I think so," Chloe replied, grabbing the trunk of a young tree to steady herself. "It's the most likely explanation given what you've said. He's called Jerry Washington. He owns the surrounding area. Apparently, a local developer has been trying to get him to sell. There were rumors about a dead hiker, land disputes, threats made . . . it's all so messed up. I initially thought he'd fallen prey to a rival of his but . . . obviously not."

"He's Alison's fall guy," Hannah said, not able to take her eyes off the old man. "She's going to blame Keren's death on him and say she shot him to get away. But that means . . ." She trailed off as she stepped closer to the body, reaching out with a shaking hand to touch his forehead before stepping back again like she'd been electrocuted.

"What is it?" Chloe asked.

"He's still warm, but I'd say he's been dead for about an hour. For her plan to work, I think she's going to have to position him inside the cabin. But for her timeline to be credible with the coroner that will have to be soon. That means Keren's time is running out . . . if it hasn't already."

"Then let's go," Chloe spat, grabbing Hannah's hand and pulling her through the clearing and back onto the path. "We're almost there."

They edged closer, moving as quickly as they could while staying under the cover of the trees. And then there it was, Jerry's rickety wooden cabin, its dark outline looming through the undergrowth. Chloe knelt behind a large rock, yanking Hannah down beside her. The front door of the cabin was closed but light flickered behind one of the windows, indicating movement inside. As she watched, she saw a streak of natural blonde hair and her pulse quickened.

"Alison's in there," she whispered. "We have to be careful. We make one wrong move and Keren's dead. And maybe we are too if she has lost the plot."

Hannah's face hardened with determination. "What do you suggest?"

But Chloe paused, her instincts kicking in. "I've been in that cabin, there are like ten hunting rifles in there, plus knives and an axe. Follow me. I've got an idea."

Staying low she headed away from the cabin, circling it in a wide arc until she was facing it side-on but with a view of the front and back. She waited behind a large cedar tree for Hannah to catch up.

"See that?" Chloe's whisper was barely audible as she gestured toward a smaller outbuilding a stone's throw from the main cabin. "Looks like an outhouse, but more importantly . . ." She leaned around the side of the tree, craning her neck to get a better look. "Yes! Look! The back door."

She hadn't taken much notice of it before, but then her attention had been taken up with raw meat and freaky newspaper clippings – but it was another way into the cabin. It was also hanging slightly ajar.

"I see it," Hannah whispered. "And over there, through the trees. Is that a jeep?"

Chloe followed where she was pointing. Yes. It was an old army jeep, camouflaged but just visible behind a row of fir trees. It likely belonged to Jerry.

"We can use it to get away if we need to make a quick exit."

Chloe nodded. It was a good find, but they needed to get Keren to safety first. She shifted back behind the cover of the cedar tree as a plan began to form in her mind. "Okay, here's what we'll do," she started. "I'm going to approach the cabin from the front and draw Alison out. I'll tell her I mean her no harm, try to reason with her."

"Do you think she'll listen?" Hannah asked.

"I'm not sure."

"Great. And what if she shoots you?"

Chloe swallowed back a knot of emotion. "I'll just have to hope she doesn't, but I have to do something, and fast. I can't let Keren die."

The truth was, Chloe was worried Alison might start shooting the second she became aware of her presence. But she'd come too far now to back down. And there was no doubt in her mind now that Keren was going to die unless they intervened. She had to stop Alison. Or try to at least. She was sick of being afraid. Of always looking for an 'out' in any difficult situation. For too long, her past had controlled her future. What had happened to Sam had kept Chloe meek and playing it safe with life.

But that stopped today.

Because life wasn't safe. Most of the time it was scary and messy and damned unpleasant, but you had to deal with it as best you could. Chloe wasn't always a timid person, plagued by indecision. In fact, she never was. She'd just told herself that because it was a good self-defense mechanism.

The truth was she was strong. She was brave.

And she could do this.

"I'll see if I can reason with her, keep her occupied at least," she told Hannah. "The thing is, she knows I'm here. But she doesn't know about you. You're our secret weapon."

Hannah swallowed. "Weapon? I don't think I'll be much use against a hunting rifle."

"It won't come to that," Chloe said. "While I approach the cabin you circle around some more and approach from the rear. Stay out of sight, but if you see an opening, if you can save Keren, take it. I'll distract Alison as best I can. Understood?"

Hannah nodded, tears glistening in her eyes. "Be careful, Chloe."

"I will. You too."

Chloe took a moment to gather her thoughts. Her heart was threatening to thump its way out of her chest but she took a deep breath like the books told you and focused all her attention on what she had to do next. She wasn't going to let the past or her fears dictate her actions any longer.

It was time to take charge, for Keren, and for herself.

Chapter 44

Chloe stepped cautiously out of the undergrowth, branches snapping beneath her feet as she approached the cabin. Glancing back through the trees she saw Hannah still standing in the clearing, seemingly frozen.

"Go on," Chloe hissed, waving her hand. "Now." She waited until Hannah vanished into the foliage, maneuvering towards the cabin's rear, and then with her breath tight in her throat, Chloe approached the front door.

Up close, the cabin's weathered façade looked more sinister than she'd remembered. But she mustn't let her imagination or her dissenting inner voice – now screaming at her to turn back and let the cops handle the situation – throw her off track.

Focus Chloe.

One step at a time.

You've got this.

Once in front of the cabin she stopped. "Alison?" Her voice trembled but it was loud enough to be heard. A few seconds ticked by. Nothing happened. Chloe's hands constricted into fists. She was about to try again when the cabin door creaked open to reveal Alison standing in the doorway, holding one of Jerry's rifles.

The once picture-perfect princess now resembled a wild, cornered animal. Her blonde hair was a tangled mess, and her blue eyes were now glassy and bloodshot, a terrifying emptiness in them where there was once energy and excitement.

"Why did you come back?" Alison's voice was chilling in its softness and lack of emotion as she trained the rifle on Chloe's midsection. "You should've left when you had the chance."

"I couldn't leave Keren. Or you."

Alison snorted. "Do you not understand, Chloe?" she said, her tone shifting to a mixture of amusement and menace. "If you hadn't run back to the other cabin earlier, you'd be keeping Jerry company in that clearing right now. I'm guessing you've found his body?"

Chloe nodded, pressing her lips together as she watched Alison, not daring to look away. "You're going to tell people Jerry killed Keren – then you killed him and saved the day?"

"That's the way we're going to spin it, yes. But this isn't about Jerry, Chloe. It's about Keren. My beautiful Maid of Honor. It's about what she did, how she tried to destroy me. She deserves everything she gets."

Chloe risked a step forward, releasing her hands and holding them up in a show of surrender. "I know you're hurting, Ali. And it's not fair what happened to you. At all. But Keren doesn't deserve to die. No one does."

She lifted her head, trying to catch a glimpse inside the cabin. Over Alison's shoulder, she saw Keren, tied to a chair, her face smeared with dirt and tears. As their eyes met, Keren whimpered through her gag, nodding frantically, urging her to do something. The sight of her – bruised, bloody, her sweater ripped, her muddy jeans around her ankles – sent a chill through Chloe.

"Jesus," she whispered to herself.

Alison glanced back over her shoulder. "Pitiful, isn't she? My *best friend*. What an evil bitch. But this is the price of betrayal you see, Chloe. You can't mess with people's lives and expect to get away with it."

"But you do expect to get away with it?" Chloe asked. "Seriously? You really think if you kill Keren and me the police will believe it was Jerry?"

"Why wouldn't they? The creepy old bastard's reputation is well-known around these parts. All those rumors . . . there has to be some truth in them. And you know me, Chloe, I can spin a good tale. I might not have made it in Hollywood yet, but I'm a damn good actress."

"Yes. You are. So don't waste that talent." Chloe took another cautious step forward, raising her hands higher. "Alison, this isn't you," she pleaded. "Look at what you're doing."

Alison stepped back into the cabin but kept the rifle aimed at Chloe. "I know what I'm doing," she said. "Do you?"

Chloe shuffled closer as Keren glared at her, straining at the rope tying her to the chair. Chloe gave her what she hoped was a reassuring nod. She couldn't do much more currently. She was desperate to glance down the side of the cabin, to check if Hannah was in position, but to do that would alert Alison to their plan. If she knew Hannah was here, then it was all over.

"Can I come inside?" Chloe asked. "Please? Can we talk about this?"

Alison laughed. "You think you can talk me down like in the movies? I don't think so. There is no *down* anymore. But sure, come in. It'll be easier that way, anyway."

Alison stepped back into the main space of the cabin, flicking her head back to indicate Chloe should follow. Warily she did so, closing the door behind her and leaning against it as Alison backed into the center of the room. Behind her, Keren groaned and whined behind her gag, tears streaming down her face.

"Have you . . . hurt her?" Chloe asked, assessing Keren's disheveled state of undress.

"Not yet." She side-eyed Keren, a cruel sneer twisting her lips. "I still need to set the scene. I'm going to make her sorry for what she's done. Because despite what you think, Chloe, I'm not the bad person, here. She is."

Chloe remained by the door, her eyes darting from Keren to Alison to the back door in the far corner. It was still hanging slightly ajar and through the gap she could see the edge of the outbuilding and a row of trees. But no Hannah.

Where the hell was she?

Chloe shifted her attention back to Alison and the rifle, still pointing at her stomach. There was no way she could disarm her without it going off. To try would be suicide.

"Listen, I know you're hurting," she tried, again. "And what happened . . . it isn't fair. But killing Keren isn't the answer."

"Yes! It is!" Alison spat. Her voice was shrill, her eyes wild with rage. "I have to get her out of the way. She slept with my fiancé. More than once. I've seen the messages – her telling him how much she loves him, how she can't wait to be riding him again. It's disgusting what she did. She has to pay for her actions." A single tear ran down Alison's face, trailing through the dirt on her cheek. "I'm the victim here. Noah will see that. He'll come back to me once he's rid of her. And I'll tell everyone that I was trying to save her. I'll be the heroine, Noah will realize his mistake and fall in love with me all over again."

Chloe remained where she was, eyes not leaving Alison's. The fractured logic, the desperation in her eyes; it was clear now how deeply her friend had spiraled. This wasn't really about Keren or even Noah anymore. It was about a broken heart trying to mend itself through destruction.

"Alison, you're not thinking straight," Chloe tried, reaching out to Alison with a flat palm, hoping she might hand over the rifle. "This won't make it right. You can't change the past, but you can choose how you act in the future. I realize that now. Please, don't make a choice you can't take back."

Alison tightened her grip on the rifle, her finger caressing the trigger. Behind her Keren's cries grew louder and more despondent.

"Please put the gun down," Chloe continued. "You're better than this, Ali. Let's find another way – a better way. We can talk it out. Get you some help."

Alison swung the rifle toward Keren. "No! She knew what she was doing. She wanted to break me, to shame me. She couldn't bear it that I was getting married first, that I had a wonderful fiancé like Noah. She had to ruin it." She sounded more frantic and desperate by the second. She poked the end of the rifle into Keren's cheek, eliciting more muffled screams. "I don't need help, Chloe. I need this evil force out of my life so I can patch things up with Noah and move forward."

Just then, Chloe noticed movement through the crack in the door. Hannah. She was inching closer, slowly easing open the door.

"Alison, please," Chloe said, determined to keep her talking. "You're a good person. You don't want to kill anyone."

"She slept with Noah! She took him from me," Alison cried. "She deserves this."

"And what about you?" Chloe asked, voice shaking, heart pounding. "What do you deserve? A lifetime of guilt? To spend the rest of your life in jail?"

That seemed to catch Alison off guard. She faltered for a second and lowered the rifle. In that moment, Hannah lunged forward, tackling her from the side. There was a deafening bang and Chloe screamed as Keren jerked back and the chair she was tied to toppled over.

"Keren!" Chloe cried out, rushing to help her.

There was blood up the wall. Had Keren been shot? Was it fatal? Chloe couldn't tell but, for now, she was alive. She was struggling to get free, to get upright. On the floor in front of them, Hannah was on top of Alison, trying to grapple the rifle out of her hand. The two women screeched at each other, gnashing their teeth with effort. But Alison was stronger, driven by vengeance and fury. Swinging wildly, she caught Hannah with a sharp elbow, that sent her reeling off her. Using the rifle like a crutch, she attempted to heave herself up.

No. This can't happen.

Chloe scrambled to her feet. With an agility that surprised even her, she leaped on Alison and tackled her to the ground.

"Get the fuck off of me!" Alison yelled. She thrashed and screamed; her features contorted with rage. But Chloe leaned forward with all her weight, grabbing Alison's wrists and restraining her. Now recovered but with a bleeding lip, Hannah leaped back into the fray, prying the rifle from Alison's grasp and sliding it away across the floor.

"Go to hell!" Alison screamed. But it was useless. Hannah and Chloe held her down until she ceased struggling and let out a heavy sigh before bursting into tears.

"Keep hold of her," Chloe instructed, turning her attention to Keren, who had managed to wrestle one of her hands free and was propped up awkwardly against the fallen chair. There was a bloody furrow across her shoulder where the bullet had grazed her but that seemed to be her only injury. Physically, at least. She was shaking, no doubt in shock.

Chloe knelt beside her and removed the gag from around her mouth. "It's okay," she said. "You're safe now."

Keren gasped for air and tried to speak but she was so jittery and teary she was hard to understand. Chloe held her hand and made reassuring noises to try to calm her. In front of them, Alison appeared to have given up. She too was shaking and crying and was pliable enough that Hannah was able to roll her onto her stomach.

"We need to tie her up until the cops arrive," Hannah said.

Chloe nodded, reaching over and picking up a coil of rope on the floor next to Keren. There was plenty of it about, no doubt to be employed in the grim scene Alison planned on constructing once she'd killed Keren and dragged Jerry's body into position. Together, Chloe and Hannah bound Alison's hands and feet.

"She's crazy," Keren murmured, her voice barely above a whisper, her gaze vacant. "I never . . . I would never . . ."

Chloe looked down at Alison, her once vibrant and joyful friend now reduced to a broken, quivering mess. In the distance, she heard a siren – possibly the cops on their way. She met Hannah's gaze and nodded.

"It's all over," she said, speaking to herself as much as Keren. She let out a long sigh and it felt as if ten years of pent-up emotion had been released. But she was right. It was over. It was all finally done with.

Chapter 45

Chloe stood with Hannah in front of the cabin, hugging herself to keep warm as police officers and medics hustled around in a flurry of activity. Over to the west, the sun was now disappearing beneath the tree line, painting the sky in vivid shades of orange and fuchsia. It was a stark contrast to the darkness that had just unfolded here – the beauty of the natural world versus the jealousy and torment of human nature.

Once they'd established the police sirens were indeed getting closer, Chloe and Hannah had hustled Alison out of the cabin and into the back of Jerry's old jeep. Finding the keys resting on the front tire – an apparent concession to the old man's paranoia – Hannah had driven them back down the track towards the main cabin, Chloe riding in the back with Alison and Keren up front with Hannah.

They arrived back, moments before a police patrol car and an ambulance pulled into the clearing, their flashing blue and red lights creating a strobe effect through the trees. Hannah jumped out and waved them down while Chloe remained in the jeep with Alison and Keren, both of them silent except for the occasional sob or jittering intake of breath.

Chloe was surprised to see Jess emerge from the back of the police car, limping and visibly in pain. Jess saw Alison and her already red eyes widened with anger, and something else Chloe couldn't quite place. As the cops escorted a handcuffed Alison away, and Keren received attention from a medic, Jess explained to Chloe and Hannah what had happened.

She told them about Alison only pretending to drink alcohol and how she became enraged, shoving Jess over the edge of the quarry when she confronted her about it. Luckily she'd hit an outgrowing bush on the way down which broke her fall, and while she was knocked unconscious, she only had cuts and bruises and a sprained ankle.

"Geez, it could have been so much worse," Chloe said, glancing over at Keren who was sitting in the back of the ambulance having a light shone in her eyes. She was as white as a ghost and her eyes had a distant quality. She was traumatized, the poor girl. But who could blame her – if they hadn't disrupted Alison's plans she'd be dead.

Jess followed Chloe's gaze and sniffed. "Yeah, tell me about it. I wish I could say I'm surprised about Alison flipping out. But I've seen this coming for years. She needs to be in control of every aspect of her life, and when that doesn't happen, she can't cope. She goes crazy. You ask me, she needs to be locked up."

Chloe nodded but couldn't help feeling that was a little harsh coming from Jess. She didn't condone anything Alison had done – or had planned to do – but she was very obviously unwell. She needed help. Professional help. She said this to Jess but received a stern look in response.

“You can’t help some people,” she replied. “That bitch left me for dead. I could have been eaten by wild animals. I had to walk for like five miles on a bad ankle before a car came past and picked me up.”

“I’m just glad the cops took you seriously,” Hannah said, coming over after speaking with one of them. “I called them as I drove up here, but they didn’t sound as if they were in any rush to investigate.”

“That makes sense,” Jess said. “They said they’d already received a call – and then with me showing up all messed up they jumped into action.”

Chloe shivered as two cops appeared from out of the trees carrying a body bag on a stretcher, no doubt with Jerry’s body inside. Through the open door of the cabin, she could see a female officer wheeling Alison’s suitcase from her room.

“The cops want us to stick around and give statements once they’re finished in the cabin,” Hannah said. “But I don’t think there’s much more we can tell them. I just heard Alison talking with one of them, she’s admitted everything. But she’s still talking about winning Noah back.”

Jess snorted derisively. Chloe puffed out a breath. What a mess. And what a shame. But it just went to show, you never really know anyone.

But maybe that wasn’t entirely true. Because at that moment Rob’s blue Honda appeared from around the bend and Chloe’s stomach fluttered – much more than she’d expected it to. Rob saw Chloe as soon as he climbed out of the car and rushed over to her, a frantic look on his face.

"What's going on?" he asked as she went to him. "Are you okay?"

They hugged. Chloe didn't want to let him go. "It's been awful," she whispered. "Alison had organized this whole weekend just to get back at Keren for sleeping with her fiancé."

"What the . . . ?" Rob asked, his expression growing more confused as Chloe stepped back to take him in.

"I'll explain on the ride home," she told him. "The cops want me to make a statement but then I can't wait to get out of here."

Rob looked around at the bustling scene, staring open-mouthed as an officer left the cabin carrying Alison's make-up case in a plastic evidence bag. "I see . . ." He looked at Chloe. "But you're okay?"

She smiled at him, her cheeks burning slightly as she did. "I'm okay now," she said.

"Great. I know you might not feel like it, but I was wondering if you wanted to get some food when we get back. We should still have time and I doubt you feel much like cooking."

Chloe shrugged. It was a tempting offer. But she was also exhausted. "Maybe."

"Fair enough. Your call." Rob backed away to his car. "I'll wait here until you're ready."

"Thank you. Hopefully not too long now."

She wandered back over to wait alongside Jess and Hannah. Hannah looked as tired as Chloe felt, but Jess had a strange look in her eyes, almost mischievous.

"So that's lover boy, is it?" she asked.

Chloe couldn't help smiling. "It's . . . Rob," she said. "He's great."

"He looks it," Jess said with a smirk.

"Listen, guys," Hannah said. "I'm going to go get a blanket and sit down on the cabin steps, I'm beat. Give me a shout when we're needed."

They waved as she staggered away and then Jess turned back to Chloe, that same mischievous expression on her face.

"Well, I hope you're luckier in love than Alison was."

Chloe raised her eyebrows. "Isn't it a bit soon for jokes?"

But Jess laughed. "I don't think so. That spoilt bitch never knew how good she had it. You see, that's the problem with girls like Alison, they get everything they want their entire lives and then the one time they don't, their entire world crumbles around them. It's kind of pathetic."

Woah.

Chloe opened her mouth and closed it again, searching for a decent response. But Jess wasn't done.

"I'm Alison's oldest friend," she said, narrowing her eyes at the back of the police car where Alison was talking to one of the local cops. "I should have been her Maid of Honor. But you know what, I wasn't surprised. She always took me for granted. It was always the amazing Alison and her boring sidekick, Jess. Me in her shadow the entire time." She lowered her head, along with her voice as she continued to eyeball Alison. "She never deserved Noah. She treated him like shit, you know that? She took him for granted. Bossed him around. He's a good guy, he doesn't deserve that. My beautiful Noah."

Chloe screwed up her face to focus herself.

Did she hear that correctly?

"What did you just say?" she asked.

Jess chuckled. "You heard me. Me and Noah, we had a thing. Well, it was more than a *thing* . . . or so I thought."

"Jesus . . . So it was—wait! What about this Ethan guy you told me about, the one who broke your heart?" She stared into Jess's eyes, who grinned back at her, presumably noticing the realization in Chloe's face. "That was Noah you were talking about."

"After he broke things off I told myself I wouldn't think about him again, but seeing Alison brought it all back. All the pain and heartbreak. All the anger and jealousy. I needed to speak to someone about him, to make it feel real again. I just changed his name."

"So, Keren didn't do anything. She was innocent. Alison was going to kill her for no reason."

"Yes, because poor mousey little Jess couldn't possibly have been the one having an affair with Mr Right, could she?" She sighed. "We were great together Noah and me. I loved him. I thought he loved me back. He told me he was going to break up with Alison and call off the wedding. And he did do that. But he also broke things off with me at the same time."

Chloe glanced over at Hannah. She was sitting on the steps of the cabin, wrapped in a throw from one of the couches. She looked tired but snug, oblivious to these sickening revelations.

Well, lucky her.

"Hannah said something about Alison seeing messages between Noah and someone called 'K'. That's why she thought it was Keren."

"He called me his little Kitty," Jess said, still grinning. "I used to do this thing where I'd meow and . . . well, it was a thing we did. He liked it. He must have saved me as 'K' in his phone because of that and – you know – because it was an affair and everything. Even if he did tell me that it was more than just sex." Her grin faded, replaced by a bitter expression. She was still glaring at Alison.

"You don't seem bothered that Keren was nearly killed because of what you did," Chloe said. "I know you're hurt too, but things could have gone a lot worse here."

Jess shrugged. "It wasn't my fault. I'm not Alison. I never was – was I?"

Chloe frowned, unsure how best to reply. She regarded Jess for a moment, trying to find some semblance of regret or humanity in her expression. But she saw nothing but self-pity. These young women; Alison, Keren, Jess; these selfish little rich girls – they were all as bad as each other. Completely self-obsessed and only caring about others if they were of benefit to them.

Perhaps Chloe was being harsh in her estimation, but it helped her to think this way – because she was moving on. And she'd already vowed to never have anything to do with any of these people again. She might catch up with Hannah for a coffee at some stage, but it was unlikely.

Now, all she wanted to do was get back to New York and restart her life.

Stepping away from Jess she wandered across the clearing to where Rob was leaning against his car. He saw her approaching and smiled and, in that moment, she felt more alive than she had for a long time. She decided there and then to stay in New York, to make a go of things whatever the outcome.

Because she was done running away from her problems. She was done second-guessing herself and worrying what other people thought. Even if she supported herself with three, four, or seven different income streams – so what? At least she was making a go of her life, doing what she loved. And if she could get through this weekend, she could do anything.

So, yes, maybe she would take Rob up on his offer of a meal, after all. It would be nice to be looked after for once. And who knows what might happen later?

She smiled at him and a shiver ran down her back. But the chill of the evening was no match for the warmth in her chest. Because some adventures were worth feeling a little scared about, she realized. Sometimes, being a little scared was good.

It was exciting.

About the Author

M.I. Hattersley grew up in Yorkshire, UK, and has spent the last couple of decades balancing creative work with a long list of mind-numbing day jobs. He's toured Europe with a rock 'n' roll band, trained as a professional actor, and founded a theatre and media company. He now writes psychological thrillers and domestic suspense novels, drawing on years of experience with intense people and unpredictable situations.

About Embla Books

Embla Books is a digital-first publisher of standout commercial adult fiction. Passionate about storytelling, the team at Embla believe our lives are built on stories – and publish books that will make you 'laugh, love, look over your shoulder and lose sleep'. Launched by Bonnier Books UK in 2021, the imprint is named after the first woman from the creation myth in Norse mythology. Embla was carved by the gods from a tree trunk found on the seashore; an image of the kind of creative work and crafting that writers do, and a symbol of how stories shape our lives.

Find out about some of our other books and stay in touch:

X, Facebook, Instagram: @emblabooks
Newsletter: https://bit.ly/emblanewsletter